Readers love *Finding Family*
by Connie Bailey

"If you are looking for a captivating sweet romance with a touch of mystery, and like stories where the kids have a good part I recommend this."
—TTC Books and More

"…it was an adorably sweet, men with children plotline that I enjoyed. Everything was practically perfect in every way, but it wasn't annoyingly so."
—The Novel Approach

"Overall this was a great story…"

—Inked Rainbow Reads

By CONNIE BAILEY

A Case of Mistaken Virginity
Catman's Reward
Golden
Human After All
Initiation
Insert Here
Kaji Sukoshi & The Shining One
Miles to Go
Moonlight, Tiger, and Smoke
One Pulse (Dreamspinner Anthology)
Ragged Dick
The Raw Prawn
Return of the Sun
Revenant
Rusty American Dream
Serendipity Kit
Smoky
Something for Nothing
Suspension of Disbelief
Table for One
Thoroughbred
Three Wise Men
True Blue
Until It's Time to Go

DREAMSPUN BEYOND
With Alix Bekins: #11 – Song and Key

DREAMSPUN DESIRES
#11 – Finding Family

Published by DREAMSPINNER PRESS
www.dreamspinnerpress.com

CONNIE BAILEY

TABLE FOR ONE

DREAMSPINNER
PRESS

Published by
DREAMSPINNER PRESS

5032 Capital Circle SW, Suite 2, PMB# 279, Tallahassee, FL 32305-7886 USA
www.dreamspinnerpress.com

Table for One
© 2017 Connie Bailey.

Cover Art
© 2017 Aaron Anderson.
aaronbydesign55@gmail.com
Cover content is for illustrative purposes only and any person depicted on the cover is a model.

ISBN: 978-1-64080-082-3
Digital ISBN: 978-1-64080-083-0
Library of Congress Control Number: 2017949837
Published December 2017
v. 1.0

Printed in the United States of America
∞
This paper meets the requirements of
ANSI/NISO Z39.48-1992 (Permanence of Paper).

Thank you, Anne Regan, Lynn West, and Danielle Mauragis

CHAPTER ONE

COPELAND SHORE'S phone chimed and jarred his concentration. He glanced from his laptop screen to his wristwatch. He wore the atrociously expensive timepiece because it was a gift from his best friend and because it was a damned good watch. He registered the fact that it was now six minutes past seven just as his phone reminded him he'd received a text message.

It is now xactly 7:05, Cope. Where the hell r u?

A smile formed on Cope's full lips as he read the message from his boss, William Donnelly. Will was as subtle as a chili sauce colonic and always assumed he was in charge, but they'd been friends since college, and besides, Cope genuinely liked him. William played the sophisticated alpha male to perfection, but Cope knew it was just an act, and the competition kept him on his toes.

He took his charcoal-gray silk suit jacket out of the closet, slipped it on, and gathered his long, espresso-dark hair into a neat ponytail. Being chic wasn't just a personal choice; it was a prerequisite of his job at Collezione di Gio. The New York–based clothing company he worked for sold stylish sportswear for affluent young adults and expected its executives to dress with flair, but Copeland was more than just a sharp-dressed man. He was one of CdG's top troubleshooters, spending most of his time getting new store locations up and running. His reputation was that of a no-nonsense organizer with a crushing work ethic, and he used that well-crafted image to do half his work for him.

Cope's phone chimed again, and he automatically switched it to Vibrate. A new text message from Will informed Cope that it was now eight minutes after seven and that Cope was demonstrably not in the lobby. Cope considered begging off with the excuse that he was worn out from the transatlantic flight and the half day at the office.

It had been four months since he'd slept in his own bed. Milan had been nice, but he longed to reacquaint himself with his king-size mattress. He veered away from the thought that he had no one waiting for him at home. At one time, he'd been a romantic who hoped for true love, but now he settled for a warm body with a modicum of good manners. He hadn't given up on love completely, but he'd stopped waiting for his prince to come. He had a fairly steady stream of good-looking strangers to satisfy his sex drive, and he had Will for company.

Cope's phone vibrated, and he looked at the screen again.

Do I have your attention? If this phone isn't up your butt, get down here now!

Cope pocketed the phone and walked out of his eleventh-floor office to the elevator.

"What the hell?" Will greeted Cope as the elevator doors opened on the lobby of CdG's flagship store on Fifth Avenue. "I got us reservations at Bento Hadaka. If we aren't there on time, we'll be shunned." He looked for confirmation from the two men standing with him.

"Let me guess," Cope drawled. "It's the most exclusive restaurant in town."

"Too right!" said Drew Cooper, an Australian import known affectionately as Drooper. "Harder to get into than a nun's knickers. I've been desperate for a rez, but so far, they've not yielded to my manly charms. Welcome back by the way."

"Good to see you too," Cope said as he shook Drew's hand. "How are things Down Under?"

"That sounds like a double entendre," Will said with a laugh.

"Everything sounds like a double entendre to you," Cope said.

"Don't be jealous." Will grinned at Cope before he introduced the fourth member of the party. "This is Thompson Wells—Tom to you—straight out of Hotlanta, Gee Ay. He came on board as my assistant about two weeks after you left. I emailed you about him."

Cope nodded. "I remember. The whiz kid. Good to meet you," he said. He and Tom shook hands, and there were a few moments of silence before Cope spoke again. "Why are we standing around? I thought you were in a hurry."

"Asshole." Will grinned as he punched Cope's shoulder. "If you weren't a fucking genius *and* a world-class fuck, I'd—"

"Come on. Let's go," Drew interrupted. "I worked through lunch, and I could eat the ass end of a dead dingo, no lie."

"Yeah, let's go," Tom said. "I can't wait to see this place."

Will started for the door before Tom finished speaking, leaving the others to follow at their own pace. Tom fell into step with Drew as they crossed the lobby, and Cope strolled along in their wake, unabashedly eavesdropping.

"What did Will mean by that last remark?" Tom asked.

"About Cope being a world-class fuck?"

"Yeah."

Drew shrugged. "He probably means that Cope makes him come like a freight train with no brakes. The way Will tells it makes *me* want to give Cope a root."

"They're gay?" Tom's shock goosed his voice up a half octave.

"Mate, if you have a problem with poofters, let me suggest another line of work."

"I'm not a homophobe," Tom said quickly. "I just haven't been around very many gay people."

"You have now," Drew said. "When it comes to shagging, I'm equal opportunity."

"Good one," Tom said. "But this isn't really my kind of humor."

Cope stopped listening in on the conversation, and a lazy smile dimpled the corners of his lips when his gaze fell on Will, who was striding along as though he owned everything under his feet. As always, Will was impeccably put together, and his tall, long-limbed frame was the perfect rack for his suit. As Cope assessed Will's clothes with an expert's eye, he noticed little touches that showed how much he'd influenced Will's taste since they'd met. The boy Cope had met at freshman orientation would never have worn that shirt with a suit, no matter how well the black turtleneck flattered his fair hair and skin. The pearl-gray jacket was anything but conventional either; it ended at Will's waistline, displaying his toned buttocks and long legs in black silk serge trousers.

"So I'm a great fuck, am I?" Cope said as he caught up with Will at the curb.

"I believe the term I used was 'world-class.'" Will smiled. "Best I've had anyway." He cleared his throat. "Hey, listen, Tom isn't into the whole man-on-man thing."

"What was your first clue?" Cope fell easily back into the teasing, brotherly relationship as though he'd seen Will yesterday, instead of four months ago. "So what's the deal? You usually hire based on the applicant's looks and how quickly they can get on all fours with their cheeks spread. Tom's a looker, but I don't think he meets your second criterion."

"He *is* a good-looking kid, and you know I like the lanky ones." Will winked at Cope. "But he's as straight as the straightest thing you can think of. He's immune to innuendo, and gayness is so far out of his worldview that he assumes any mention of it is meant as a joke."

"That could make for an interesting evening." Cope shook off his jet lag and made up his mind to enjoy the night. "What are you doing later?"

"You." Will laughed at Cope's blank expression. "Isn't that what you were asking?"

"Not really, but I could use a little quality time between the sheets."

"You know I'm happy to get busy with you anytime. I wasn't kidding about you being a great fuck."

"You're not so bad either." Cope gave Will the sideways smile that he knew never failed to jump-start Will's libido.

Though they weren't a couple, they slept together from time to time. What had started out as curiosity in college had become a comfortable habit when each was between lovers. There was no question of them falling in love, but they knew each other's likes and dislikes, and in the bedroom, all trappings and façades were set aside, allowing them to simply be themselves, to take what they needed without strings.

Cope couldn't place a high enough value on the energetic sessions that left him drained, glowing, and content to just *be* for a little while. That didn't happen often in his world, and more and more, he found that what he really craved was peace—not wealth, not success or status, but peace and the time to enjoy it. Lately the words of poems he'd never got around to writing had been beating in his brain like the wings of moths around a lamp. Maybe he'd outgrown his ambition to be a force in the fashion industry. Maybe he should take a long, hard look at his life and ask some tough questions about where he was headed and whether it made him happy. And maybe he was just creating a little drama because this was his thirtieth birthday, the big Three-Oh, a supposed milestone in a person's life.

"What are you brooding about?" Will asked as he poked Cope in the ribs. "The car's here. Get in."

"A limo?" Cope stared at the long shiny car that came to a stop in front of them.

"Thirty is a significant age in a man's life and should not pass without proper notice being taken. Tonight is my present to you. We will celebrate in appropriately Roman style."

"Now I'm scared," Cope said in the joking manner he knew Will was expecting.

"Don't be silly. What's there to be afraid of?"

"The name, for one thing. *Bento Hadaka*? *Naked Lunch Box*? Really?"

Will grinned. "You're going to love it. I know what you like, and you'll love it, trust me. Now get in the damn car. I'm paying by the hour."

Cope smiled at Will's bluster. He climbed into the back of the limo, and the others followed. Will sat next to Cope, while Drew and Tom took seats on either side.

"The restaurant sounds really cool," Tom said. "Atlanta's a big city, but I bet you won't find anything like Bento Hadaka there."

"That Tokyo sales rep who had that luscious antique slubbed silk told me this place does sashimi and all kinds of sushi," Drew said. "He said if I went there I *had* to do the body shots."

"Sounds like we have no choice." Will smirked and nudged Cope.

Cope knew Will was waiting for him to ask, so he did. "So what's so special about this sushi bar anyway?"

"You'll see." Will's eyes gleamed gleefully. He was almost vibrating with happiness, overjoyed at having a chance to give his friend something truly special, and that was one of the reasons Cope loved him so much and indulged his less attractive qualities. "But let's just say, you can take something out of the dream box and add it to the scrapbook."

"I'm in your hands," Cope said. He sat back against the leather upholstery, prepared to enjoy the ride. He idly wondered which dream box wish would come true tonight, but he was content to wait and see.

By six o'clock, the evening staff of the fashionable Bento Hadaka restaurant had arrived to get ready for work. In the employee locker room, two men were talking over the sound of a shower in the background as one dressed and the other undressed.

"Harlooooow?" Daimaru Tanaka crooned as he set his running shoes in the locker. He turned a winning gaze on friend and coworker Masahiro "Call me Harlow" Nakamura, big doe eyes melting under jet-black bangs.

"What?" Harlow asked suspiciously. Whenever Dai gave him the puppy-dog eyes like the little prick-tease from his favorite movie *Carrie*, he tensed a little, wondering what outrageous thing his roommate might ask for. He was pretty sure Dai wasn't going to ask him to humiliate Carrie White at the prom, but you never knew with this guy. "What do you want?"

"We were going to play rock, paper, scissors for the shift tonight. Remember?"

Harlow stopping fussing with his tie and left it draped around his neck. The black silk was the color of his eyes and contrasted sharply with his platinum-blond hair. He paid dearly to touch up the dark roots once a week, but the hair was part of his signature look, and he was convinced that a signature look was essential to an aspiring dance star. He'd only left Tokyo two years ago, but he'd assimilated the local culture so quickly that strangers took him for a native New Yorker. "Why are we even talking about this? It's your turn."

"Come on, Harl. Be a sport."

Harlow narrowed his eyes. "Why do I let you get away with stuff like this? You got to wait tables last night. By rights, I should get my turn tonight. Plus, I'm already dressed."

"I gave you a ride home last night, remember? I asked if we could trade places tonight, and you said we'd play rock, paper, scissors for it."

"I must have been delirious with exhaustion. You give me a ride home every night."

"Yeah, because it's really tiring lying around for hours."

Harlow stuck out his lower lip. "You know it's not the work that tires me. It's the…." His voice trailed off as he searched for the right word.

Dai waited silently for Harlow to start talking again. Idly, he admired Harlow's compact gymnast's body in the crisp white shirt and black trousers. A toned physique was a requirement where they worked, and though neither Harlow nor Dai was planning on making a career of this job, they took pride in looking their best. Being gym partners was just another perk of their friendship.

"It's a strain," Harlow said. "You know?"

Dai nodded his understanding. "Yeah, it *looks* like all we do is just lie there, but it *is* a real strain having all those eyes on you. And the way they talk about you like you're not there."

Harlow nodded. "Sometimes I want to jump up and yell at them to have some common courtesy."

"But you grit your teeth and wait for it to be over."

Harlow nodded again. "Yeah."

Dai put an arm around Harlow and gave him a squeeze. "It won't be for much longer, man. The way you save money, you'll be able to quit soon."

"I hope so. I'm never going to get anywhere if I have to work full-time. I came to New York to dance on Broadway not to literally be furniture."

"I know that, and you'll get there."

"I need to practice, and I need to go to every audition. I need enough money in the bank to pay my bills for at least a year so I can concentrate on getting into a show."

"That's why you should switch places with me tonight. You'll make better tips."

"Let's settle it now." Harlow held up a hand and made a fist.

Dai brought his hand up at the same time, fore and middle fingers extended in a V.

"Ha!" Harlow shouted gleefully. "I win!"

"Fine," Dai said, opening his locker. "I'll just give you my tips."

"Don't be ridiculous. I'm not taking your hard-earned money."

"It's not as hard for me as it is for you." Dai's grin disappeared for a moment as he pulled his shirt over his head. "Honestly, I don't mind it so much."

"Exhibitionist."

Dai's grin reappeared. "I'm not a show-off," he said. "I'm just not as self-conscious as some people."

"Not now, but I remember your first night. You blushed so much the customers thought you were sunburned."

Dai chuckled. "You'd only been here two weeks when I signed on."

"Well, you know, when you've danced naked in front of an audience...." Harlow shrugged.

"Are you considering that stripper job again?"

"Very funny. You know it was an avant-garde ballet."

"I know I enjoyed it, but honestly, any time there are a half-dozen naked men I can stare at, I'm going to enjoy it."

Harlow shook his head. "Even when you're saying something like that, you have this air of... innocence, I guess is the word. You could be giving someone a blow job under the table and still look virginal."

"Yes, but we know differently, don't we?" Dai shucked his underwear and stepped out of them, leaving him completely naked. Even in the wan lighting, his skin glowed like satin draped over sculpted marble.

"You really are gorgeous," Harlow said.

"Come on. You see me naked almost every night. I'd think you'd be bored by now."

"No way. I'm knocked out every time."

Dai threw a towel at Harlow. "Knock it off, you big tease. You always compliment me, but you never do anything about it."

Harlow shrugged. "You're not my type."

"Bullshit," said Kei Ito as he came out of the shower room. "Dai is everyone's type." With a sly smile, Kei sidled up to Dai and nuzzled at his shoulder. "You have skin like a baby's butt," he said. "And you smell like cherry blossoms."

"Cherry blossoms don't have a scent." Dai brushed Kei off. "Quit screwing around. You just got clean."

Kei shrugged. "If I'm not sanitary enough for work, I'll take another shower. Want to join me?"

Dai rolled his eyes. Kei was a hottie, but he was a kid, and Dai wasn't interested in him at all. He wanted someone more sophisticated, which was the main reason he'd taken this job. Bento Hadaka's clientele was mainly wealthy businessmen who were much more refined than the guys Dai was used to. He wasn't a gold digger; he just wanted someone who'd take him somewhere besides arcades and cheap bars, someone whose conversation didn't revolve around the latest pop star or sports champion, someone who wanted a relationship that was more than a series of one-night stands. Maybe it was because he'd just turned twenty-four and being a quarter of a century old made him think about how he was spending his time. He was still young, but he didn't want to waste a single minute he had coming to him.

"Why won't you go out with me?" Kei persisted. "Harlow had no complaints."

"But no repeat performance," Dai retorted.

"Not after I realized Kei was systematically sleeping his way through the staff," Harlow said.

"But I'm doing the hottest ones first," Kei said, completely unrepentant.

"I'm going to take my shower," Dai said, as he walked away. "See you guys up front."

"Come on," Harlow said, pulling Kei away. "Let's get to work."

Kei took one last look at Dai's heart-shaped ass and went with Harlow to get ready for opening time. There was always more side work to do.

"STREWTH!" DREW said as he and his friends entered the restaurant foyer. "This is real class."

"Would I take my friends anywhere that wasn't?" Will asked.

"Well, you know, considering the type of place this is, I thought it might be a little *flashier*," Drew said.

"Why?" Cope asked.

"This is a nantaimori restaurant," Will said.

Tom's eyes bugged out, and surprise made his Southern accent more pronounced. "You mean this is one of those places where you eat off a nekkid lady?"

"You've heard of them?" Drew sounded just as surprised as Tom.

Tom shrugged. "You know how it is when you're researching recreational pornography."

"Indeed I do." Drew patted Tom's shoulder.

"This place is a little different," Will said as he moved around Tom and Drew to speak with the host. A few minutes later, his party was being shown to a private dining room by their waiter. Will smirked as the server rolled back a rice paper screen. "Happy birthday, my friend." He clapped Cope on the shoulder.

Cope grinned. "You devil," he said to Will as the waiter gestured to them to enter the room.

They had to go around Tom, who was frozen in place. Tom was staring at the exceptionally attractive young Asian man lying on his back with food arranged artistically over his smooth body. "That's a guy," Tom said.

"You were right," Cope said to Will. "Tom is really sharp."

Will laughed softly and shook his head.

Drew gave Tom a little shove. "It's called nyotaimori if it's a girl and nantaimori when it's a guy," he said. "Now you've learned something, sit down, mate. You're blocking the view."

"I… I'm not really hungry." Tom took a step back and nearly collided with Will.

"Don't be such a baby." Will squeezed the back of Tom's neck. "Sit."

"But he's completely naked," Tom protested.

"Not *completely*," Cope said. "All the really good bits are covered."

Tom's gaze went to Cope, and it was obvious from his expression that he'd just realized a couple of things. Will had made the reservation at this restaurant to please Cope, which meant that Cope really did like guys *that way*. It wasn't an inside joke at all.

"Are you all right?" Cope asked. "You look a little green."

Will made an impatient noise. "Sit down, Tom. It won't kill you. You know, a *real* man who's secure in his masculinity wouldn't be bothered at all."

Cope left Will to deal with Tom and followed the handsome server to a cushion at the head of the table. He was vacillating between being horrified and delighted by Will's present. On one hand, the idea of eating his dinner off an attractive young man was an exciting prospect, but on the other, he was nervous about getting too excited. He was surprised by the Asian's effect on him, but he couldn't deny the instant attraction; it was too strong to be dismissed. And it was a little disconcerting. Cope's reputation as a killer kick-starter was due in part to his almost unnatural unflappability. Nothing threw him—nothing. He faced undelivered shipments, imminent deadlines, and angry contractors with the same stone calm. He wasn't unfeeling, but he had his emotions under tight control… until now. Cope dragged his gaze away from the delectable buffet as their server spoke.

The waiter said his name was Harlow and politely explained the proper procedure for consuming the food. He pointed out the different types of sushi and sashimi arrayed on the human table, Dai's body, extolling the qualities of each eye-pleasing creation. Bands of dark green nori seaweed sectioned off the offerings, striping Dai's legs and arms, outlining his abs and pectorals, and forming an edible triangle over his crotch. Islands of nigirizushi were artfully arranged within these boundaries: sunset-pink salmon, velvety eel, vermilion pearls of flying fish eggs, tiger shrimp on small beds of pressed rice tied up with ribbons of nori. Dai's nipples were covered by mounds of wasabi paste accented with petals of pickled ginger slices, and pools of soy glistened in his upturned palms.

"Everything looks delicious," Will said in answer to Harlow's inquiring look. "We were told to ask about sake shots."

Harlow mentally rolled his eyes. "Yes, sir. It's possible to drink sake from the table if you wish."

"I wish," Will assured the server.

"I can pour for you, or you may choose to pour for yourself," Harlow said, gesturing to the sake bottle and tiny cups on a tray of inlaid wood.

"I think we can manage on our own," Will said.

"Would sir like me to stay, or shall I return when it's time to make the tea?" Harlow asked. "Of course, I will come back to replace what you eat, but—"

"We'll have a few drinks first while we appreciate the beautiful table setting," Will said.

Harlow bowed and backed out of the room. He glanced at Dai as he closed the screen behind him, but Dai was very professionally staring at the ceiling. Harlow paused for a moment to appreciate the way Dai's dark hair fanned out over the small red silk pillow that supported his neck, the way the deep black lacquer of the table made his skin look like alabaster. If these four businessmen were gay—and Harlow couldn't imagine why they'd choose a male table if they weren't—then they were going to have the best meal of their lives.

"Cope, my friend," Will said as he picked up the stoneware bottle of warmed sake. "You drink first because it's your special day."

"I think I'd rather have a cup," Cope said.

Will gave Cope an incredulous look. "You have to be kidding me." He swept his eyes over Dai's decorated form and met Cope's gaze. "Look at him and tell me you don't want to drink from—"

"You can count me out," Tom said. "I can't believe you guys are doing this."

"It's all in good fun, sport," Drew said. "The latest trend and all that."

"I don't want to know," Tom said. "Like I said, I'm not a homophobe, but what people do in private is their own business and none of mine."

"That's not a bad policy," Will said. "Now let's have a drink to get this party started."

Tom broke etiquette and took a cup from the tray without waiting for Will to offer him one. "You guys do what you want," he said. "Belly buttons are too close to other body parts for me."

"So you're familiar with the technique of body shots," Cope drawled.

Bright red flared in Tom's cheeks, but his tone was unapologetic when he answered. "I've been to clubs where the waitresses did body shots."

"So you've seen it." Will joined in the teasing.

"Yes." Tom refused to be baited further. He held out his cup. "Are you keeping all the sake for yourself?" he asked.

"Maybe," Will answered. "I'm tempted to order another bottle for you guys while I drink all of this one off our table."

"You'll be blind drunk," Drew commented.

"It would be a real shame to be blind in the presence of so much beauty," Cope murmured.

Dai didn't react, but the remark was the corniest and most romantic thing anyone had ever said about him, and the timbre of the speaker's voice was an almost tangible caress. The one called Cope hadn't been speaking directly to Dai, of course; that would be very bad manners. However, Dai knew the words were meant for him. They fell as softly as snowflakes onto fresh snow, but they echoed in Dai's head like the lyrics of a favorite song. A warm glow spread in his chest, and he had a hard time keeping his face composed in a neutral mask.

"Are you ready?" Will asked Cope.

"I think I need a couple of shots to loosen up first," Cope said.

"It's your party," Will said as he poured Cope a drink. "I'm going to have a body shot if you don't mind."

Cope let his eyes rest directly on Dai for more than two seconds. "I envy you, but I'm not as uninhibited as you are."

"Bullshit." Will grinned as he poured a neat puddle of clear liquor into Dai's navel. Placing his lips against Dai's taut belly, Will sucked up the small shot of sake, cleaning up the last drops with a swipe of his tongue.

A shiver ran down Dai's spine and set up a sympathetic vibration in his groin. It wasn't the first time someone had licked his stomach, and he'd thought he was used to it, but a powerful surge of arousal shook his detached demeanor. He'd never had a problem maintaining his equilibrium, but his reaction to Cope's voice and Will's touch was turning into a problem. Clearing his mind of distractions with an effort of will, Dai composed himself again.

"I'll have one of those," Drew said. "With the birthday boy's kind permission."

Cope raised his cup to Drew. "Cheers," he toasted and then downed his second shot.

"Let's do this right," Will said, keeping a firm grip on the bottle. "You drink while I pour."

Drew happily leaned over the table with his mouth near Dai's belly button. Will poured slowly, and Drew did his best to drink all the sake before it ran under Dai's seaweed thong. Abruptly, Drew grabbed Will's wrist and tilted the bottle up. "Enough," he said between chuckles. "Are you trying to get me drunk?"

"You've discovered my evil plan." Will grinned at Drew. "I'm hoping for a three-way with you and Cope."

"Gah," Tom sputtered as he choked on a mouthful of sake. "Come on, man. A joke's a joke, but you're taking it too far."

"No, taking it too far would be asking *you* to join us." Will broke into laughter at the look on Tom's face.

"Now I've lost my appetite for good," Tom said.

"Does that mean you have an appetite for bad?" Cope asked.

Tom stared at Cope for a long moment, and then a wide grin spread slowly over his face. "Good one," he said, saluting Cope with his empty glass.

"Relax," Cope said, letting his voice drop into a lower gear that was like hot fudge poured over pure gold nuggets. "We're just having fun."

Dai tried to ignore the effect of Cope's bedroom voice and concentrated on the humor of the situation, but it turned out to be a mistake. He had a lot of practice in keeping still and not reacting to the customers, but these guys were testing him to his limits. If this kept up, Dai was afraid he was going to burst out laughing at the teasing Tom was enduring. A second later, all fear of breaking into giggles was driven from his head.

Drew poured a shot for Will, and Will's lips grazed Dai's abs on their way down to Dai's navel. Heat bloomed at Dai's core as Will's mouth moved on his skin, sucking and licking at the warm sake as it ran down Dai's lower belly. When Drew finally stopped pouring, Will came up with a strip of nori between his teeth. Dai was certain he'd get hard if this kept up. *Where the hell was Harlow?* The server was supposed to keep things from getting out of hand. They weren't quite there yet, but they were definitely headed in that direction.

Cope bumped Will with his shoulder and held out his cup. "How about saving a little for me?" "Sorry." Will smiled as he wiped his mouth. "I think we need another bottle."

"I think you're taking advantage of the...." Cope paused. "Table? I'm not sure what to call him."

"You're not supposed to call him anything," Drew interrupted. "He's furniture."

"Damn, I wish I could get one for my apartment," Will said, making Drew and Cope chuckle. "Come on, Cope, I think there's just enough left to pour you a shot."

Cope knew that tone in Will's voice. It would be easier to go through the embarrassment of drinking sake off a gorgeous guy's stomach than to argue with Will in this mood. "Sure," he said. "My birthday only comes once a year. I might as well go all out."

"That's what I like to hear," Will said. "Ready?"

Cope's shoulder was pressed against Will's side as Will held the bottle over Dai's stomach again. Taking a deep breath, Cope leaned in, and Will dribbled some sake over the satiny skin of Dai's drumhead belly. When Cope hesitated, Will took hold of his friend's ponytail and pushed his head down. Cope gulped sake out of necessity to keep it from going up his nose and felt Dai's muscles contract in response. It was simultaneously one of the most uncomfortable and arousing moments of his life. Jamming an elbow backward into Will's midsection, Cope convinced him to let go of his hair. He started to raise his head, but before he did, he pressed his tongue once against Dai's smooth skin.

"Will, you just don't know when to stop," Cope said as he straightened up.

"Thank you," Will said. "Ready for another?"

"I think we might have already crossed a line," Cope said. "Just because our… table isn't allowed to react doesn't mean we should take advantage. Why don't we have something to eat?"

"I know what I'd like," Will said, "and it's right under here." He touched his chopsticks to the seaweed draped over Dai's crotch.

"Seriously," Cope said. "I think you're being a little too bold."

"It's his middle name," Tom said and looked surprised when everyone laughed.

"I can't argue," Will said, looking up as the screen slid aside. "Good. Here's the waiter. We need another bottle of sake."

"No, we don't," Cope said. "We're going to eat now."

"Shall I make the tea?" Harlow glanced discreetly at Dai to make sure everything was all right. Aside from a piece of nori missing from the modesty covering, all was as it should be. Sometimes these groups of self-assured young businessmen could turn into snickering little boys with the application of alcohol. He'd had to put the brakes on at least two parties since he'd started working here. The shine of wetness from the sake shots went rather low on Dai's groin, but Dai didn't seem to be in any distress.

"Thank you. Tea would be very nice," Cope answered before Will could.

"Is everything all right so far?" Harlow asked as he set about making the tea.

"Couldn't be better," Will said. "Unless I could get our table's phone number."

"I'm sorry, sir," Harlow said. "That's not on the menu."

"I had to try." Will plucked a rice cake topped with shark off Dai's upper thigh. He teased a dab of wasabi from Dai's chest, tweaking Dai's nipple with his chopsticks.

Dai's cock stirred under the cool patch of nori, and he sincerely hoped no one noticed, but he didn't see how they could miss it.

Will nudged Cope and tilted his head toward Dai's crotch. "I think the table likes us," he whispered. "They're trained to stay still as statues, but I knew I could get him to react."

Cope glanced down, and two patches of red appeared high on his cheekbones. Again, his feelings were divided between arousal and embarrassment. In an attempt to distract Will from his game, Cope lifted a tiny octopus from between Dai's collarbones and brought it to Will's lips. "Try this," he said.

Will opened his mouth and took the eight-armed treat from Cope's chopsticks. He chewed and swallowed, nodding in approval. "That's good. Wonder what they pickled it with. It has a really different taste."

Cope relaxed again. He could usually count on distracting Will with food, but their table was hard to ignore. Cope had never seen anyone so beautiful, and before he got a grip on himself again, he wondered if the young man's personality matched his looks.

"Thank you," Cope said as the waiter set a cup of tea in front of him.

"Is there anything else I can get for you?" Harlow asked. "Would you like me to bring another selection of nigirizushi? Or perhaps some sashimi?"

"No, the food is fine." Cope smiled. "We just haven't got around to eating much yet."

Harlow bowed and moved on.

"It's the table's fault," Will said. "The setting is so beautiful that it seems a shame to ruin the design by eating it."

"We take great pride in our décor," Harlow said. "I will pass your compliment along to the appropriate people."

"I'm hoping to give my compliments to the table personally," Will said.

Cope touched Will's forearm. "Have some tea," he said. "The flavor is very delicate."

Will turned to Cope. "I know you're being a good friend and trying to keep me from embarrassing myself, but you can't tell me you don't find this man attractive."

"Of course I do," Cope said, "but I don't feel it's fair to him to discuss his looks as though he really was a piece of furniture."

"It's his job," Drew said as he chose a cake of rice that formed a nest for a quail egg.

Tom looked up as Harlow served his tea. "Would it be too rude to ask you a personal question?"

"I'll do my best to answer, sir," Harlow said.

"Do you just do a waiter's work or do you also… act as a table?"

"The staff rotates between serving and serving as a human sushi tray."

"Why would a man—even a gay man—do this job?" When Harlow didn't answer right away, Tom continued. "I'm just trying to understand. To me, this is very close to being a stripper. After all, you take your clothes off for money, right?"

"I can only speak for myself," Harlow said, keeping his voice neutral. "It's my ambition to be a professional dancer, and I'm trying to earn enough money to take a year off so I can practice and audition. I've worked as a server in ordinary restaurants, but it would take me a week to make the amount of money I make in a night here. I hope that satisfies your curiosity, sir."

Tom nodded. "Thanks for explaining."

Harlow nodded politely as he left the dining room.

"Could you try and be a little less insulting?" Will asked Tom.

"I didn't mean to insult anyone. I really wanted to know what would make a man take a job where people eat food off his naked body."

"I could have answered that question for you," Will said. "They do it for the money. Why else do people work?"

"Not everyone," Cope contradicted gently. "Some people work because they love what they do. Not all work is just a job. I know you're familiar with the idea of a vocation."

Drew nodded. "Like artists and singers."

"Not only performers," Cope said. "What about doctors and nurses? Or teachers."

"All right," Will said. "You've made your point. Maybe our table's great ambition is to provide a graceful setting for vinegar rice and raw fish."

Cope sighed. "I think it's more likely that he took this job for the same reason as our waiter."

"He wants to be a dancer?" Drew said.

"While I don't see anything shameful in this job, I doubt this is his goal in life."

Will plucked another blob of wasabi from Dai's nipple. "Maybe not, but he's really good at it. Can we talk about something else now? Where would you like to go after dinner?"

The talk turned to nightclubs, interspersed with compliments for the food, and Dai began to relax. His half a hard-on had subsided and his heartbeat had slowed down. He was able now to take the long steady breaths that kept his chest movement to a minimum. As he listened to the four men making plans for the rest of the night, he wished he could join them, even though he knew that was an utter fantasy. He'd lie here until they were gone, and Harlow would come to help him clean up. At least it was his last booking, since this party had reserved him for a full two hours. He could take a shower and wait for Harlow to get off work, maybe share a bottle of wine with him and talk about their dreams. He had managed to get himself back into the tranquil state that allowed him to ignore the brush of chopsticks, and of course, that's when Harlow returned.

Deftly, Harlow replaced the food that had been consumed and refreshed the tea. Instead of leaving, he took up a station near the tea-making table in case the diners had requests. In his experience, once the customers got over the novelty of eating off a human body, they settled down and enjoyed the meal at a normal pace. At this stage their hunger was satisfied, and they were merely nibbling at the delicacies. The presence of a server no longer felt intrusive, and Harlow had several small tricks designed to keep things moving along in case the guests showed an inclination to linger. No one else had a reservation for this dining room, but Harlow had his way of doing things, and he stuck to his routine.

When Harlow judged the time was right, he went around the table with the teapot and offered dessert. As he expected, there were no takers for the sweets he mentioned. To judge from their physiques, the men in this group exercised frequently and took care what they put in their bodies. He approved of their fitness and considered that every man needed to indulge in a wild night every now and then. All in all, he'd call the evening a success, which held an importance for him that Dai often scoffed at. Dai took pride in his work but not to the extent that Harlow did. Maybe it was because Harlow was raised in Japan, and Dai had lived in the US all his life. Whatever the reason, Harlow took his job no less seriously than a brain surgeon.

"I suppose it's nearly that time," Will said as he turned to Harlow. "Would you prepare the bill, please?"

"I don't want to go," Drew said. "But I couldn't eat another bite."

"Me either," said Tom.

"That's the first time I've heard you say you were full," Will marveled.

"I didn't say I was full," Tom told him. "I said I couldn't eat another bite. The only food left is too close to his… you know… his privates."

Will grinned. "I have to hand it to you. You endured it like a man."

"I just hope you aren't taking me to one of those clubs with male strippers," Tom answered as Harlow presented Will with the bill.

Will ignored all offers to help with the payment and handed Harlow his credit card. "You can all leave a cash tip," he said. "But this is my present to Cope."

Harlow left and returned with four jackets. His eyes bulged a bit at the amount of money the men had piled on their placemats. As a team, he and Dai usually commanded large tips, but this was twice as much as the biggest gratuity they had ever received. It was almost equal to the price of the entire meal. There was no way he was letting Dai give him all of it.

"Thank you very much," Harlow said as he gave Will his card back. "I'll hang your jackets just over there. Please sit for as long as you like, and I hope you will visit again."

"You can count on it." Will winked. "What nights do you become a table?"

"You can request me anytime, sir." Harlow bowed. "Ask for Masahiro Nakamura ."

"I'll look forward to it," Will said before looking around at his friends. "Who's ready to go clubbing? Which one did we decide on?"

"We didn't, mate," Drew said. "We narrowed it down to Best's and Black Velvet, but we never chose one."

Will turned to Cope. "Which would you prefer?"

"You know, the whole time I was in Milan, I really missed Wild Ginger."

"We can't take Tom there."

"Oh what the hell," Tom spoke up. "If I can make it through a dinner with a naked man spread out in front of me, I think I can take whatever you throw at me."

"You're taking all the fun out of Will's teasing," Cope told him. "Good for you."

Will smacked the back of Cope's head. Cope smacked Will back, catching him completely off guard. Will lurched in his chair and sprayed green tea across Dai's abdomen. Dai flinched before regaining his composure. Without thinking, Cope began blotting the wetness away with his napkin.

"If you ever get tired of the fashion industry, you could get a job here cleaning up," Will said.

Drew grinned. "I'd be happy to do the washing up if all the dishes look like this one."

"Shit! I'm surrounded." Tom stood up. "Let's go before the three of you make complete fools of yourselves."

"You're only right, son," Drew said good-naturedly. He picked up one of the blossoms from the black lacquered table and placed it in the center of Dai's chest. "Cheers!"

Not to be outdone, Will chose a white lily and tucked it into the top of the seaweed triangle that covered Dai's crotch. "I've eaten in fine restaurants all over the world, and I can honestly say I've never enjoyed a meal as much as I've enjoyed this one," he said with mock-solemnity.

Cope hesitated and then picked up a spray of tiny white flowers. Sliding it into Dai's hair, he ran his fingertips over the delicate blossoms in lieu of stroking the fall of dark silk as he wished to. He didn't say a word as he rose from his cushion and moved toward the door.

Tom dithered for a few seconds before he took up a bright yellow flower and tossed it toward Dai. The bloom landed on Dai's thigh and slid down to the table. "I hope that isn't bad luck or anything," Tom said.

"I don't think so," Will replied. "But I'll bet you'll think twice before inviting yourself to one of my dinner parties again."

Tom bowed to Will. "I've learned my lesson, boss. Now let's go."

Amid a flurry of remarks that were half insult, half joke, the four men put their jackets on and left the dining room. Harlow was waiting at the end of the short corridor to escort them to the front and wish them a good evening as the host held the door for them. As soon as they were on the sidewalk, Harlow bustled back to check on Dai.

"Are they gone?" Dai asked as Harlow came in.

"The last I saw, they were getting into a limo and talking about going to Wild Ginger."

"Expensive night out," Dai said as he sat up.

Harlow tilted his head to the side. "The flowers in your hair are pretty."

Dai reached up and pulled the spray from behind his ear. Gently, he stirred the ivory bells of the small flowers with his forefinger. "Maybe I should wear them every time I table."

"Good idea. Ready for your shower?" Harlow asked as he plucked the uneaten food from Dai's lap and the tabletop.

"Yeah. It was a long dinner."

"Really? I would've thought you'd enjoy being surrounded by four good-looking guys."

"They were fun, but…." Dai sighed as he got off the table.

"But what? You can't leave me hanging like that."

"I had a boner."

"You're kidding!" Harlow almost dropped the teapot.

"They were all hot and a couple of them were… let's just say they were my type."

"No kidding," Harlow said wryly. "It couldn't have been the tall skinny one. He's as straight as they come or I'll turn in my het-detector. Out of the other three, I can see you going for the one that oozed alpha male essence like sweat."

"Which one?"

"Are you kidding?" Harlow frowned. "The one who paid. The one in charge. Who else?"

"How could you miss the one with the smoky voice and bedroom eyes? He was quieter but definitely all man. He made my toes curl when he talked."

"He didn't say much when I was in the room." Harlow handed Dai a wet wipe to wash off the wasabi and the soy. "He *was* sexy, though. You didn't get to see him walking, but he moves like a panther on the prowl." He paused. "A poker-faced panther," he revised.

"I can picture that," Dai said as he peeled away the seaweed strips.

Harlow took a folded robe from under the tea table and tossed it to Dai. "So he's one of the two you thought were worthy. Who was the other one?"

"You're right about the other one. When he touched me, I thought I was going to lose it."

"Oh yeah. I can see that." Harlow nodded. "He was kind of arrogant, but I'll forgive him because he was so insanely hot—like a prince posing as a commoner."

"Very poetic of you." Dai's expression was wistful as he tied the sash of the robe. "Why can't I meet guys like that when I'm not dressed as a buffet?"

"You will." Harlow patted his friend's shoulder. "If that's what you want."

Dai sighed. "I don't want to be alone."

"You're not alone. You have friends."

"Yeah, but I want someone just for me, you know?"

"I know." Harlow patted Dai's shoulder again. "You'll find him."

"You'll be on Broadway by then."

"I could do without the sarcasm."

"I wasn't being sarcastic!" Dai protested. "I was being serious. You're a really great dancer. You were born to dance. Who *knows* what I was born for?"

"You were born to be loved." Harlow hugged Dai and then pulled away. "Come on. Let's get cleaned up and cut out early. I'll buy you a drink."

Dai gathered the tips into a pile and threw the bills in the air like autumn leaves. "Bullshit. The drinks are on me." He paused and grinned. "*Literally.*"

"That would be hilarious… if you didn't make the same joke every time," Harlow said. "Now go take your shower."

"Hang on." Dai divided up the money and held out half to Harlow. "I know you won't take all of it, but you'll take half, right?"

"There was a tip for me on the bill."

"Yeah, but this is cash. Take it. Come on," Dai coaxed. "You can use it to buy me drinks."

Harlow took the bills, folded them, and put them in his pocket. "All right, but just this once. Now go. Get clean and put on some clothes. I'll meet you in the locker room."

"Okay." Dai smiled over his shoulder as he left. "Our luck is going to be good from now on; I can feel it."

Harlow smiled back and kept his doubts to himself. He hadn't been joking about Dai's air of innocence, and he didn't want anything or anyone to break Dai's heart. He was realistic enough to know Dai was bound to get disappointed by someone or something eventually, but he hoped it happened when Dai was a little older and a whole lot wiser. Harlow couldn't see the future, but he knew one thing for certain. Luck played a part in making dreams come true; however so did hard work. He wasn't sure Dai understood that yet.

"TAKE THE car," Will said as the limo stopped at the curb outside his apartment building.

"I don't need it," Cope answered. "I can easily walk the three blocks to my place. I've done it a thousand times."

"It's paid for," Will said dismissively as he climbed out of the car. "Enjoy it."

"Well… I am a little drunk."

"Ha! We were drunk off our asses by the time we left the second club. Seriously, I'd feel better if you let the limo take you home."

"Fine." Cope gave an exaggerated put-upon sigh. "For you, I'll do it."

"Damn right, you will." Will put his hands in his pockets and tilted his head back to look up at the stars. "Man, what a gorgeous night."

"It was rather spectacular." Cope smiled. "Thanks for the birthday present."

"My pleasure." Will smiled back and pulled Cope out of the car. Wrapping his arms around Cope's lithe frame, Will hugged him fiercely. "I don't say it much, but you know I love you, right?"

"Yeah." Cope swallowed hard, feeling the prickle of salt water on his eyelids as tears formed. "Love you too, maniac."

"Hey, if you want to come up…?" Will let the question dangle.

"I'm too drunk to be any good, but I appreciate the offer."

Will let go of Cope and stepped back. "That guy was really something, wasn't he?"

Cope didn't pretend he didn't know who Will was talking about. "Beautiful," he said. "I started thinking that I might like to know him better."

"No shit." Will slapped Cope's cheek lightly. "Why didn't you go for it?"

"Ah, you know, the situation was awkward, and he probably gets hit on every night. It was just too cheesy."

"Whatever. See you tomorrow, stud."

"Not if I see you first," Cope answered as he slid back into the car.

Will laughed as he shut the door and stepped back from the curb. Cope gave the driver his address, and the limo pulled away from the curb. His head spinning with alcohol and visions of making love on an edible bed, he sat back against the leather upholstery and spun a few naughty dreams for the duration of the ride.

CHAPTER TWO

COPE WOKE, gave thanks for the lack of a hangover, and got out of bed. Not only did he *not* have a hangover, there was no trace of jet lag either. He felt fantastic and not just physically. Everywhere he looked, his eye fell on some familiar object that was now imbued with ineffable beauty and profound meaning. Instead of analyzing it, he went with the flow, the way he did when he was a high school poet, before he got on this track to success.

Cope showered and dressed with markedly less pomp and ceremony than usual, eager to be on the move for no discernible reason. By quarter to eight, he was in the elevator to the eleventh floor, and in three more minutes, he was seated behind his desk. Beyond the floor-to-ceiling window opposite him, New York was the shining El Dorado of legend, its spires gleaming in the sun. Still gazing at the splendid view, he picked up his Conway Stewart fountain pen with his left hand and pulled open the stationery drawer with his right. His fingers touched bare wood and broke his trance.

Cope looked down and saw he was out of stationery. Obviously no one had thought to replace it while he was in Milan, and he hadn't needed it until now. Somehow a notepad wouldn't do for what he wanted to write.

Still holding the pen—another gift from Will—he went into the hall. There was a supplies closet behind the reception desk. On the other hand, Will's office was right next door. Cope didn't hesitate to enter Will's space and borrow three sheets of the creamy paper CdG so generously provided to employees at this level. It didn't matter that Will's name and title were on the stationery. He'd cross it out of the letterhead with a few flourishes and sign his name at the bottom—problem solved.

Cope sat back down at his desk, pictured the man who'd served as his table last night, and put pen to paper. When he was satisfied with the words he'd written, he set the sheet aside, called his favorite florist, and placed an order before he could talk himself out of the impulsive extravagance. He wrote a note for Sophie, their shared executive secretary, and picked up the piece of stationery. He read the words once more before he picked up his pen to sign the sheet. Before he could do that, his phone chimed.

"Hey, Will. What's up?" he said when he answered.

"Come to my office?"

"Sure. Give me five?"

"Make it two."

"Okay, drama llama. Sheesh." Cope hung up, put the letters in envelopes, and wrote a quick note for Sophie in case the messenger showed up while he was with Will. In exactly two minutes, he opened the door to Will's office.

"Do you ever knock? What if I was choking the weasel?"

"I'm always hoping to catch you at it." Cope shut the door and repeated Will's final words as a question. "Choking the weasel?"

"I'm running out of colorful ways to say masturbating. What do you think of that one?"

"Um... weasel? I don't know. It's kind of a negative connotation."

"You got a better one?"

"Buff the banana?"

Will was silent for a moment before he answered. "You know, that's not bad."

"Badger the witness?"

"Yeah, that's good too."

"Liquidate the inventory?"

"All right. Enough. I get it. You know more ways to say jerking off than I do."

"True, but I'm almost sure that's not why you called me in."

"Coffee?"

"I'll get it." Cope poured himself a cup from the Krups machine on the table behind Will's desk. "Need yours warmed up?"

"No, thanks. Hey, you've always wanted to go to Hong Kong, right?"

Cope sat down. "Am I going to Hong Kong?"

"You can say no. You just got back from Italy, for Christ's sake."

"It's fine."

"This is Drooper's fault. He talked you up to a buyer who knows some big-money guys who want to finance construction of a high-end casual couture store. They want you to give them an informal presentation of your methods."

"Not a problem. The timing could be better, but I'm assuming this is going to be a short trip."

"Couple of days, tops."

"I guess I'll go on home and pack."

"Sophie will send the flight and hotel details to your phone." Will stood and pulled Cope into a hug. "Have a safe journey."

"Will do, and when I get back, see if you can get reservations at that nantaimori place again."

Will grinned. "My pleasure." Cope picked up his workbag and laptop from his office and went directly home. As promised, Sophie sent his electronic tickets and hotel reservation information before he actually got inside his apartment. In less than an hour, he was on his way to the airport in a Lincoln Town Car with his minimal luggage on the seat beside him. As usual when he traveled, he felt the curious sensation of entering a sort of limbo. For the duration of the flight, things would effectively be out of his hands. He accepted this, and instead of cramming in as many calls as he could before boarding, he used the time to relax.

Two hours later, pleasantly buzzed on premium vodka from the Sky Lounge, he boarded his flight. As the nose of the jet tilted up and he felt the familiar lurch in the pit of his stomach, he was visited by a vision of a gorgeous man with eyes and hair as black as ink. He kissed the vision goodbye for now. That dream would have to wait just a little while longer.

"DAI!" HARLOW was hanging out the back door of the restaurant when Dai pulled up on his scooter. "Park that Day-Glo piece of shit and get in here."

"What's going on?" Dai asked as he lifted the shocking pink scooter—who would steal something that color?—onto its stand and walked to the door.

"You're not going to believe it. Look!" Harlow said, his voice bubbling with delight. "Come and look. The staff has been gossiping for hours."

"About what?"

Harlow grabbed Dai by the upper arm and hustled him into the employee lounge. Dai stopped in his tracks and stared at the biggest flower arrangement he'd ever seen. It was standing on the floor because it wouldn't fit on any of the horizontal surfaces without touching the ceiling.

"Where did this come from?" he asked. He inhaled deeply, enjoying the mingled fragrance of roses, lily of the valley, and hyacinth.

"Look at the card." Harlow was all but bouncing.

Dai took the small envelope from the bouquet. He opened it and stared at the piece of pasteboard with a stunned expression. "It's my name."

"Yeah. They're for you."

"What? Why? Who?"

"Read the back of the card."

Dai turned the card over. *From your sincere admirer.* "I'm overwhelmed."

"You should be, but that's still not everything." Harlow dragged Dai across the room. "This is for you too."

Dai took the rolled sheet of stationery Harlow handed him and untied the red silk ribbon. After a moment, he realized the two handwritten lines on the creamy paper formed a poem.

Your dark hair against your skin like shadows on the snow.
Has brushed my soul with ink that will never fade.

"This—" Dai swallowed as the words caught in his throat. He turned the paper over. "There's no signature."

"Let me see." Harlow grabbed the paper, his eyes scanning the words. "Wow. I'd die if someone wrote something like that to me. We have to find out who he is. We know the company from the letterhead, but the name's been scratched out. There could be thousands of people working there."

"Hang on," Dai said. He took a pencil from the apron hanging on a hook behind him. "I hate to do this, but I have to know."

"What are you going to do?"

Dai held the sheet sideways to the light, and a smile dimpled his cheeks. "This sheet was under another paper that he signed." He put the stationery flat on a table, held the pencil parallel to the paper, and rubbed the lead across a small area at the bottom. As he worked, a ghost signature appeared. After a few minutes of peering at it, Dai and Harlow deduced that the sender's name was William. Not exactly an uncommon name, but they also knew where he worked from the letterhead. If they wanted to track him down, it shouldn't be too hard.

"The guy who paid for dinner last night was named William. You remember. The blond alpha male."

"You think he sent me the poem and flowers?"

"So it would seem. What are you going to do now?" Harlow asked.

"I'm going to thank him, of course."

"Lucky William."

Dai smiled a trifle smugly and went to get ready for work.

CHAPTER THREE

DAI PAID the driver and got out of the cab in Manhattan. Half a block down was the building that housed the offices of Collezione di Gio. On the ground floor was a boutique version of the standard CdG store model. Dai looked in the display windows for a few minutes to admire the clothes that were cut on classic lines enhanced by touches of whimsy. He particularly liked a white dinner jacket printed with larger-than-life poppies.

"May I direct you, sir?" asked the uniformed man at the door.

Dai smiled at the doorman and gave him the name from the credit card receipt. "I'm here to see William Donnelly."

"Please come in. You'll find reception on your right."

Dai walked into the lobby and glanced around. A bank of four elevators with brushed aluminum doors were set into a wall of black marble trimmed with malachite. Directly ahead was an atrium with the company's logo displayed above a miniature waterfall that fed a miniature rainforest. The air in the lobby was pleasantly cool and had a green smell. So far, so good. Like Harlow said, what did he have to lose? *Besides my self-respect?* Dai shook his head. It wouldn't be the first time he had looked foolish in pursuit of romance.

"Good morning, sir," said the young man who was one of three employees behind the reception counter. "I'm Kevin. How may I help you today?"

"I'm here to see Will Donnelly."

"Just one moment, please." Kevin glanced down at a screen, and Dai heard him typing. "I don't have any appointments listed for Mr. Donnelly."

"I don't have an appointment, but I'd like to see him, if possible."

"I'm sorry, sir, but CdG executives don't see people without an appointment."

"Could you maybe call him?"

Kevin smiled. He had a nice smile. "I could call my supervisor and ask her to ask someone to call Mr. Donnelly. I assume this is important?"

"It is to me."

Kevin leaned toward Dai. "If you're trying to get on as a model, you don't want Mr. Donnelly. He's in charge of the acquisitions department. I could call up to personnel for you."

"Wow, that's really nice of you, but I came here to see Mr. Donnelly specifically."

"I wish I could help." Kevin's rueful smile looked genuine. "Sorry."

"It's not your fault. Anyway, it's person—"

"Excuse me," said the man waiting behind Dai. "If you've finished your business, would you mind stepping aside?" He gave Dai's black jeans and white button-down shirt a scornful glance. "I'm late for a meeting with a client."

"Sorry." Dai turned back to Kevin. "Thanks."

"My pleasure, and now it's time for my break." Kevin gave Dai a brilliant smile and walked away from the counter.

Dai walked in the opposite direction, ignoring the muttering of the rude man as he passed by him. It wasn't until he was back on the sidewalk that it occurred to him he should have found out how to make an appointment. "Dumbass," he whispered fiercely and drew a sharp look from the doorman. He moved a little farther down the block and pretended to look at the gleaming wares in the window of the Bulgari store. He had just formulated a vague plan of hanging around the area in case Will Donnelly came out for lunch when someone stopped beside him.

"Strike me pink! It's the table," said Drew Cooper.

Dai recognized the man's accent immediately. The butter-yellow curls were familiar as well. "You had dinner at Bento Hadaka a couple of nights ago."

"Believe me, mate, I hadn't forgotten." Drew gave Dai a warm smile.

"I'm trying to get in touch with Will Donnelly. Can you help me?"

"That I can, but I'm not sure I should."

"Why not?"

Drew chuckled. "Just a poor attempt at humor." He took out his phone. "Wait a tick," he said as he touched the screen. "Yeah, it's me, mate. I'm standing here with someone who wants to meet you." He gave Dai the side-eye and a smile that was little more than a reflex. "Does the word *furniture* mean anything to you?" He chuckled again. "I thought it might. Tallyho." Drew put his phone back in his pocket. "He'll be right down," he told Dai. "We only have a few minutes, so if you wouldn't mind satisfying my curiosity—why Will?"

"I came to thank him for the flowers." Dai didn't mention the poem. It was personal.

"He sent flowers?" Drew laughed. "The sly bugger."

"I wanted to say thank you, but he didn't include his number. I had to track him down."

"Will has a stalker." Another laugh from Drew. "He'll be bragging about this for donkey's years." He glanced at the building. "He should be here any mo. I'd like to stay and watch, but I can't be late for another meeting. It was a pleasure to see you again."

"Thanks for your help," Dai said, but Drew had already turned away. Dai barely had time to run his hands through his thick black hair before he saw Will come out of the door.

Will saw Dai at the same time and smiled as he came toward him. "Nice to see you again," he said, holding out his hand as he reached Dai. "William Donnelly. My friends call me Will."

Dai smiled. "I'm Daimaru Tanaka. My friends call me Dai."

"Does that mean something in Japanese?"

"I've heard different things from my elders. One granny says my name means someone who struggles. If you take it apart, *maru* means circle and *dai* means… it's kind of hard to explain. Mom always told me I was named after Daimaru department stores."

Will grinned. "This is great. We're getting to know each other better already."

"I just wanted to—"

"Have you had lunch?" Will started walking, pulling Dai along with him like a wood chip in a stream. "There's a great place just a couple of blocks away. Whatever you want to say to me will sound even better over some good food."

Dai followed breathlessly until Will ducked into the Stage Door Deli. The place was packed, but the old-school New Yorker at the door found them a tiny table in the back left corner. They were right in front of the restrooms, but beggars couldn't be choosers. The waitress looked like she was barely on the sunny side of one hundred and sounded like she smoked a couple of cartons a day. Will quickly ordered a Reuben and a stout. Dai dithered for a few seconds before the waitress's glare prompted him to order the same.

"So," Will said when the waitress had gone. "What did you want to see me about? Not that it matters. I'm just happy to be sitting across from the prettiest man in the Big Apple."

"Thank you," Dai said. "And thank you for the flowers."

Will hesitated for just a second before he spoke, choosing his words carefully. "Did you like them?"

"They're beautiful! I love them."

"Then you're welcome." Will grinned as he blithely took credit for someone else's gesture.

"I also wanted—"

"Here you go!" The waitress set down two beer bottles and two chilled glasses. "Your food will be right out."

"Thanks," Will said as he picked up his glass and bottle.

Dai watched Will pour the dark beer down the side of the glass and imitated him. He was impressed at the lack of foam. "This is good," he said after taking a drink. "Never had it before."

"It's from a local boutique brewery. Goes great with corned beef."

"I don't drink a lot of beer… or eat a lot of sandwiches."

"I hear you." Will patted his flat abdomen. "Gotta keep the girlish figure." He chuckled. "Especially in your line of work, right?" He chuckled again. "Be embarrassing if the food rolled off you, I bet."

"Yeah, that would be frowned on."

The waitress returned and put their plates in front of them. "Pay on your way out," she said and hustled off like someone a third her age.

Will took a huge bite, chewed, and swallowed. "That hits the spot," he said.

"It's good," Dai agreed. "I'm not sure I can eat the entire sandwich, though."

"Eat what you want and take the rest home. It's on me."

"You don't have to buy me lunch."

"I invited you."

"All the same, I'll pay for mine."

"Okay, if you won't let me buy you lunch, how about dinner?"

"I'm working."

"Right." Will took another bite and chewed it while he thought. "Are you at all interested in going on a date with me? It's just that I'd hate to waste my time if you weren't interested."

"I'm interested, but I really am working tonight."

"How late? I know lots of places that stay open all night. Or would you be too tired?"

Dai hesitated. *What would Harlow do?* "All right," he said. "I can be ready by ten thirty."

"Yeah?"

"Yeah." The smile on Will's face reassured Dai he'd made the right decision. Lunch was no time for discussing romantic matters. That kind of talk would go down much better around midnight with a few glasses of good wine under his belt. He was intensely interested in getting to know the man who'd written that poem, and a few hours' sleep was a small thing to sacrifice. "Where should I meet you?"

"Are you kidding? I'll pick you up. It's not like I don't know where you work."

Dai thought Will's smile edged close to a smirk, but maybe it was just a trick of the way Will's lips curled at the corners. So Will was a little cocky. So what? "That *was* a pretty strange way to meet," he said.

"You think so?" Will drained his beer and picked up the check. "As far as I'm concerned, I lucked out. There's no chance you're a pig in a blanket." He laughed at the expression on Dai's face and then sobered instantly. "That was a stupid thing to say. I'm a little nervous, and when I get nervous, I make bad jokes."

"No harm done," Dai said not quite truthfully.

"I hope this isn't going to be a problem, but it's not possible for me to forget that I've seen you naked. You have to know what an amazing body you have."

"I got lucky in the genetic lottery. My dad is tall for a Japanese man, almost six feet. My mom is half Japanese, one-quarter Caucasian, one-quarter black. She's, like, five eleven."

"So they're about the same height?"

"Yeah." Dai chuckled. "That's true. Don't know why I didn't say that instead of giving you ancestry dot com." He took the check out of Will's hand. "I've got this."

"I'll leave a tip." If there was one thing Will knew, it was when to capitulate to a client. Not that he thought of Dai as a client exactly, but he *was* trying to woo him. Will's antennae were at full extension, and he was already picking up on Dai's body language. There was a good reason why his ringtone was the eighties hit "Hungry Like the Wolf." Will knew more than one thing about seduction; it was a skill that got him promoted to the top of his division at the age of twenty-nine.

"Meet you on the sidewalk," Dai said as he headed for the cashier. He glanced at the bill and gave a mental shrug. It wasn't expensive, but it was more than he'd planned to spend today. He had intended to eat the leftover pad thai in the fridge, but that couldn't be helped. Most likely it was in Harlow's belly by now anyway. After he paid, he decided he'd let Will buy dinner after all.

"Thanks for lunch," Will said when Dai joined him. "I'd love to hang out awhile, but duty calls and all that."

"I understand. I'll meet you in front of the restaurant at ten thirty."

"Be prepared to have a good time."

"Always." Dai gave Will a self-deprecating little grin.

Will stretched out his hand as though snatching something from the air. "I'd like to keep that smile until I see you again," he said.

Dai's return smile indicated he was properly charmed. "See you tonight," he said.

Will pretended to tuck Dai's smile into his pocket before he walked away. Dai watched him for a few seconds and then went to the corner to hail a cab. And that used up the last of his mad money for the week. But he wasn't going to regret it. Though Will had struck one or two false notes during lunch, he was attractive and personable, not to mention sexy, and he was definitely interested. It was just a first date. What could go wrong?

"SO WHERE have you been, and why wasn't I invited?" Harlow asked as soon as Dai entered their below-ground-floor apartment. The landlord referred to it as a garden apartment. Dai and Harlow referred to it as the dungeon… jokingly, of course. It was tiny—two rooms with a kitchenette and closet-sized bathroom—but they got along well and the rent was fair. The bedroom was Dai's because he'd found the place and leased it. Harlow slept on the futon in the living room area, but he had the use of Dai's bed for sexual purposes as long as he sought permission beforehand and washed the sheets afterward… immediately afterward. This was a roommate rule never to be broken since its inception in the aftermath of the devastating Whose Goo? incident of the winter of last year.

"I had some errands to run."

"Dressed like that?" Harlow scoffed. "You look like you're interviewing for a job as a waiter at a high-end nightclub."

"Tell me you're just fucking with me. Do I really look like that?"

"Why do you care? You were just doing some errands."

"Forget it." Dai went into the kitchen area and opened the refrigerator. As he'd suspected, the pad thai had disappeared. "Want water?" he asked.

"No thanks." Harlow turned on the couch to watch Dai. "What were you really doing?"

"I told you." Dai took a long drink from a bottle of water.

"I know what you told me, but I don't believe you. Your skin is all pink like you've been drinking. Since when do you drink in the middle of the day?"

"Are you going to keep picking at me until I tell you?"

"Of course."

"I met Will Donnelly."

"Shut *up*! The stud who sent the flowers?"

"We had lunch. With beers."

"This sounds serious."

"Shut *up*!" Dai mimicked Harlow. "Don't make a big deal of this, okay? We're going on a date tonight."

Harlow bounced off the futon. "That's fantastic!" he crowed.

"We'll see." Dai smiled. "But I have hopes."

Harlow hugged his friend. "That's great," he said. "But do you have anything worth wearing on a date with this heavy hitter?"

Dai squeezed Harlow before letting him go. "How is it you've only been in the US for two years but you talk like a native?"

"Because I hang around with you too much. You've completely corrupted the English I learned in school. Now, let's get serious. What are you wearing on this date?"

"He's picking me up after work, so I guess I'll wear whatever I wear to work."

"You'll wear the jeans you have on. They make your ass look like two cantaloupe halves under a tablecloth."

"That's the nicest thing you've ever said to me. What shirt do you think I should wear? I'm not saying I'll wear it; I'm just curious."

"Only one choice." Harlow pulled out the drawer under the futon where he kept his folded clothes. He took a rose-pink T-shirt and tossed it to Dai. "My beloved baby tee. The color is perfect for your skin tone, it fits like a second skin, and you've got the body for it. But the clincher is that it's as soft as it looks. It's almost impossible to resist stroking it."

Dai stopped stroking the fabric. "You have a point," he said. "But am I trying to seduce him?"

"Life is seduction."

"I thought life was pain?" Dai threw out a *Princess Bride* reference.

"True, but I am in fact trying to sell you something." Harlow grinned when Dai broke into laughter. "And I bet Prince Charming Will wants to sell you something too."

"So, you're saying sex tonight is inevitable?"

"Well, you have been going through a dry spell."

"It hasn't been that long." Dai absently petted the T-shirt. "Has it?"

"It's been long enough. Just shoot me a text if you bring him home, and I'll clear out."

"To where?"

"There's always Kei's *standing* invitation."

"I can actually hear the innuendo in your voice. I think you're the one who needs to get laid."

"He's a hound, but he's good in the sack."

"He's a kid."

"He's got skills."

"He's… a… kid," Dai repeated.

"You're only twenty-four."

"He's only twenty. There's a big difference."

Harlow cackled. "Keep telling yourself that."

"You sure you don't want to wear this shirt?" Dai held it out.

Harlow shook his head. "Don't need it. Kei's a sure thing." He covered a yawn. "Did you eat? Oh, wait, you said you had lunch with Mr. Wonderful. Good, because I ate your leftovers."

"I knew you would."

Harlow continued as though Dai hadn't spoken. "And after work you're going out for what will undoubtedly be a fabulous night on the town, while I will be eating Doritos out of the bag in Kei's room while we guzzle beer and watch that cartoon porn he likes."

"Stop. You're making me jealous."

"Eat me."

"Would that be fair to Kei? What if he's looking forward to some Harlow crème filling for dessert?"

Harlow snorted. "I'm authentic Nihonjin, not the watered-down American version. I can produce sperm at will."

"Who's this Will you speak of? Better not be my Will."

"Lame," Harlow pronounced.

"Are you quoting Will Arnett in *Blades of Glory*? Or are you just calling me lame? Because one would be kind of clever, but the other one is just dickish."

"First of all, it was Will *Ferrell*'s character who called Will Arnett's character lame. Second, I wish I could say it was intentional, but I really was just calling you lame because you were being lame at the time."

"I'm glad we got that straightened out. What do you want to do until it's time to go to work?"

"I kind of want to watch *Blades of Glory*."

Dai made a face. "I'm not in the mood for Will Ferrell."

"Bullshit. Since when?"

"If you really want to watch it, go ahead."

"Why would I do that when I can spend the time compulsively searching the listings for something that catches my interest enough to watch it instead of clicking *add to watchlist*?"

"You're cute when you pout. I'll make some popcorn. You pick a movie." Dai put a bag in the microwave and waited while he listened to the sounds of Harlow sampling movie trailers. When Dai came back to the futon with the big bowl of popcorn, he saw Harlow had chosen *Trading Places* with Eddie Murphy and Dan Aykroyd. "Change your mind?" he asked.

Harlow grabbed a fistful of popcorn. "I haven't seen this one in a while. But if you don't want to see it, how about *Dirty Rotten Scoundrels* or *Roxanne*?"

"You know I'll watch anything with Steve Martin in it, but this is good. Hit Play."

"Are you sure you want to waste two hours? We could go to the gym or jog or something."

"You should've said that before. We have popcorn now."

"True." Harlow pressed Play, and he and Dai spent a restful afternoon laughing at some great comic actors until it was time to get ready for work.

AT NINE thirty, Drew stuck his head in Will's office door. "Burnin' the midnight oil?" he called out.

"Come on in," Will beckoned without taking his eyes off his laptop screen. "You gotta see this."

Drew came around the desk and leaned in over Will's shoulder.

"Jee-zuss!" Will exclaimed. "Easy on the cologne next time, big guy."

"Too much?"

"You smell like you fell into a vat of whatever it is you're wearing."

"Mate, my new girlfriend gave it to me. She likes it."

"It's more likely she's trying to keep other girls away from you. That is foul."

"Fuck you, Donnelly."

"Not until you wash off a gallon of that jungle juice."

"Get stuffed. What am I supposed to be looking at?" Drew squinted at the screen. His contacts were dry and blurry, and his eye drops were in his desk down the hall. He blinked several times, and the image swam into focus. "Strewth!" he exclaimed in surprise. It wasn't as though he and Will had never shared porn with each other, but this was the first time he recognized one of the participants. "Is that our table?"

Will shook his head. "Sadly, no, but he looks a lot like him, doesn't he?" He clicked the mouse and the image moved. On the screen, a bearded blond muscleman pinned a buff young Asian man to some sort of faux-fur rug. Hot Asian Guy feigned a struggle, but he was being paid to fuck, not win an Academy Award. After a few seconds of obligatory tussling, Viking Dude had Hot Asian Guy's legs in the air and was thrusting like he meant it. "With elegant simplicity, it's called *Viking Fucks Samurai*. What do you think, Drooper?"

Drew licked his lips. "He really looks like the kid from the restaurant." He reached down and adjusted himself. "I shouldn't keep Toni waiting."

"This is hot stuff, though, right?"

"No doubt." Drew lingered for another moment. "What are you doing tonight?"

"I have a date too."

Drew bugged his eyes. "Are you pullin' me leg? Never tell me you're going out with the sushi bar, you lucky bugger!"

"Come on. You knew I had to at least *try* to bag him. He's def, as they said in my grandad's day."

"They're saying that again, you know."

"No, I didn't know." Will shrugged. "Whatever the word is, he's got it all. He's beautiful from his head to his feet and sexy as hell. Plus, he's got that thing, you know?"

"What thing?"

"He talks and acts like an American, but he looks so... exotic. Those eyes...."

"I think someone has a fetish."

"You don't think he's sexy?"

Drew heard the warning in his boss's voice and dropped the taunting tone. "Yeah, he's sex on toast, no doubt. What about those lips?"

"Are you picturing what I'm picturing?"

"What else would I be picturing? But that's just a fantasy. You're going out with the real deal."

"That I am, my boy."

Drew rolled his eyes. "So, are you going for it, as if I didn't know?"

"I was born going for it."

"Ha-ha." Drew paused. "So are you?"

"Yes, if you must know, I'll be accepting your standard wager."

"I'll need proof."

Will shook his head. "You'll take my word that I made sweet love to sweet, sweet Dai."

Drew growled. "You don't want me to have any fun at all. I should go." He went to the door. "See you Monday, sport. Hey, did you pull that routine where you pretend to catch his smile and save it for later?"

"You know I did. Custom-made for guys like Dai. I keep telling you; try some romance."

"Not my style. I'm off."

After Drew left, Will shut down his laptop and straightened his desk. He went into his private bathroom and looked in the mirror. Deciding his hair was fetchingly tousled rather than simply unkempt, he straightened his pearl-lavender tie as methodically as he'd cleared his desktop. As he was slipping into a navy shantung jacket, reception in the lobby rang to let him know his car was waiting. Will smiled at his reflection in the mirror beside the door. Everything was on schedule. He just had to make sure Dai delivered.

CHAPTER FOUR

"Scram," Dai said again. He loved Harlow, but he didn't want him hanging around when Will showed up.

"The sidewalk is public property," Harlow said again.

"Please take my scooter and go home."

Harlow shook his head. "No way. I'll get out of sight when he shows up, but I want to see his entrance."

"Just don't embarrass me."

"Have I ever?" Harlow said with overstated sincerity.

"Yes, you have, but that was a good *Buckaroo Banzai* quote. You get points for that."

"It *was* good, wasn't it? I've been waiting for an oppor—" Harlow stopped talking as something down the block caught his interest. "Nice. That's the latest-model Maserati sedan. Supposed to be incredibly comfy."

"I think you're going to get a closer look," Dai said as the sleek black car pulled over to the curb.

The driver got out and walked around the car. He opened the rear passenger door, and Will got out.

"Hi," Dai said. "I hear that's a really comfy car."

"As a matter of fact, it is. Why don't you get in and find out for yourself?"

Dai looked around, but Harlow must have ducked behind one of the big wooden pillars that held up the covered entryway. "Sounds like fun," he said.

"I hope we're not going to argue about money tonight," Will said when he sat next to Dai on the back seat. "I asked you out, so I'll be paying."

Dai nodded. "That's acceptable to me."

"I went ahead and made some reservations, but if you don't like them, we can go somewhere else."

"Where are we going?"

"Assuming you'd be hungry after working all night, I got a table at this tapas place that does amazing cold plates. The chef is from

Barcelona. After that, I thought we'd go to Wild Ginger. It's a nightclub I hang out at sometimes."

"I've heard of it."

"So… acceptable?"

"Absolutely."

"Outstanding. Would you like a drink?"

Dai looked around. It was a big car but not as big as a limousine, and he didn't see a bar anywhere. "What are you offering?"

"The car company provides a basket of goodies with the rental."

"Oh good! I was afraid this was your car."

"Afraid? That's an odd choice of words." Will looked up from rummaging in the basket.

"I was judging you. Not in a bad way," Dai said quickly. "I was feeling a little overwhelmed that you could afford a car like this."

"I probably could, but why bother when the corporation leases this one?" Will looked down at the basket again. "Aha! I can offer you tiny bottles of assorted liquors and tiny cans of mixers. Vodka, tequila, gin, whiskey, rum, and scotch. Coke, ginger ale, OJ, spicy V-8—"

"Is there any water?"

"Sparkling or still?"

"Either. I'm parched."

Will handed Dai a chilled can of club soda and then mixed himself a scotch and soda. If Drooper was here, he'd call Will out for desecrating scotch by diluting it, but Drooper wasn't here and besides, it was hardly what you'd call a "fine" scotch. "Here's to the evening," he said before he took a sip.

"To the evening." Dai toasted with his can of club soda. He was going to relax and enjoy whatever the night brought. As Harlow was fond of saying, at least he was getting dinner and maybe some dancing, and if he was lucky, he might get lucky. But Dai wasn't Harlow, and he'd had enough one-night stands. If he was moved to sleep with Will, that was one thing, but he wasn't going to give it up automatically. "I feel underdressed," he said, just to be saying something.

"Are you kidding? You look fantastic." Will toasted Dai. "I can barely resist stroking that shirt. Do you mind?"

"I guess not."

"Am I being too bold?" Will smiled. "It's in my blood. My ancestry is British and Russian. One of my great-great-grandparents fled to

England during the Russian Revolution. There's a family saying passed down from that time. 'You don't ask, you don't get.'"

"It's all right if you touch the fabric."

Will ran a hand over Dai's shoulder and down his sleeve. "That's nice," he said. "I was going to guess silk cotton blend, but it feels more like bamboo."

"I have no idea."

"Do you mind?" Will gestured to the back of his shirt collar. "Hazard of working in the rag trade."

"No, go ahead and look." Dai leaned forward. He felt Will's fingers on his nape, and warmth spread from the point of contact. The back of the collar was lifted away from his neck, and he felt Will's breath as he leaned in.

"Bamboo," Will said triumphantly before he sat back in his seat.

"So, I guess you know your fabrics," Dai said.

"Boring, right? Do you like to dance?"

"Yeah. Harlow and I go out dancing sometimes. It's fun and it's great exercise."

"It's not the only thing that's good for burning calories." Will smirked.

"True, but I'm not going jogging with you tonight," Dai said, ignoring the implied meaning of Will's remark.

Will laughed. "Dancing it is."

The driver pulled into a parking lot and got out to open the door for Will and Dai. He got back in the car, put his earbuds in, and settled back to wait. Will and Dai walked around the corner to a two-story restaurant called *Sabore*.

The hostess showed Will and Dai to a small table with a view of the Avenue of the Americas and took their drink order. They had barely settled in before a waiter arrived with a bottle of tempranillo. He poured two glasses of the red wine, made food suggestions, and pronounced their selections excellent. After he bustled away, Will picked up his glass and held it out.

"Another toast to a good evening," he said.

Dai touched his glass to Will's and took a sip. "I haven't had this wine before. It's nice."

"A little dry," Will said. "But it will be perfect with the food."

Dai smiled. So far Will was fulfilling all the requirements on Dai's Perfect Man list. Will was tall, handsome, ambitious, and refined. Dai had yet to see the poetic side that had touched him, but then again, maybe he was embarrassed to show his softer side. When they knew each other a little better, Dai figured Will would open up and let him see the soul that had created the lovely little poem. Meanwhile, Dai was enjoying some very good wine in a really nice restaurant. He should feel underdressed in his black jeans and pink T-shirt, but he didn't. The way Will looked at him, he might as well be wearing Prada.

"I hope you don't mind me asking," Will said, "but how did you get into your line of work?"

"It's not a very interesting story. After high school, my parents wanted me to go to college. I took a few classes, but honestly, I was tired of school. I dropped out after three months, but I was still living on campus to save money. It was this big conspiracy in the dorm to keep admin from figuring out I was still there."

"Cloak-and-dagger," Will joked, twirling a pretend mustache.

"I picked up a little money modeling for the art department, but it was nowhere near enough to live on." Dai smiled. "That's when I met Harlow."

"Who's Harlow?" Will asked.

Before Dai could answer, the waiter returned and served platters heaped with sliced meats, various types of cheeses from waxy to runny, mounds of shelled nuts, and elegant little ramekins with fig preserves, hot mustard, and fresh horseradish. The waiter made a little production of slicing a pear and fanning out the pieces. After sprinkling the slices with bleu cheese, he set the plate in the middle of the table. He poured more wine, asked if he could bring anything else, and then glided away. There was silence for a few moments as they sampled some of the charcuterie.

"You were telling me about Harlow," Will prompted.

Dai swallowed a bite of goat cheese drizzled with crystallized honey. "You met him, sort of. He was your server at Hadaka."

"How could I forget him? What a hottie. But what's with the bleached hair?"

Dai shrugged. "It makes him different. He wants to be on Broadway… but you know that because he talked about it when your friend asked him why he worked at Hadaka."

"Right." Will scrambled for something neutral to say because he truly didn't remember the waiter mentioning Broadway. "He's got the looks for it."

"No kidding. And he's a great dancer, plus he can sing."

"How'd you meet?" Bored, Will steered the conversation to the past, which was usually safer. After a few minutes, he'd be able to steer the conversation back to himself or sex. Either would suit Will.

"At a party on campus. He was invited by someone in the theater department. He'd only been in America a few months, but he already had the lingo down pat. I've never seen someone work so hard to fit in. Anyway, he approached me because he could see I'm at least part Japanese, and we hit it off. When the subject of me needing a job came up, as it always did back then, he told me about the restaurant where he worked. The next day, I was working there."

"How's the pay?"

"I feel adequately compensated." Dai gave Will an impish smile. "And the tips are good."

"You should never have to worry about money," Will said. "Not with a face like that."

"You'll make me blush."

"Is that a challenge?"

"Of course not. This is a date, not a boxing match."

"Sometimes it's hard to tell the difference, though it's more like fencing, really."

"I don't feel that way about it." Dai took a sip of wine to stop his tongue. His mother had never allowed disagreements at the table. She said it was bad for the digestion.

Will was a little jarred by Dai's statement, which came close to ruining his fantasy. It didn't fit with his preconceived image of Daimaru Tanaka, which was half-geisha/half-anime prince, and based on nothing more than Dai's looks. "How's your dinner?" he asked.

"Fantastic!" Dai was relieved to have something positive to say. "This is easily the best prosciutto I've ever tasted."

"I love how thin they get it." Will held up a nearly transparent slice. "Melts in your mouth." He gave Dai his patented naughty schoolboy grin. "Like me."

Dai chuckled. He was expecting the risqué double entendres. He and Will might be gay, but they were still guys, and guys had a tendency to become snickering fourth-graders from time to time. "We might have to test that theory," he answered in kind.

"I'll be your lab rat anytime."

"Hm, let's see how you dance first. Harlow says you can tell how good a guy is in the sack by the way he dances."

"Anytime you're ready." Will held up a hand to call for the check. "We can be at Wild Ginger in ten minutes."

As soon as they got into the Maserati, Dai took his phone out. "Sorry. I need to text Harlow. It'll only take a minute."

"No problem. Hey, why don't you ask him if he wants to come to the club?"

"Because I don't need the competition."

Will laughed. "Seriously, though, if—"

Dai looked up from texting. "It's really sweet of you to think of him, but Harlow's busy tonight," he said. He looked back down at the phone. "And this is a first date."

"I like to think our lunch at the deli was our first date."

"I have no objections to that, but I don't want a third wheel on *this* date, okay?"

"Absolutely." Will grinned. "But can you blame a guy for trying for a three-way?"

Dai hit Send and gave Will his full attention. "I'm not big on blame, or guilt, or shame. I don't have any right to judge."

"Really? That's pretty remarkable, actually."

"If you say so. Wow, look at the line!" Dai gazed past Will's shoulder at the line of people on the sidewalk outside Wild Ginger. "It's all the way around the block."

"I've got this," Will said, and he wasn't wrong.

His cachet and a one-hundred-dollar tip got them past the velvet rope at Wild Ginger a little after midnight. The dance floor was packed with all manner of glitterati, from young professionals gyrating earnestly in Ralph Lauren suits to bare-chested young men in bicycle shorts and heavy makeup. It was exactly the way Dai had pictured it: a mélange of color and sound and the almost palpable humidity of sex. When Will put a hand on the small of Dai's back to steer him effortlessly through the crowd, Dai decided his dry spell was over—perhaps not permanently, but tonight, at least, it was going to rain.

WILL MOVED as well in bed as he did on the dance floor, Dai decided. The past half hour was a blur of tangoing foreplay: hungry kisses and gentle groping in the back of a moving car, deep kisses and stealthy caresses in the elevator, and being pinned against this foyer wall for kisses that strayed ever lower and fondling that didn't stop at clothing. Dai couldn't remember when he'd been this turned on, if ever. It was a heady feeling to be so desired and desiring.

"Are you as turned on as I am?" Will asked, his lips moving on Dai's ear.

"Shut up and fuck me."

Will took Dai's mouth again, running his tongue along the seam of Dai's lips. His tongue flirted with Dai's, licking and twining, as they tasted each other. He groaned into Dai's mouth when Dai's hand slid under his briefs and grasped his bare cock. Quickly, he unzipped and shoved trousers and underwear down his thighs.

"Better," Dai breathed as he felt Will's hands working at his jeans, and then Will pushed his trousers and underwear to his ankles. Cool air caressed his bare ass and crotch for a second before Will pressed against him again. Dai reached around to squeeze Will's toned ass as Will pulsed his hips, rubbing their dicks together, stoking the fire.

"You ready for more?"

Instead of answering, Dai turned, put his hands against the flocked wallpaper, and spread his feet. He was more than ready. He didn't think Will would mind the blatant hint that he preferred to bottom, and all his instincts told him he was right.

"Perfect," Will said under his breath as he ran his hands over Dai's sculpted cheeks. "Hold that thought."

Dai waited impatiently, hand on his cock, as Will made rummaging noises behind him. "Come on," he said. "I don't mind spit."

"Shhh. Just getting into my raincoat." Will shushed Dai as he gently kicked Dai's feet farther apart.

Will put an arm around Dai's waist and took hold of his hard-on. Dai shivered when Will ran a slippery finger around his hole. Will squeezed Dai's cock, pumping his hand on the hard flesh as he teased Dai's opening with his fingertip. Dai pushed back against the prodding and took Will's finger to the second knuckle. Will eagerly took the hint, applied more lube, and slid his finger into Dai. Aroused even further by the small sounds Dai made, Will shunted his finger in and out, rubbing at the walls of Dai's sheath as he stretched it.

"Ah fuck yeah," Dai gasped. "Come on. Come on. Fuck me."

"Not yet."

Will applied more lube and eased two fingers into Dai. Dai mewled and drew his fingernails down the wall as he was penetrated. Will shuttled his hand on Dai's cock while he used his curled fingers to stroke Dai's prostate.

"Fuck! I'm on fire," Dai said in a strained voice.

"Cum for me." Will twisted his fingers inside Dai and thumbed precum from the head of Dai's dick. "Cum for me, baby." He stroked to a faster tempo and was rewarded by Dai's cry of completion. "Good baby," Will whispered.

Dai sagged a little as the powerful orgasm lifted him up and held him helpless while the tide of bliss rolled through him. He had one coherent thought—*Why can't they all be like this?*—and then Will's supporting arm tightened around his waist. He felt the head of Will's latex-sheathed cock at his opening.

Sensitive flesh puckered as Will applied pressure, and then the tip popped through. The ring of muscle tightened just behind the head of Will's dick, and he groaned in reaction as he thrust. Half his length slid into Dai, and he gripped Dai's flanks with both hands as though restraining himself from another thrust. He looked on his most treasured fantasy made flesh, and a surge of arousal urged him to take what he wanted. This beautiful, submissive boy was waiting for him to claim his prize. It was a scenario he'd jerked off to too many times to count.

Will drew back to the brink and then filled Dai's sheath in a smooth, gliding stroke. He shifted his weight, tickling Dai's ass with his bush, balls slapping lightly against Dai's inner thigh. He wanted this so badly, he thought he might explode. It had too much power over him, he decided. He needed to know how long he could wait for it.

Dai gasped softly and whined low in his throat as Will pulled out. Will slotted his hard-on in Dai's crack and reached around for Dai's lolling dick. He pushed Dai's T-shirt up to his neck and nuzzled his back as he stroked him. Dai whimpered and moved his hips suggestively as Will coaxed his hard-on back to life.

Will was disappointed that it took only a few seconds of Dai's ass rubbing against his cock to make a mockery of his test. Taking hold of his dick at the root, he thrust into Dai again, his breath catching at the exquisite feel of heat and pressure. No more holding back. Will kept hold of Dai's cock and slid his other hand up to cradle Dai's neck. Rolling his hips, he rocked into Dai in powerful strokes.

Dai braced his hands and met Will's stroke with solid resistance. He could feel another orgasm coiling at his core and hoped he survived it. He could hear himself moaning and whimpering, and he didn't care. All he cared about at this moment was the skillful, passionate way Will's long cock filled him and the way Will's long fingers were wringing another release from him. The world outside this melting bubble of fire and ecstasy might as well not exist. He was lost in the blessed oblivion of all-consuming sex.

Despite the air-conditioning, a drop of sweat fell from Will's chin to Dai's back. Will licked a cool stripe up Dai's spine and slid his free hand around to pluck at Dai's nipples. He nipped and sucked at the skin of Dai's back, never slacking the rhythm of his hand or cock. Abruptly, Dai gave a strangled little cry and spilled a small amount of cum into Will's fist.

"You beauty," Will breathed as Dai shuddered through his orgasm.

Will wrapped an arm tightly around Dai's middle and thrust into him. The soft slap of flesh on flesh filled the small space as Will rode out Dai's release and stoked his own. He was nearly undone by the rhythmic contractions of Dai's sheath, but he held on a bit longer. He didn't want this fever dream to end just yet.

"Turn around," he said.

As Dai turned, kicking his jeans and underwear away, Will swept the brass bowl off the foyer table. He kissed Dai as he lifted him onto the table and pulled Dai's legs to his shoulders. Quickly, he thrust back into Dai's enthralling tight, wet heat and churned his hips. Each stroke slammed the table against the wall and rattled the mirror.

"Oh God, man, I'm coming apart," Dai gasped out.

An electric thrill zinged down Will's spine. He thrust a final time, and his release unspooled deep inside Dai. He clutched at Dai's thighs, kissing the insides of Dai's knees, as his heartbeat calmed and his breathing returned to normal. He looked down into Dai's dewy, satisfied gaze, and his cock pulsed in its snug burrow. Dai made a soft sound, and Will's dick stirred again.

Will shook his head in bemused wonderment. "Well, whaddaya know about that?" he said.

"Where am I?" Dai asked weakly.

Will chuckled. "Could be the middle of next week for all I know. Goddamn, that was good."

"Tell me something I don't know." Dai grunted when Will shifted his weight.

"Sorry. Hang on." Gently, Will disengaged and lowered Dai's feet to the floor. "You all right?" he asked as he removed his condom.

"Huh?" Dai gave Will a dazed look. "All right? I'm great. I'm better than great. I've never felt this good before in my life."

"You're a little scrambled, aren't you?" Will smiled indulgently. After Will pulled up his trousers and got rid of the rubber, he led Dai to the bedroom. "Bathroom's there," he said.

Dai quickly cleaned off the cum and lube and returned to the bedroom. Will was undressed and lying down. He gestured for Dai to join him. Dai pulled the T-shirt over his head and got into bed.

"Seriously," Will said. "I wasn't too rough, was I?"

"You're cute." Dai kissed Will.

"I couldn't help myself."

"I get it." Dai kissed Will again. "Neither could I. No one's ever got me so hot so fast."

"Really?"

"No lie. I'm boneless."

"Same here. You lit me up like a shuttle launch." Will smiled as he kissed Dai. "I hope you don't mind, but I'm not much of a bottom."

"No problem. I'm not much of a top."

Will grinned happily. "I'd like to do this again."

"Now?"

Will chuckled. "I'm not sure that's possible." He lifted the sheet. "But then again…."

"Are you kidding? You can't possibly be hard."

"Hang on. I'm thinking about how your skin turns pink when you cum."

Dai put a hand on Will's crotch.

"And there it is!" Will crowed. He surged up from the mattress and covered Dai's body with his. "Round two?"

"I don't believe this." Dai grinned as he raised his arms and legs, making a cradle of his body.

"Hang on." Will reached over and snagged a condom from the night table. After he rolled it on, he seated his rod, leaned in, and filled Dai's channel like a log sinking into quicksand. "How can anything feel this good?"

"Years of practice," Dai groaned, but Will didn't appreciate the *Ferris Bueller* reference. No big deal. What Will was currently doing with his dick made up for any number of flaws.

"Practice makes perfect," Will said. "Not that I think we need any."

"Let's keep doing it anyway." Dai bit at his bottom lip as the head of Will's cock bumped against his prostate.

Will brought his cock across the same spot at a different angle and smiled smugly when Dai squirmed against the sheets. It was a long time before they got any sleep.

COPE GAZED at the harbor from his seat on his host's luxury "junk." The craft outwardly resembled the working boats that plied these waters, but it was much bigger, and the interior rivaled any yacht for the sheer richness of the furnishings. All the fabrics were manufactured in plants owned by his host's father. For the entire time since Cope had landed in Hong Kong and was whisked to the harbor, he'd been wooed as though he was a wealthy heiress with big boobs and three months to live.

"Ah, there you are," said Tommy Chong as he walked onto the deck.

Immediately after greeting Cope at the airport, Tommy had announced he was well aware that he had an American namesake who was a comedian, and yes, he'd seen the movies. Cope had been both taken aback and relieved that he didn't have to wonder about it.

"Thanks," Cope said as he took the iced drink Tommy offered. It was mostly rum mixed with a mélange of fruit juices, pineapple coming on strong. Cope shrugged; it was a cold liquid, and that was good enough for him right now.

"Cheers," Tommy said before he took a sip of his drink. "Are you having a good time?"

"Your hospitality is excellent."

"Good, good. My father will be pleased."

"When will I be speaking with Mr. Chong Senior?"

"Not until Monday, I am afraid."

"I have a flight out of Hong Kong tomorrow evening."

"I am happy to change it for you—at our expense, of course."

"I'm terribly sorry to tell you that my schedule won't allow me to stay another day." This wasn't strictly, or even loosely, true. What was true was that Cope hadn't been able to stop thinking about Daimaru

Tanaka. It now seemed like a mistake to have sent the extravagant flower arrangement and the romantic poem. It was too much. He grew certain he had frightened Dai off. After years of exercising tight control, he'd picked now to be impulsive. Cope sighed.

"Please reconsider. This meeting is very important to us."

"You have my respect, but I also understand your father. He's old-school, learned everything about business at his grandfather's knee. A real gangster, that one." Cope nodded in response to Tommy's surprised expression. "Yes, I did some research on your family, and I understand that your father is pulling a classic power play on me. Normally I would make allowances, but the timing is bad. Perhaps we can talk again in the future."

"I will do my best to convince Father to see you tomorrow."

"Before 6:00 p.m."

"*Shi!*" Tommy agreed with a sharp nod of his head.

Cope took another sip of the drink that now seemed sickly sweet. He didn't like resorting to his own power check, but he was uncharacteristically impatient. It wasn't the first time he'd been homesick, but it was the first time he'd used his authority to bring a client to heel because of it. However, the fact was that Cope couldn't wait to get back to New York. Whenever he thought about getting home and finding out what Dai thought of the poem, he felt a fluttering in his heart, a stirring as of a thousand tiny wings, a dizzying mix of anticipation and anxiety. It was putting him off-balance, and he wasn't sure if he liked it or not. He needed to know, one way or the other, just what it presaged.

"GOOD MORNING." Will sat down on the side of the bed. "I let you sleep as long as I could, but I have to leave for work soon."

Dai pushed the sheet down and stretched. "Okay," he said and yawned in the middle of the word. "Do I have time for a shower?"

"A quick one. Sorry about kicking you out, but—"

"No explanation necessary." Dai got out of bed. "I'll be fast. Lightning."

"A shame. Wish I had time to join you."

"Didn't you tell me you were in charge of your department? Who's going to bitch if you're late?"

Will smiled. "You're dangerous, Daimaru Tanaka."

"I don't know about that, but I do know I'd like a little more of that sizzling sex we had last night."

"It *was* good, wasn't it?"

"Good?"

Will chuckled. "You're right. Good isn't the word for it. How about volcanic?"

Dai smiled over his shoulder as he walked into the bathroom. He turned on the shower and got under the hot spray. His smile got bigger when he heard Will come in.

FORTY MINUTES later, Will and Dai walked out of Will's apartment building together. Will put Dai in a cab and then walked the eight blocks to CdG. The first thing he did was call Drew and inform him that he needed to pay up on the bet. Only then did he look at his calendar for the day before diving into his emails.

A knock at the door startled Will. He had no appointments, and Sophie hadn't pinged him to let him know anyone wanted to see him.

"It's Drooper," Drew called through the door.

"Come in."

Drew walked to the desk, took a hundred-dollar bill from his clip, and handed it to Will. "Now that the formalities are out of the way, I need details."

Will sat back in his chair, and Drew leaned against the desk. "First, let me say that Daimaru Tanaka not only looks like a dream, but he fucks like one too."

"Go on."

"It was like living a fantasy."

"That's pretty vague."

Will smirked. "You're right, but instead of me describing it to you, wouldn't you rather watch?"

"Of course, but you said—"

"I'm not going to let you hide in the closet like this is some lame teenage rom-com. However, I did make a recording."

"You dog!" Drew said admiringly.

"It's just for my personal use, but the next time we have dinner, I'll let you see a few minutes."

"I'm free tonight."

"I'm not. Cool your jets. Anything good is worth waiting for."

"What a cocktease!"

Will shook his head. "Not me. I always deliver."

"So you do, mate." Drew went to the door. "Let me know when you *are* free," he said before he left.

AFTER A three-hour wait in one of the plushest rooms Cope had ever seen, Mr. Chong Sr. sent a courier with his regrets. Tommy was all abject apologies; Cope was cool but unrelenting.

"I can't control Father," Tommy burst out in an uncharacteristic display of emotion.

"I knew that, actually." Cope hit Send and closed his laptop to give Tommy his full attention. "I just sent you a document. Deny it if you like, but I know that you have the power to sign the contract, and I have the lawyers to make it stick. Put your electronic signature on it, and we're in business, or you can decline and remain under your father's thumb." He stood. "I don't mind at all that you've made me wait around when you had power of attorney all along, but I do mind that you thought I wouldn't be conscientious enough to catch you at your game." He went to the door. "Tell your father that he needs to adopt more modern methods and that he'll be paying for one more day at my hotel. I feel the need for a good massage and detox. I hope I'll hear from you soon."

Tommy replied, but Cope didn't hear him. Cope was halfway down the hall to the elevator. He was serious about the detox and made an appointment with the hotel spa as soon as he returned to his room. Buying the deluxe package ensured the spa would fit him in on short notice, and he was soon relaxing in an herbal bath while looking forward to the sauna. After some aromatherapy and a deep tissue massage that verged on torture, he sipped buckwheat tea in a dim, quiet room designed to let the mind relax along with the body.

Cope closed his eyes, but his brain insisted on focusing on textures. The terrycloth robe. The thin rim of the porcelain cup and the silky feel of the tea on his tongue. The slight breeze from the air-conditioning that caressed his face. Behind his eyelids, he saw a vision of Daimaru Tanaka, naked and perfect, arms open wide to welcome him home.

Cope opened his eyes. Clearly, he wasn't going to be able to forget Daimaru, and if that was the case, he should start moving forward instead of sitting in neutral. He finished his tea, got dressed, and went to speak to the concierge.

Cope was shown to the hotel's business center and the materials he requested were provided. He sat down at one of the cubicle desks with a sheet of fine stationery in front of him. After a few seconds of tapping his bottom lip with the pen, he began to write.

Though I'm far away,
I walk under the same sun
That shines down on you

Cope read it once and then took it to the concierge. He was assured that his message would be delivered with a live Boston fern as quickly as possible to the address he provided. The concierge explained that the poem would be scanned and sent to a florist in New York. Cope paid for the express service, thanked the man lavishly for the care he'd received from the hotel staff, and went back to his room to order dinner in. He still couldn't quite bring himself to commit to a courtship from a distance, but sending the poem took the pressure off until he could talk to Dai in person.

CHAPTER FIVE

AT TEN thirty New York City time, the morning after Dai and Will's third date, Dai and Harlow were awakened by the doorbell. Harlow answered the door, took the enormous potted fern and the card, yawned in the deliveryman's face, and shut the door. He promptly set the plant down and went back to the futon.

"Harlow?" Dai called softly from the door to his room.

Harlow opened his eyes. "Yeah?"

"What's with the humungous plant?"

"A guy brought it." Harlow slapped at the sheet. "Here." He held up an envelope. "It's probably for you."

Dai opened the envelope and took out the folded paper.

"Read it somewhere else, please. The crinkling is way too loud."

"Sure." Dai went into his room and closed the door gently behind him. He turned on the lamp and sat down on the bed. After reading the three brief lines, he lay back down and stared dreamily at the ceiling. So that's how Will wanted to play it—keeping his softer side a secret. That was all right. Dai was willing to put in the time to earn Will's trust. Under the cocky, self-absorbed façade was a vulnerable soul who yearned for things money could not buy. Dai was willing to give him those things to show him he didn't have to be afraid of showing his true self.

Dai slipped his phone into his sweatpants' pocket, went to the kitchen area, and made coffee as quietly as possible. He poured a cup and went out the back to the eight-by-eight slab of concrete bounded by the walls of neighboring buildings. He unfolded a beach chair and sat, careful not to spill the hot liquid on himself. As soon as he was settled, he took out his phone.

Will answered in the middle of the third ring. "Hi," he said warmly.

"I hope I'm not distracting you."

"Of course you are, but who cares? This is my private number, and I'm having lunch at my desk."

"What a good boy you are."

Will chuckled. "That's not what you said last night."

"Well… you were very naughty last night."

"How naughty?"

"You deserve a spanking."

"Promises, promises. Excuse me." Will took a drink of coffee. "Sorry about that. So what's up? Are you working tonight?"

"Yeah, but we could do something after, if you want."

"If I want?" Will scoffed. "Of course I want."

"Any ideas?"

"Plenty."

Dai laughed. "One-track mind."

"I like sex. I won't apologize for that."

Dai laughed again. "Well, at least we have *that* in common."

"Yeah, I do enjoy your full-bore approach."

Dai hesitated only a moment before responding to the banter. "You ain't seen nothin' yet."

"You just gave me goose bumps. Been a while since that happened."

A pleased glow spread from Dai's core. "I should go before this turns into phone sex."

"Tease." Will chuckled. "Why don't you get a cab to my place after work? I'll have something good for you to eat, and we can decide whether we want to go out or not."

"I'm going to go out on a limb and predict that we'll stay in. In fact, it's becoming a habit."

"Do you mind?"

Dai spared one regretful thought for missing Harlow's costume on Carmen Miranda night at their favorite dance club. "Not at all. I'm sure we can find some craptastic movie that won't be too distracting."

"I like your style, Daimaru."

"Same." Dai looked up as the door opened behind him. "I'll say bye now."

"See you tonight," Will said before he hung up.

Harlow flopped down in a beach chair next to Dai. "Why did you let me drink so much and stay up so late?" he groaned.

"Because you threatened to teach me the secrets of a fuck master from the Far East."

"I offered to teach you if you'd give the bottle back."

"Agree to disagree?"

"Sure." Harlow sighed and raked his fingers through his pale hair, leaving it standing in tufts. "I'm not doing this again," he vowed.

"My fault for joining you when I got home. I should have said no."

"Yeah. It's all your fault." Harlow lifted his shades and winked at Dai. "Seriously, I can't keep doing this to my body. I'm in peak condition right now. It's all downhill from here."

"Wow, that's not depressing at all."

"Maybe if I had a gorgeous new boyfriend who couldn't get enough of me, I'd have the energy to be sarcastic."

"Want some coffee?"

"No." Harlow held up the bottle of water in his hand.

"It only works if you actually drink it."

"Got any aspirin?"

Dai went inside and returned with two extrastrength headache tablets. Harlow chased the pills with gulps of cold water while Dai watched him.

"If you're serious about not drinking," Dai said, "I'm happy to help. I don't have to drink in the house, for instance."

"I'm not talking about quitting completely. I just need to cut down." Harlow pressed the bottle to his forehead. "When I was a teen in Tokyo, how much liquor you could hold was a mark of how manly you were."

"You don't have to prove anything to me."

"Fuck you. I know that. What time is it?"

Dai looked at his phone. "Just a couple of minutes after eleven. How would you feel about brunch at the Lennon Closet? Around one or so."

"I think I could pull myself together by then." Harlow drank more water. "So how are things going with Mr. Suave McSuaverson?"

"Fine."

Harlow opened one eye. "Fine?" He sat up and turned to look Dai in the face.

"Don't start."

"Oh, but I must. How could I possibly let you get away with a bullshit answer like *fine*?"

"You could respect my privacy."

"How?" Harlow frowned. "Are you even serious right now?"

"Maybe I don't want to talk to you about Will."

Harlow looked stunned. "What? Why not?"

"Maybe because you never call him by his name."

Now Harlow looked mystified. "You'll have to be a little more specific."

Dai sighed. "When you talk about him, you call him things like Mr. Suave McSuaverson or Dr. Handsome Goodcock."

"Handsome *Big*cock," Harlow corrected. "You're the one who mentioned his less-than-tragic endowment to me. Let me see. How did you put it?"

"Never mind. In fact, things are going great with Will."

"Sure." Harlow nodded. "Things are *fine*."

Dai sighed again and wondered if it was too early to add Baileys to his coffee. Then again, maybe he ought to cut down on his drinking too. "If you must know the truth," he said. "I just don't feel completely comfortable with him yet." He glanced over at Harlow. "You know what I mean. I still feel like I'm putting on a little performance when I'm with him."

"The audition date. I know it well."

"We've gone out three days in a row, and we've had sex...." Dai paused. "Well, more than three times, anyway. The sex is good. Really good. And I enjoy going out with him. He's the kind of guy who's always in charge, you know?"

"Yeah, and I know how that turns you on."

"True...."

"True but what?"

"I'm not sure really, but sometimes Will strikes me as arrogant."

"Sometimes? Dai, if you look in the dictionary under arrogant, there's a picture of Baron Wilhelm von Whitebread."

Dai gave Harlow a sharp look.

"Sorry," Harlow said. "I'm a little grouchy. But I could see how arrogant he was the first time I met him. He was having a good time because he was the one providing the good time for everyone else. Guys like that—"

Dai gave Harlow another cutting look. "I didn't know you didn't like him this much."

"I know he's good-looking, and rich, and sexes you good, but no, I don't like him. I didn't say anything because I thought he'd show you a good time and we'd never see him again. But now it looks like you're dating him, and I can't—" Harlow shut his mouth for a few seconds before he spoke again. "I know I'm stupid for saying this stuff. I just wanted you to know that I know how stupid it is, and then I'm going to say it anyway. Even if you throw me out."

"Don't be silly. It's not that serious."

"Good, because I think you should dump him."

"Just because he's arrogant? I think it's endearing."

"It's not just that. He's a control freak and probably a narcissist. Worst of all, he doesn't see you as a person. You're the classic sex object."

"Go ahead and flaunt your college education at me, but it doesn't explain why I should dump him out of hand."

"Because he'll never love you." Harlow met Dai's gaze. "And you don't love him. I can't think of a better reason for two people to part ways."

"Well, you're not wrong about me not loving him, but maybe I will."

"Fair enough, and I get it. Like I said, he's good-looking, rich, and sexy. I'm probably just jealous."

"I doubt it. You don't do jealousy."

"You're not mad at me?" Harlow made a puppy-dog face.

Dai shook his head. "I agree with you." He smiled wistfully. "But he sure is a lot of fun when he wants to be."

"So have some fun, but listen to your Uncle Harlow.... Don't fall in love with him."

"That's your advice? Hm, tell me again how you keep from falling in love?"

"Focus on his faults. That's how I keep from falling for you."

"What a brat!"

"Don't hit me. I'm fragile."

Dai chuckled as he stood up. "I'm going to take a shower and put on some clothes," he said. "I'll leave you to brood on your sins."

"For such a sweet guy, you have an awfully acid tongue."

"Delusional," Dai said over his shoulder as he went into the apartment.

AFTER A couple of hours at his desk, Will went to pick Cope up at the airport. It wasn't necessary—Cope could have easily taken a cab—but both of them enjoyed the tradition.

"Welcome back." Will embraced Cope and held him close for a few seconds before letting him go. "Sorry to hear you had to play some hardball."

Cope shrugged and didn't protest when Will picked up his carry-on bag. "Sometimes you have to put a guy's brakes on for him," he said. "Comes with the territory."

"You're only right," Will said. "And you know what I always say."

"It doesn't matter what bait you use, as long as you get them into the bucket," Cope responded.

"That's my boy." Will patted Cope's shoulder. "You did a good job. Feel like celebrating?"

"Not particularly. In fact, there's something I need to do."

Will started walking. "Car's this way. What is it you need to do?"

Cope easily kept pace with Will's long-legged stride. "Just some personal business to take care of," he said.

"Anything interesting?"

"Never you mind."

"Since when do we have secrets from each other?" Will glanced at Cope as they walked through the automatic doors and onto the sidewalk.

"Since always." Cope spotted the company sedan idling illegally a hundred feet ahead of the taxi queue. "Over there," he said. "Let's go or that cop's going to beat us to the car."

Will and Cope slid into the back seat of the big car, and the driver pulled away from the curb just as the policeman blew his whistle. Will glanced out the rear window and then smiled at Cope. "I'm thinking of sending young Wells over to Hong Kong to liaise as soon as the foundation is poured."

"They're planning on renovating an existing building. Do you even read my emails?"

"Sophie reads them. So what do you think of Wells?"

"Is he ready?"

"No. That's why he'd be working under you."

"I didn't much care for Hong Kong."

"There's my answer, then. We'll have to discuss this further when the time comes, but if you don't want to go back to Hong Kong, we'll figure out something else. We'll just leave that photo of Hong Kong in the dream box."

"Suits me."

"How about dinner? You hungry?"

"Actually, they fed me well on the plane. Just drop me at home."

Will studied Cope's profile as his friend looked out the side window. "You okay?"

"I'm not sure." Cope turned to give Will a reassuring smile. "But it's nothing dire and nothing you can help with."

"You might be underestimating me."

"Probably, but let it go, okay?"

"Sure. Want to go out tomorrow night?"

"I'll let you know tomorrow."

Will held up his hands as though surrendering. "Okay. I can take a hint."

"Not so far," Cope replied.

Will chuckled. "What do you want to talk about?"

"What's new with you?"

"It's only been three days since I saw you."

"Yeah, but you're you. So who are you currently banging?"

"I'll let you know tomorrow."

"All right." Cope met Will's eyes. "What happened to us?" he said.

Will darted a glance at the driver before meeting Cope's gaze again. "You'll have to be more specific."

"Is it really impossible for us to have a conversation that isn't about business or fucking?" Cope sighed. "We used to talk about Mackintosh, Tony Duquette, Helmut Newton, Tom Clancy, Hitchcock, Dior, Chanel…." His voice trailed off. "Remember?"

"That was college. We have jobs now. You don't get to be head of acquisitions by sitting around talking."

"Your words have the ring of truth. Are you happy, though?"

"Yeah. Hell yeah, I'm happy. What kind of question is that? I'm successful in my chosen field. My yearly salary is six figures. I have a killer crib and a posse of sharp-dressed handsome guys to hit the clubs with. I'm catnip to women and men. And I have the best wingman who ever lived."

"I'm touched." Cope smiled to show he wasn't being sarcastic. "But I think I'm ready for more."

"Of what?"

"More than an endless cycle of work and play. I want someone to share my life with."

"What am I?"

"The second-best wingman who ever lived."

Will laughed and then sobered. "So what are you telling me? You want to find a special someone, get married, and settle down?"

"Would that be as awful as your tone suggests?"

"I'm a player." Will shrugged.

The driver pulled into the porte cochere of Cope's building. A doorman stepped over and opened the back door.

"To be continued," Will said as Cope slid out of the car.

"Absolutely," Cope answered. "Enjoy your evening."

"That's my plan," Will said, and then the doorman shut the door.

Cope went up to his apartment and dumped his bag on his bed. He stripped down, took a quick shower, and went into the kitchen in a white terrycloth robe. His wet hair hung in ringlets to his shoulders, dripping water on the counter as he made a drink with the vodka and grapefruit juice from the fridge. He carried his cocktail out to the balcony and watched the sun set on the city, on the yellow cabs and mounted policemen. The neon signs came on and filled the night the way tropical blooms light up the jungle. It was never quiet, but the sound of the car engines, car horns, and sirens had become like waves on the beach to him.

"Just do it," Cope told himself under his breath. He managed to get to the couch and his phone and started to key in a number before he lost courage. Instead of making the call, he got up, went into his bedroom, and got dressed. In the middle of putting on a white silk T-shirt and a pair of royal blue gabardine trousers, he decided to go out. His destination was already stored in his phone's map app. All he had to do was go outside and start the journey. After dithering for a few minutes, he slipped his feet into a pair of oxblood loafers and went downstairs.

The doorman hailed a cab for Cope and shut him into the back seat. Cope gave the driver the address and spent the ride talking himself out of turning around and going back home. The taxi dropped him on the corner of the block and sped away. Cope checked his phone and then started down the sidewalk. Daimaru Tanaka paid rent on an apartment on this street, and Cope was determined to find it. He knew it was crazy to just show up, but he didn't want to talk to Dai on the phone. He didn't want to take the chance that Dai would refuse to meet him. He thanked God he hadn't signed the poem. He could always disavow any knowledge if it turned out Dai thought he was a stalker.

A burst of laughter jolted Cope from his thoughts. He would know that laugh anywhere. He looked around and spotted Will at a café across the street. Will held a pilsner glass in one hand, and he was smiling at his companion across the small table. A shock ran down Cope's spine on cold lizard feet as he recognized Daimaru. His heart lurched, and he felt abruptly as though he was going to throw up. This was ridiculous. He

had no relationship with Dai; he hadn't actually met him yet. And yet....
Cope didn't know how to account for the feeling that he'd lost something
precious before it was even his, but that's how he felt.

For another couple of minutes, Cope stared at the couple, who
appeared to be having a wonderful time. He didn't blame Will for making
a play for Dai, but he couldn't help feeling a little betrayed, even if he
didn't have cause. It was ridiculous to expect Will to read his mind, but
somehow, he always had in the past. Will had always known when Cope
was interested in someone. So what was Cope to think about all this?

With dragging steps, Cope walked back down the block and hailed
a cab. Feeling very badly done by, he went home. Though logically he
knew he had no good reason to feel this way, he did. He made another
drink, gulped it down, and went to bed. It was some time before he
managed to fall asleep.

CHAPTER SIX

COPE TOOK the day off, but nothing he did distracted him from his problem. He just couldn't get the image of Dai and Will out of his head. That evening, he went over to Will's apartment to talk to him like he should have done in the first place. In retrospect, he should have been prepared, but he wasn't.

"Hi!" Dai said cheerily as he opened the door of Will's apartment. "You're Cope, right?"

"Hi. Yeah." Cope paused to regain his equilibrium. "Is Will here?"

"He'll be right back. Come on in. Want to give me your jacket?"

"You seem at home here."

"I told Will I would answer the door until he gets here. He decided at the last minute he needed a haircut to look his best." Dai grinned. "I call him Primp Daddy."

Cope laughed in spite of his unease. "I hope you don't mind if I steal that."

"Not at all. I'm Dai Tanaka. Do you remember me?"

With every fiber of my being, Cope thought as Dai hung up his jacket. What he said was, "I'm going to have a drink while I wait. Do you have one already? Or can I make you one?"

"I'm good." Dai sat on a barstool and watched Cope pour vodka and brine into a martini glass.

"I feel a little awkward," Cope said. "I'm not sure how to ask this without just coming out and asking. How are you and Will involved?"

"Involved?" Dai frowned. "He hasn't said anything to you about me?"

Cope shook his head before he took a sip of his drink.

"Weird."

"Maybe he thought I'd try to steal you away from him."

"Would you?"

"There's no way I'll answer a hypothetical question like that without having all of the hypothetical facts."

Dai chuckled. "Will says you have the best sense of humor. I think he's right."

"Oh yeah? What else does Will say? About me, I mean."

Dai chuckled again. "He talks about you quite a bit for someone as self-centered as he is."

"I see," Cope drawled. "So love isn't blind after all."

Dai grinned. "To answer your question, we're dating. We've had three dates, anyway. Tonight is number four."

"He's always been a fast worker."

"Actually… I went after him."

Cope's heart plunged, but his polite smile didn't waver. No point now in asking if Dai had liked the poems. "I must hear this story," he said, feigning nonchalance.

"It's kind of embarrassing and… kind of makes me look like a stalker."

"Lucky Will. Most stalkers don't look like you." Cope paused. "Was that crass?"

"Maybe a little, but since you were flattering me, I'll let it pass. You were at the restaurant with Will, right? For your birthday?" Dai knew very well Cope had been at that dinner. Having once heard it, he'd never forget that warm baritone voice.

"Yeah, it was my birthday. The dinner was Will's idea of the perfect present." Cope grinned sheepishly and then looked startled when his phone chimed. "Excuse me," he said. He checked the number and then let the call go to voicemail. "So where are the two of you going tonight?"

Dai answered, glad he didn't have to tell the story about tracking Will to his office. "Some place in Hell's Kitchen, but it's not carved in stone."

"I should have called first. Sorry."

"Don't be sorry. It's not my intention to come between friends."

"No, you don't seem like the type."

"You don't know me at all."

Cope smiled slightly. "Whose fault is that?"

Dai returned the smile. "Smooth," he said. "Will mentioned what a lethal flirt you are."

"Really?"

"He said if all you had was your voice, you could talk the underwear off anybody, but—" Dai looked at Cope from under his lashes.

"But what?"

"But you also have those eyes and those lips and all that style, not to mention your wit."

"Will says all that?"

"He has a high opinion of you." Dai chuckled. "I'd even say he has a man crush on you."

"Damn right, I do." Will spoke from the foyer. Neither Dai nor Cope had heard him come in. They moved apart with a guilty little start though they'd been doing nothing wrong. "If you two want a threesome, just say so." He chuckled and then stopped laughing when no one joined him.

"That's inappropriate even for you," Cope said.

"I don't remember inviting you," Will retorted.

"That's because you didn't, you rude bastard." Cope held up his drink in a salute. "Glad to see you're finally stocking decent vodka."

"As if you'd know what decent vodka tastes like."

"And you have a new friend."

Will's smile was smug. "You remember Dai from the restaurant, right?"

"How could I forget?"

"Dai, this is my best friend, Copeland Shore. Everyone calls him Cope."

Dai held out his hand. "Nice to meet you properly."

Cope took Dai's hand. "Likewise."

"You can let go now," Will said.

"I'm not sure I can." Cope made a joke of it as he let go of Dai's hand. "I came over to hang out, but Dai says you're going out, so I'll catch you later."

"We're just going to dinner," Will said. "Want to tag along?"

Cope couldn't imagine anything more depressing than watching Will with Dai all evening. On the other hand, his foolish heart wanted to spend time with Dai no matter the circumstances. "If you're sure I wouldn't be intruding…."

"Don't be ridiculous," Will said. "We'd love for you to come along."

Cope looked to Dai. "Is it all right with you?"

"You'd be very welcome," Dai said.

"It's settled." Will took out his phone and changed his reservation at the restaurant. "Let's go," he said to Dai and Cope. "I'm so hungry I might eat one of you on the ride over."

"Where are we going?" Cope asked as they got in the car service limo.

"It opened while you were gone," Will said. "According to Sophie, it's run by this 'ultimately cute' gay couple who escaped from South Korea."

"No one escapes from *South* Korea," Cope said.

"These guys did."

Cope tried again, unsure as usual whether Will was being obtuse or baiting him. "It's North Korea that people escape from."

"No, I don't think they do. That guy in North Korea is a real asshole about it." Will looked to Dai for validation.

"Sorry, but Cope's right," Dai said. "People visit from South Korea and even immigrate, but they don't escape. There aren't soldiers at the border with machine guns. That's North Korea."

"Fine, the restaurant is run by the cutest gay couple who *didn't* escape from South Korea." Will rolled his eyes. "The place is called Last Mango."

"I love it already," Cope said.

"Why didn't they go ahead and call it Last Mango in Paris?" Dai wondered.

"It's actually Last Mango *on* Paris," Will said. "Paris Avenue… or Street, maybe."

"I love it," Cope said as they stepped into the pale orange foyer of the restaurant.

A young woman with burnished mahogany skin left her post in front of a turquoise-tiled fountain to greet the party of three. Will gave her his name, and she escorted them into the small dining room. Eight tables lined a central aisle, four to a side, each with seating for six. At the end of the aisle was a wall sheathed in copper. Sheets of water slid down the polished metal to a shallow pool with arms that extended along the side walls. White water lilies floated on the surface, glowing in the dim light. A slim young man with eyes like a gazelle refilled water glasses at a table on the left. He nodded when the woman signaled and followed to fill the glasses after Will, Cope, and Dai were seated. The hostess left, but the young man stayed to take their orders.

"Good evening," he said haltingly. "My name is Minho. Please excuse my English. Staff is low tonight, so I will be your server. I am also part owner of Mango."

"Way to hustle," Will said. "What do you recommend?"

"We have two menus tonight. One with meat and one without meat."

"Well then," Will said. "I'll have the meat, definitely."

"Why don't we get two meat and one without?" Cope said.

"Without meat is the same as with meat but without meat," Minho said.

"I see." Cope glanced at Dai, and both smiled. "I'll have mine with meat, then."

"So will I," Dai said.

"Beer, beer, beer." Minho pointed to each man in turn as though confirming an order rather than making a suggestion.

"Yes, beer, of course," Will said.

"Soju?"

"Is it alcohol?" Will asked.

"It's alcohol the way a sequoia is a tree," Dai said. "Do we want to get that drunk?"

"We have a ride home," Will pointed out.

"I'm trying to cut down on my drinking," Dai said.

"Does that mean you aren't doing shots with me?"

"Probably."

"Ruin my fun, then." Will gestured to Minho. "Soju, *s'il vous plaît*," he said.

"*Oui, monsieur*," Minho replied crisply. "*Immédiatement*."

As Minho left the table, Dai glanced at Cope, and both chuckled.

"What?" Will asked.

"We're not laughing at you," Cope said. "It just struck me funny when the waiter answered you in French."

"A lot of South Koreans speak at least a little French," Dai said.

"I thought you were Japanese," Will said.

"For the last time, I'm A-mer-i-can," Dai said slowly.

"Whatever. Why do you know so much about South Korea?" Will asked.

Minho returned with three large bottles of Cass beer and a green bottle of soju. He opened the beers and poured them into lager glasses. He unscrewed the top of the soju bottle and poured three shots into small clay cups. He bowed to the three men. "*Kampai!*" he said and mimed tossing back a shot. Everyone drank as Minho left to check on their orders.

"Nice," Will said in a strained voice as he set his cup down.

"Your eyes are watering," Cope observed.

Dai set his cup down and picked up the bottle. "I'm the youngest, so I'll pour," he said.

They drank another shot and then turned to their beers.

"Seriously, though, why do you know so much about Korea?" Will asked again.

Dai sighed. "Okay, you asked. My best friend in high school was this great chick who was crazy about Korean music and movies. I spent a lot of time reading subtitles and eating kimchi."

"It doesn't seem to have done you any harm," Cope joked.

"Are you flirting with my boyfriend?" Will joined in.

"Are you saying I'm your boyfriend?" Dai retorted.

Both Dai and Cope burst out laughing at the conflicted expression on Will's face. "No fair ganging up on me," Will said.

"Are you saying you couldn't handle the two of us?" Cope asked archly.

The opening was all Will needed to regain his equilibrium. "You bet I could," he said.

Before Will could speak again, Minho returned and set out several small dishes. Will, Cope, and Dai picked up their chopsticks and sampled the various pickled, fermented, and spicy side dishes of vegetables and seafood. Talking dwindled to remarks on the food, and after the main course arrived, ceased altogether. Not until the last bite was gone did anyone speak.

"This is my new favorite restaurant," Cope said while Dai was pouring the last of the soju.

"To South Korea," Will said as he raised his cup.

"To good food with interesting people," Dai said before tossing back his shot.

Minho came over to ask if anyone would like tea or coffee but got no takers. After the bill was paid, he urged his guests to take their time and relax, and then he moved away to take care of his other customers.

"What should we do now?" Will said.

"I love how you make it seem like we have a choice," Cope said. "Why don't you just tell us where we're going?"

"I was thinking we could go back to my place for dessert." Will winked. "I have three kinds of cheesecake sitting in my fridge, thanks to Sophie. And Dai makes a terrific cup of coffee."

"It's true," Dai said when Cope looked over at him. "I have a way with the bean."

"Is it settled, then?" Will asked. "My place? Coffee? A plethora of cheesecake?"

"A plethora?" Dai said in a cheesy Spanish accent. "Oh yes, you have a plethora, señor."

Will looked mystified, but Cope broke into laughter.

"Come on, man," Cope said, smacking Will on the shoulder. "*Three Amigos*? Ring a bell?"

"I remember the movie. It was dumb."

Dai didn't correct Will, but his smile faded a trifle, enough for Cope to notice.

"Dai was quoting a line from the movie," Cope explained to Will. "See, El Guapo says he has a plethora of piñatas and—"

"I still don't get it," Will said. "Can we stop talking about it and get out of here?" He rose as he finished speaking and headed for the door.

"He's not much of a movie buff," Cope told Dai as they got up from their chairs.

"I know," Dai answered. "But I keep hoping."

"Ah yes, hope. The small thing with feathers."

"Yeah, I know, you have to be real careful with it because it's so fragile."

Cope looked over at Dai as they joined Will on the sidewalk. Will was on his phone to the driver. "I didn't mean to start a deep and meaningful conversation," Cope said. "Unless you feel like having one, in which case, I did mean to."

Dai smiled. "You're nice," he said. "And I know I say weird stuff sometimes. Just ignore me."

"How would that be possible?"

"Cut it out. Or I'll start to think you're flirting with me too."

"And we wouldn't want that."

"No, we wouldn't." Dai glanced up as Will put a hand on the back of his neck. "Since I'm apparently taken."

"You'll be taken and properly too, as soon as I get you home," Will said.

"Surely not right away," Cope said. "I was promised cheesecake and sublime coffee." He paused. "But I can take a rain check."

"No way," Dai said quickly. "You have to eat some of the cheesecake. If it stays in the fridge, I'll end up eating it. Will has the power of self-denial when it comes to food, but I don't."

Cope raised his eyebrows at Will. Will threw his arm around Cope's neck and dragged him to the car. Dai opened the door before the driver could get out, and Will threw Cope into the back seat. Will shoved Dai in after Cope and laughed at the ensuing tangle of limbs.

"You kids settle down," Will said as he got in. "Don't make me turn this car around."

"You heard Dad," Cope told Dai.

"That's right. I'm your daddy," Will shot back.

Dai finished buckling his seat belt. "Am I the only one concerned with safety?" he asked.

"Yes," Will and Cope said simultaneously.

Dai decided Will was undeniably more fun when his friend was around. He acknowledged his attraction to Cope, but he could deal with it. He'd worried a bit that Cope might be jealous—given how close he was to Will—but after spending an evening together, he still couldn't find any traces of resentment in Cope's manner. That would be a factor if he planned to date Will long-term.

At Will's apartment, Dai busied himself with the coffee maker. Will led Cope to the bar and insisted on pouring him a finger of brandy. When Dai came out to say the coffee was almost ready, Cope asked if he could help with anything.

"Forget it," Will said. "Dai's got it handled. Anyway, he doesn't really like anyone in the kitchen with him."

"That's not strictly true," Dai said. "I just don't understand how a man can live in a place and not know what's in the drawers and cabinets."

Will spread his hands. "I rest my case. He gets cranky if I even talk about it."

"Is there anything I can do?" Cope asked again.

"As a matter of fact, you could pick out your cheesecake. I already know Will wants the mocha."

"I can do that," Cope said. "I don't even need special tools."

"Come on, then." Dai turned and went back into the kitchen.

"Be right back," Cope told Will and then followed Dai.

Dai glanced over his shoulder at Cope as he laughed at the line from the movie *Scream*.

"You know what?" Will said to the empty living room. "I think he *is* flirting with my boyfriend." He finished his drink in one long swallow. "And I think my boyfriend is flirting back."

Cope came back and set his cup and plate on the coffee table. As Will joined him, Dai came out of the kitchen with a tray. Dai set the tray down, and Will reached for a plate and a fork.

"This really is great coffee," Cope said.

"Told you," Will said around a bite of cheesecake. "Dai's a keeper."

Cope took another sip of coffee to cover his sudden change of expression. He was getting annoyed with himself for letting the situation affect him. It wasn't as if he had an understanding with Dai. Dai was fair game when Will bagged him, but still, Cope felt somehow betrayed. It wasn't fair that he'd had to go to Hong Kong and miss his chance.

"What the hell are you thinking about?" Will asked. "You should see your face."

"It's nothing. I—I was just thinking I could have handled Hong Kong better."

"No work talk tonight. Nothing but fun." Will stood. "Who wants a shot of Courvoisier in their coffee?" He took his cup to the bar and poured a generous measure.

"No, thanks," Cope said. "I'm pretty buzzed from the cocktails at dinner."

"Same here," Dai said. "Plus, I think there's a quart of Kahlua in my cheesecake."

Will came back and sat on the couch next to Cope, shoulder to shoulder and hip to hip. "Are you okay to go home by yourself? You can always sleep here, you know."

"I know, but I think I can manage to get myself in a cab."

"Why bother? It's not like any of us have to work in the morning. You could get up, have a shower, and go home to change. Then we can decide where to have brunch."

"I love the way you never oversell." Cope smiled at Will, their faces inches apart. "But why do I feel like you're selling something?"

Will met Cope's gaze. "Because you're the suspicious type. Whenever something good is about to happen to you, you start wondering what's wrong with it."

"Is *that* my problem?" Cope mused, not fazed at all by Will's proximity.

"At least one of them." Will smiled, still looking unwaveringly into Cope's eyes.

"Stop it, please!" Dai said. "The sexual tension in here is three feet deep and rising."

Will looked over at Dai, eyes glittering. "Maybe you'd be safer over here." He patted the cushion on his right.

"I doubt it," Dai said.

"But you're not scared." Will's words were a clear challenge.

Cope picked up his cup and drained it. "Damn! Is that the time?" he said. "I really need to get going."

Will put a hand on Cope's arm. "Stay," he said.

"Not this time," Cope said. His gaze brushed Dai and moved quickly away.

"It'll be fun," Will coaxed, his voice thick with promises.

Cope's gaze flickered over Dai again. "Don't beg," he said to Will. "You're no good at it."

"Beg? Me?" Will scoffed. "If you want to turn down the night of your life, go ahead and be a fool, but I'm not going to beg you." He moved slightly away from Cope. "Mind telling me what the problem is? Just for the sake of my curiosity?"

"The offer seems to be coming strictly from you."

"Dai's in, aren't you?" Will turned to Dai.

Dai abruptly found himself the focus of Will's and Cope's eyes. "What?"

"Will has invited me, I think, to have a threesome with the two of you."

Dai's eyes widened fractionally, the only sign of his surprise. "He does things like that," he said in an overly bright voice. "You get used to it. If he says anything else like that, just ignore him. If he doesn't get attention, he'll stop."

Will's brows drew together even as his lips drew back in an automatic smile. The sound of Cope's laughter was unaccountably irritating. Suddenly, all Will wanted was for Cope to be gone as quickly as possible. "I'll take that as a no," he said. "Well, if you really have to go, I won't try to stop you."

Cope stood up. "Thanks for the coffee, Dai. Will, it was entertaining, as always. See you Monday morning."

Dai gathered up cups and plates while Will walked Cope to the door.

"Good night," Cope said as he shrugged into his jacket.

"It could have been a good night—a great night. You should have backed my play." Will cuffed the back of Cope's head. "You're going to lose your top wingman status."

"I'll try not to get any tears on you when I cry my eyes out."

"We good?"

"Yeah, we're good." Cope hugged Will tight before letting him go.

After closing the door behind Cope, Will joined Dai in the kitchen. "Well, that was embarrassing," Will said.

Dai looked up from loading the dishwasher. He didn't pretend he didn't know what Will was talking about. "What did you expect when you spring something like that on a person?"

"Excuse me for thinking you were more sophisticated than that."

"Are you starting a fight over this?" Dai didn't sound mad, just curious.

"Of course I don't want to fight, but I think I have a right to express my disappointment."

"*You're* disappointed in *me*?"

"Yes, I am. You've led me to believe you're sexually adventurous, but when I invite my best friend—my brother—to have some fun with us, you turn into a choirboy. What's the deal? I thought you liked him. You sure got along like gangbusters at dinner."

"First you're mad because I wouldn't sleep with your friend and now you're jealous because I like him?"

"Who said I was jealous?"

"You sure sound jealous."

Will took a deep breath and let it out. "Maybe we need some ground rules."

Dai leaned back against the counter, suddenly worried his legs wouldn't hold him. He had the impulse to babble an apology and clenched his teeth to keep the words from escaping. He could hear Harlow's voice in his head telling him he hadn't done anything to be sorry for, but still the urge to give in and smooth things over was strong. "I'm listening," he said calmly.

Will was impressed. The other low-income pretty boys he'd let this far into his life would have been anxious at the thought of losing a good thing. Dai was cool as ice cream. Will licked his lips as a pulse of desire tightened his groin. When he spoke again, it wasn't about rules, as he'd intended. "Maybe I *am* a little jealous," he said, testing the water.

"Well, don't be." Dai bit his lower lip as he thought about his next words. "I do like your friend Cope, but I'd never cheat on you or anyone else. If I'm with you, then I'm with you and you alone. Call me old-fashioned, but that's how I am."

"I believe you." Will tried a small smile. "But it's not cheating if I give you permission."

Dai smiled back. "You're too much," he said indulgently. "I guess I'm just not as... spontaneous as you."

Will sighed. "I know you're a man because you have a penis," he said. "But sometimes…."

"What?"

"A guy is always ready for sex. Everyone knows that. Comedians make jokes about it."

Dai chuckled. "Okay, you're right. I *can* get a hard-on at any given moment, but that's just half of it." He sobered. "I know it's weird, but I have to feel something for a guy before I have sex."

"And you don't feel like you want a ménage with me and Cope? Are you kidding me?"

Dai shook his head. "You're so cute," he said. "I admit, you're both hotties, but I can't just do something like that without thinking about the, you know, repercussions."

"Okay, why don't we drop it for now? We missed the opportunity, but there'll be others."

"Yeah, let's drop it." Dai sighed as he turned to wash his hands at the sink.

Will came over to embrace Dai from behind. He nuzzled Dai's nape, breathing deeply of the mingled scents of shampoo, cologne, and Dai's skin. He slid a hand down Dai's flat belly, under his waistband. He spread his fingers, gently massaging as he nipped and sucked at Dai's earlobe.

Dai grabbed the edge of the sink as Will worked his hand lower and touched his cock. The brush of fingernails against sensitive skin detonated a blast of need that spread from his core. He'd always been a responsive lover, but Will's confident, greedy touch aroused him as swiftly as a lightning strike. In an eyeblink, he was gripping the stainless steel so hard his fingertips ached and grinding his ass against Will's crotch.

"Why don't we take this somewhere horizontal?" Will asked, his breath hot on Dai's ear.

Dai turned in the circle of Will's arms and took his face between both hands. Hungrily, he sought Will's lips and pushed his tongue between them to taste coffee, brandy, and the lingering sweetness of the cheesecake. A tingling thrill ran down his spine as Will's tongue slid over his, and Will took control of the kiss.

"I want you now," Will said when their lips parted.

"Me too," Dai answered eagerly. He toed off his shoes, shoved his trousers down, and stepped out of them. Before he could peel down his briefs, Will stopped him, cupping a hand over Dai's cock and balls. "Fuck, that feels good," Dai whispered.

Will took Dai's lips in a torrid kiss while he rubbed, squeezed, and stroked Dai's crotch. He groaned into Dai's mouth when Dai unzipped him and took hold of his cock. Following the tug of Dai's hand, Will moved forward until Dai was pressed between him and the table. "Lube," Will gasped.

"Spit," Dai said. "Or use the olive oil." He laughed breathlessly. "It's extra virgin."

Will grinned as he watched Dai drop his underwear and climb onto the table. Dai rolled up onto his shoulders and took hold of his knees. For a long moment, Will paused at the threshold. Dai's delicate Eurasian features, lean, hard body, sweet submission, and unfettered enjoyment of sex were the stuff of Will's wet dreams. Dai was so close to perfect he made Will's jaw ache.

Leaving the olive oil where it was, Will sat on a kitchen chair with Dai spread like a banquet before him. With lips, tongue, teeth, and fingers, Will took his time preparing Dai. He nipped, licked, and sucked, savoring the tastes and scents of his lover. He flirted the tip of his tongue in and around Dai's hole until Dai was squirming on the table. Will wrapped his arms around Dai's thighs and thrust his tongue as far as it would go.

"Come on." Dai panted and caught his breath. Whiskers prickled the skin of his inner thighs, and the thrusting tongue made his insides melt. By contrast, his dick was as hard as the hardest thing that ever existed. "Come on. I want you in me now."

Will shoved a hand in his pocket and grabbed a foil packet. He tore it open with his teeth and rolled the condom onto his aching cock. He took hold of the shaft where it emerged from his fly and nuzzled the tip against Dai's glistening hole. "You sure you're ready?"

Dai nodded. "Yes. Yes. *Yes!*"

Will worked the head of his cock into Dai, eyelids drooping drowsily as the tight ring of muscle gripped his shaft. Rolling his hips in a small circle, he rocked into Dai by degrees, sinking deeper with each pass, until Dai gave a small cry that trailed off in a moan. Given his cue, Will pulled out and pushed back in at the same depth and angle.

He was rewarded by the same shivery sound of pleasure, and a rush of pride surged through him. Never did he feel more complete than at this moment of utter control; at a whim, he bestowed ecstasy or withheld it, depending on his mood and needs. The beautiful man at the end of his dick was on fire for him, a slave to lust in this moment. With a feral drawing back of lips from teeth, Will wrapped his hand around Dai's hard cock. His breathing grew shallow as he thrust and shuttled his hand on Dai's dick to the same rhythm.

"Fuck, that's good!" Dai managed to say between gasps for air. "Faster!"

Will obliged, pumping his hips, buttocks clenching as he quickened the tempo. "You feel so good," he said. "I'm gonna cum."

At Will's words, the sweet tension at Dai's core uncoiled in a streamer of pure pleasure. His cock jerked against Will's palm and shot a jet of cum between his fingers.

Will laughed the way he used to when something delighted him, and then, freed for a few moments from responsibility, he thrust with abandon. He loved the way Dai's inner muscles yielded so grudgingly and the dewy look of Dai's dark eyes, as though they'd melted in the heat of orgasm. He loved the way Dai's belly quivered, the way the muscles of his abs rippled, the way Dai's entire body undulated to the stroke of his cock. He wanted to do this forever, and yet, he wanted it to reach its end. "Ah fuck yeah," he said under his breath as he reached his peak. His release rolled through him to his farthest shores and filled him with glory and the peace of satisfaction. After shooting his load, he thrust lazily a few times, prolonging the exquisite feeling.

"That was amazing," Dai said weakly. "It just kept going."

Will took several long, slow breaths before he spoke. "Nuclear."

"Seriously, I think I had a meltdown."

Will eased out of Dai, dropped trousers and underwear, and went to the sink. "Hang on," he called over his shoulder as he slid the condom off. He tied off the end and chucked it into the garbage bin from where he stood. "I'll bring you a wet cloth."

"That's okay. I'm going to jump in the shower."

"As you wish."

For half a second, Dai thought Will was quoting a line from *The Princess Bride*, but his smile died before it reached his lips. Of course Will wasn't referencing a film; it just wasn't the kind of thing Will did.

In fact, it was the kind of thing Will considered silly and useless. On the plus side—a different sort of smile curved Dai's lips—he'd just had world-class sex.

WILL CAME into the bedroom as Dai came out the bathroom door with a towel around his hips. Dai's ink-black hair was spiky, and water dripped from the ends onto his shoulders.

"Man, you are in fantastic shape," Will said. He crossed the room to run a hand down Dai's chest to his navel. "Yet I never see you work out or do any kind of exercising."

"I go to the Y three or four days a week. I *do* spend time away from you, you know."

"Why is that?" Will leaned in as he palmed Dai's left nipple. "You could stay here."

"You don't mean that."

"I don't?" Will punctuated the question by pinching Dai's nipple.

Dai sucked in a sharp breath. "Ow," he said mildly.

"Sorry. Was that too hard?"

"Little bit." Dai stepped back, unwrapped the towel, and used it on his hair. "Are you still horny?" he asked as he rubbed vigorously at his damp hair.

"I love how candid you are. You don't make me guess what you want."

"Probably not a hundred percent true, but I try to be up front about what I want."

"And I appreciate that. I'm glad we didn't have a fight earlier."

"Me too." Dai put the towel around his neck as he moved to face Will. "I like you, and you're good to me."

"Ditto." Will put his hands on Dai's hips and pulled him closer. "You tuck so easily into my life; you're the thing I didn't know was missing until you showed up."

Dai wanted to be moved by Will's words, but they sounded a little too smooth, as though Will had rehearsed them. Or was he imagining things? Dai looked into Will's eyes and tried to see the man who'd written the poems to him.

Will gazed steadily back, projecting the aura of sincerity he'd perfected in years of meetings with clients and executives. It was equal parts protective and vulnerable, and he'd found it to be just as effective in the game of seduction as it was in the boardroom.

"I'll think about living with you," Dai said. "But I really don't think it's what you want right now."

"Why don't you let me decide what I want?"

"So many answers to that question." Dai smiled. "Excuse me while I get dressed."

"Are you sure you won't stay?" Will knew when to back off on the pressure. He didn't kid himself that he and Dai were going to get married and live happily ever after, but he did want to keep him around for a while. Dai was gorgeous, fit, easy to be with, and liked sex as much as Will did. Inevitably, the differences between them would end the relationship or one of them would simply get tired of the other. That's the way it happened in Will's experience, and he saw no reason for this relationship to end any differently.

"It's not even midnight," Dai said. "I can be home before one, and when I wake up, I'll be on my side of town, which means I won't have to wake up so early."

"I understand." Will let Dai go. "Call me when you're free."

"You too." Dai gave Will a quick kiss before he turned to gather his clothes. His jacket eluded him for a few minutes until he remembered hanging it on the back of a kitchen chair.

At the door of the apartment, Will gave Dai a deep, lingering kiss. "There's plenty more where that came from," Will said.

"Thanks for the warning," Dai said. He stepped into the hall. "Next time I'll wear my fireproof underwear."

Will chuckled and then sobered as Dai walked away. "Hey, Dai," he called out.

Dai turned back. "What?"

"I just wanted you to know that…." Will paused. "That I really hope you reconsider that threesome with me and Cope." He kept a straight face for a few seconds, but Dai's expression made him burst out laughing. "Sorry, I couldn't resist."

"I'm not mad. It was funny." Dai shook his head. "Good night, Will."

As he walked to the elevator, he heard Will's door close behind him. Though he still felt the warm glow of really good sex, he didn't feel an overwhelming need to stay with Will. He was just as happy heading home to sleep in his own bed. He was beginning to think Will was never going to reveal his romantic side—the side that had intrigued Dai into going out with him.

Dai stepped out of the elevator into the lobby and strode quickly to the front door. He wanted to get home as fast as possible so he could talk to Harlow. He dug out his phone and called to make sure Harlow wouldn't go to sleep before he got there. He kept an eye out for cabs, but each one he spotted already had a fare. He walked several blocks in the direction of the nearest train before he realized something was missing. Nothing was jingling in his jacket pocket. Dai put his hands in both pockets, but he already knew his keys weren't there. It wouldn't be a big deal except that his work keys and the key to his scooter were on the ring with his house key.

Dai sighed and walked back the way he had come. So much for a relatively early night. He might as well stay at Will's apartment. There was no need to be hasty in deciding Will was too withholding. They'd known each other little more than a week. Yeah. Of course Will deserved more from Dai than giving up on him so easily. Dai was pretty sure that's what Harlow would tell him.

DAI KNOCKED twice on Will's door and then tried the knob. It turned easily, and Dai pulled the door open. He was already across the foyer when he realized Will was talking to someone. It occurred to him that Will was probably on the phone, and then he heard a loud groan. Dai's heart froze and his feet stopped carrying him forward. Riveted in place, he listened to the unmistakable sounds of sex. He felt hollow, as though his insides had been scooped out. It felt horrible to know Will was screwing around, but it was somehow worse because he and Will had made love less than a half hour ago. He was crushed, but little by little the pain was being replaced by anger. *How could Will do something like this?*

Feeling righteously angry, Dai marched the last few steps of the entry and into the living room. He stopped again in stunned confusion. Will was sitting on the couch with Drew Cooper, watching television. Both had their backs to Dai and were so intent on what they were watching that they hadn't heard Dai come in. Dai's gaze went to the screen, and his knees almost gave out. Silently, stiffly, he backed away from the sight of him and Will fucking. He made it all the way to the door before he turned around. He stepped on his missing keys and reached down to pick them up with numb fingers. Careful not to make a noise, he opened the door and slipped into the hall.

The elevator door opened, and one of Will's neighbors got out. Dai passed the woman without seeing her and got into the elevator before the doors closed. He pushed the button for the lobby and moved to stand at the back of the empty car. He started to shake and couldn't stop. His mouth was sour with the copper penny taste of blood, and he realized he'd bitten his lower lip. In the polished metal of the elevator door, he could see a trickle of red on his chin. Abruptly, his eyes filled with tears that overflowed to run down his cheeks.

"Why?" he whispered. "Why did you have to do something so nasty?" His guts clenched, and he doubled over as though he'd been punched. For a few seconds, it hurt so much that he couldn't take a breath.

The chime sounded for the ground floor, and Dai forced himself to straighten up. He wiped his chin with the back of his hand and strode quickly across the lobby. Blindly, he walked away from the building and kept going until the shock wore off a little. When he looked up, he saw he'd been walking around the block and ended up where he'd started. As he was standing there in a daze, someone called his name.

"Dai?" Cope called out again. He left the corner and joined Dai in the middle of the block. "Are you coming or going?"

"I'm going. You're back?"

"I got a text from Will about half an hour ago inviting me for hot coffee. I thought it was weird, but I wasn't sleeping so I thought, why not?"

"*Fucker!*"

Cope's eyes widened. "Excuse me?"

"That wasn't for you." Dai managed a smile. "I must have zipped one of my pubes up after I took a whiz."

"Ouch!" Cope cringed.

"Well, it's not a problem anymore." Dai plucked at the front of his trousers. "I should get going. Have fun."

"Listen, this isn't a booty call or anything like that."

"I didn't think it was."

"You sure?"

"Yeah, I'm sure."

"Well… good, because it isn't."

"Fine. Good night, Cope." Dai turned and walked away.

Feeling like something was off-balance, Cope said the first thing that came to mind. "Have fun stormin' the castle!"

At any other time, the classic quote from *The Princess Bride* would have cheered Dai up, but at this moment, it seemed unkind, as though his pain was being mocked. He didn't even try to hold back his tears as he made his way home.

CHAPTER SEVEN

"WHAT HAPPENED?" Harlow cried out in dismay as soon as Dai walked in the door.

"I'm breaking up with Will."

"Without discussing it with me first?"

"It wasn't going to work out."

Harlow dropped his teasing tone. "That's all you've got to say?"

"Yeah, that's all I've got to say." Dai crossed the floor to his bedroom door.

Harlow dodged around Dai and stood barring the door. "No way. I'm not letting you be alone right now. I can see you're upset even if you don't want me to."

"Don't be ridiculous. I'm not going to slash my wrists."

"Shut! Up!" Harlow pushed Dai backward until they reached the futon. "Sit. I'm making tea and we're going to drink it."

"I don't want to talk right now."

"Too bad." Harlow went over to the kitchen area and turned on the burner under the kettle. "I'm not fucking around here. You're going to tell me what's wrong."

"I told you I don't want to talk. Why are you being such a dick?"

"Because I know you, Dai-chan. You'll pull into your shell and pretend you're fine, but you aren't. I can tell."

"Bullshit."

"Am I wrong?"

"Yeah, you're wrong. Now can I go take a shower?"

"No. You can go out back if you want, but this talk is going to happen."

"Fine. I'll tell you." Dai looked straight into Harlow's eyes and lied. The truth was too humiliating for anyone else to know. Dai knew he wouldn't be able to handle the immensity of Harlow's pity. It was much easier to let the world believe he was a garden-variety fool. "Will cheated on me."

"The bastard!"

"Right?"

"Who was it?"

"One of his friends from work. I left his apartment but had to go back for my keys, and I caught them in the act."

"*Bakayarõ!*" Harlow lapsed into Japanese.

"Yeah, he's an asshole, all right."

"Want me to break open a can of ninja whup-ass on him?"

"No." Dai smiled wearily. "I'm just glad I found out about him before I invested any more time."

"True that."

The kettle whistled, and Harlow ran to take it off the stove. He poured two cups of spearmint tea and carried them out back. He and Dai sat on the battered beach chairs and sipped the fragrant tea while they listened to the late-night sounds of the city.

"I'm really sorry," Harlow said quietly.

"Me too. I liked him. Mostly."

"Mostly?"

"Well, you know…."

"He turned out to be like all the other 'strong' men you've dated?"

"I guess you could say that."

"So he was overbearing? Entitled? Self-centered?"

"Well, yeah, but none of those is a deal-breaker for me. I can work around that stuff and even enjoy it, but I won't put up with faithlessness."

"Faithlessness?" Harlow rolled the word on his tongue. "Faithlessness."

"Yeah, it means—"

"Having no faith, yeah, I get it. And I'm glad you found out too. It would be even shittier to find out a few months down the road during the holiday season." Harlow shuddered at the thought of such a fate.

"Seriously. Breaking up at Christmas is the worst."

"No date for New Year's." Harlow looked as though he might cry.

"So… now that's out of the way, you've been quiet lately. What's been going on with you while I was lost in Mr. Will Wonderful's eyes?"

"If you must pry…." Harlow's voice trailed off.

Dai took the hint and mustered the correct quote from *Blazing Saddles*. "I must! I must!"

"I've got a big audition coming up, and I think my new ballet instructor is sweet on me."

"You think?"

"It's a little hard to tell." Harlow leaned over as though confiding a state secret. "He's Russian."

Dai took a sip of his tea before he answered. "What does that mean exactly?"

"Don't be messin' with me. You know how Russians are."

"The few I know are pretty different from each other. Sergei the sous chef isn't anything like Sasha who cuts my hair. They're night and day. Sergei broods and always smells like tobacco. Sasha is a chatterbox who has something good to say about everyone except Putin. And Albina who works at Amy's is—"

"I get the point," Harlow said. "I should have said that I can't tell if he's being touchy-feely with me because it's a cultural thing or if he wants to jump my bones."

"Is he gay?"

"Rumor has it."

"Why don't you put the rumors to bed?"

"So you think I should pounce?"

"You can always find another ballet coach, so what do you have to lose?"

"My pride?"

"Your *what*?" Dai put a hand to his ear as though he hadn't heard Harlow correctly.

"Fuck you."

"I'm just messin' with you." Dai sipped his tea. "But I do think you should go for it. Ask him if he wants to have a drink or something."

"Lame."

"But safe."

Harlow shrugged. "I'm not so worried about that. I just don't want to look like a fool."

Dai was quiet for a few moments before he spoke again. "Not for nothing, but you're careful, right?"

"I never have unprotected sex."

"I don't mean that. I'm talking about maybe getting harassed or even bashed by someone who hates gay people. We live in kind of a bubble where most of the people we see every day are gay, or at least cool with the whole gay thing. Outside the bubble, things can get ugly."

"Who are you talking to, bro? I'm from Tokyo. We're the capital of don't ask/don't tell. I've been hiding who I am since fourth grade. Don't worry about me."

"Okay. I'm not your mom. I just worry about you sometimes."

"Really?"

Dai nodded. "You're my best and only friend."

"I was touched for a second, and then I realized you were quoting from *Blade Runner*, asshole," Harlow said. "Good one, though."

"It *was* a quote, but nonetheless true."

"No. Too late. You ruined the moment." Harlow sat back in his chair. "I'm going to miss Will."

"Why would you say that?"

"I don't know what he was doing to you, but you were always in a great mood after you saw him." Harlow grinned lazily. "I assumed it was a lot of great sex."

"Yeah, I'll miss that too. I'll say this much for Will, he's got all the right equipment and he knows how to use it."

"If only that was enough."

"Damn, we're a couple of wise bastards," Dai said. "We've got this shit figured out. Our next relationships are going to be amazing because of all this stuff we've learned."

"Is that how it works?"

"Yes, Grasshopper."

Harlow finished his tea and stood up. "If you want to cry, go ahead. I'll give you privacy."

"I want a shower." Dai stood too. "But you insisted on having a talk."

"Yeah, the shower is the best place to cry."

"I'm not going to cry," Dai said, but he did.

COPE STARED at Will's door but instead of polished wood, he saw Dai walking away. Something in the set of Dai's shoulders struck a discordant note, and now Cope wished he'd called after him to make sure he was all right. Then again, it was probably nothing more than one of the spats that were a hazard of being close to Will.

Cope shook his head as he chided himself. "You hardly know the guy and he's dating your best friend." He knocked his personal code on

Will's door and then opened it and walked in. "Honey, I'm home," he called out as he crossed the foyer.

"Cope," Drew called out. "Have a seat. Will's making a pitcher of martinis."

"I could use a drink," Cope said as he sat across from Drew. "I swear I'm cursed."

"Cursed?" Will turned from the bar to look at Cope.

Cope didn't answer. The sounds from the television had impinged on his consciousness, and he looked up to see what kind of porn his friends were watching. His face froze in stunned disbelief. "That's Dai," he said.

"And me." Will came over with a martini in each hand. He gave one to Drew and offered the other to Cope.

Cope was still staring at the screen.

"Mesmerizing, isn't he?" Will commented.

Slowly, Cope turned his head to focus on Will. "What did you do?" he asked in a low voice.

"Made a little movie. You want the drink or not?" Will held out the glass.

"Does Dai know you made this little movie?"

"I'm not answering your question until you answer mine."

Cope took the glass from Will's hand and set it on the coffee table. "Does he know?"

"Probably. He knows me, anyway, so he'd have to expect it."

"Yes or no?"

"I don't know."

"Then I'll assume he doesn't know you're showing it to people."

"Just my tightest bros. What's the big deal?"

Cope stood. "If you honestly don't know what the big deal is, I've been very mistaken about you for a long time."

"Whoa, mate," Drew said as he got to his feet.

"Stay out of it, Droop," Cope said. "If you want a piece of this action, I'll get to you when I'm done with Will."

"Take it easy, was all I was going to say." Drew sat back down.

"Thanks, and for fuck's sake, will someone turn off the goddamn TV?" Cope said sharply.

Will gave a voice command and the screen went black.

"Thank you," Cope said and then took a deep breath. "How could you do something like this?" he asked Will. "I just can't get my head around it. Could I really have been this wrong about you?"

"Easy," Will said. "This is escalating quickly."

"Yeah, simmer down, mate," Drew said. He blinked when Will and Cope both glared at him. "Strewth, I didn't know it was that late. I'm off." He stood and walked toward the door. "Don't do anything lethal, chaps," he said over his shoulder.

Neither Will nor Cope spoke until they heard the door close.

"What the fuck, man?" Will spoke quickly to get in the first word.

"No." Cope shook his head. "You don't get to be indignant."

"I do when you're attacking me out of the blue. I thought we were best buds for life."

"So did I, but unless you can adequately explain yourself, I'm not sure I can be your friend."

"Adequately explain myself? What the hell? What are you even talking about? Are you saying we're not friends anymore?"

"Why are you wasting time with pointless questions? Just give me an explanation that I can swallow. That's all I'm asking."

"You know what I can't get my head around? Why you're acting so holier-than-thou."

"I didn't film my lover without permission, and I didn't show that film to a third party. I'm pretty sure that gives me the moral high ground here."

Will stared at Cope as though he'd never seen him before. "Just like that?" he said calmly. "Just because I did something millions of men do, you're going to… what? Unfriend me?"

"Will, I'm not—"

Will heard a hint of softening in Cope's voice and talked over him. "After all the years we've been as close as brothers—closer, even—I can't believe you can be so cold. How can you throw all that aside for someone you barely know?" He saw Cope's eyes narrow slightly and knew he'd made a misstep.

"How can *you* betray someone who put his trust in you?" Cope asked.

Will reached out a hand. "Come on, man," he said softly. "I was just being a guy."

"You were being a low-life guy. Even if Dai knew you made the recording, how do you think he would feel if he knew you and Drew were watching it? Did you even think about that when you invited Drew and me to watch?"

"He'll never find out."

"That doesn't make it right, Will." Cope paused, as he remembered Dai's odd manner when he'd seen him outside Will's building. "And you might be wrong about him not finding out."

"I'm pretty sure Drew's not going to say anything, and I *know* you won't, so how's he going to find out?"

Cope shrugged. "How would I know?" He picked up the cocktail off the table and drank it in one swallow. It was almost pure vodka, but he managed not to cough when he took his next breath. "Look, Will, I can see how you'd think this wasn't a fatal mistake, so I promise I'll think hard about whether I can get past it. I need some space to do that, so don't call me and try to talk your way around this."

"This is crazy." Will put his hand on Cope's arm. "Stay and talk."

Cope glanced at the television. "No can do," he said. "I don't know if you'll understand, but I feel like I fell into a dumpster. I need to go home and shower—and don't say I can take one here and you'll wash my back."

"I wasn't going to say that." Will dropped his hand. "I was going to offer to wash your front."

"Bye, Will."

"I'll see you at the office tomorrow," Will said, but he didn't.

IN FACT, Will didn't see Cope for quite some time. In the days that followed, he was informed by the CEO of his division that Cope was taking some accrued personal time. The fifth or sixth time he tried Cope's phone, he was informed the number was no longer in service. When he went by Cope's apartment, the superintendent told him Cope had sublet the unit for six months to a Milanese handbag designer. He heard rumors and some eyewitness accounts of Cope sightings, but no matter how hard he tried, Will simply couldn't manage to be in the same place at the same time. It was frustrating, and he missed his friend, but they'd been apart before, and if there was one thing Will could count on in life, it was that Cope always came back.

The day after Cope had confronted Will, Will called Dai's number looking forward to making a date for that evening.

"Hello, Will," Dai said. "I was hoping you'd call, because apparently, I don't have the guts to call you."

"Since when?" Will chuckled. "I was wondering if you want to get together tonight. I promise I'll make last night look like a preview of coming attractions."

"No, I don't want to get together tonight or any other night."

"What?" Will gripped the phone tightly; this was like déjà vu of his conversation with Cope. "Why not?"

"It's weird, I know, but I just don't like you anymore. In fact, I can't stand you."

"Did I do something?"

"Did you do something?" Dai took a deep breath. "If you think about it, you'll probably think of something you might have done, but all you really need to know is that I don't want to see you again."

"Dai, talk to me. Whatever it is I've done, I'm sure I can make it up to you."

"Listen to me carefully. There's nothing you can say or do to make me change my mind. I don't want anything you have. Not your looks. Not your money. Not your cock. Don't call me again. If you try to see me, I'll—"

"Are you going to threaten me with cops?"

"No. I'm warning you that I know some pretty tough bouncers who would love to do me a favor. Goodbye, Will."

"Wait! Dai! You at least owe me an expla—" Will looked down at the red Disconnect symbol on his phone screen. "What the actual fuck?" he said under his breath. He called Cope's phone and got a recording again. He called the office and was told Cope still hadn't shown up. He called a florist and had roses sent to Bento Hadaka. He could get Dai back; he didn't doubt it for a second. However, he did wonder why Dai had cut him off so abruptly. At first, he didn't want to consider it, but the more he thought about it, the more likely it seemed that Cope had said something to Dai. The betrayal stung, but he conceded that it was a brilliant move if Cope was interested in Dai… and what gay man wouldn't be?

Will shook his head at the quirks of fate and put another forkful of roast beef in his mouth. He had a healthy appetite and only so much time for lunch.

TWO DAYS after Cope's break with Will, he had a new living space. After enlisting the help of a friend whose husband was a real estate broker, he put down a deposit on a six-month lease on a small ground-floor efficiency. By eleven he was sitting in his presumed-temporary home, staring out the french doors at the tiny terrace. He'd already memorized the furnishings of the two-room apartment: convertible sofa bed, tasteful charcoal gray against the khaki wall covering; an aggressively modern coffee table with an asymmetrical top of cast concrete; kitchenette in the right-hand corner, desk and chair on the left; oatmeal-colored berber on the floor; tonal, nondescript art on the walls. There was nothing there to distract.

Cope closed his eyes and saw Dai, naked and open, eyes liquid with need, as Will thrust into him. He was haunted by the few seconds of film he'd seen before he'd averted his eyes. When he'd managed to sleep last night, his dreams were rated triple-X and gave him no rest. He'd had few regrets in his life thus far and was unprepared for the awful, gnawing needle teeth that never stopped chewing. *If only* he'd said something to Dai about how he felt. *If only* he'd listened to his intuition that night on the street. *If only....* Cope shook his head and sent his loose hair flying into disarray. He wondered where his scissors were.

"This is a fine thing," he said to his cold cup of coffee. "I'm having a breakdown over a guy I knew for a few hours—not that I actually *knew* him, but... I felt something for him. I really did." He looked outside again. "I still do."

Cope sighed and picked up the pen that lay beside a battered moleskin notebook. He turned to a blank page and started to write.

DAI CAME out of the shower with a white towel hanging low on his hips. He saw Harlow adjusting his bow tie in the mirror and changed course. Instead of drying his hair first, he went to his locker to get the silk robe he'd be wearing until it was time to be a table. He dropped the towel on a bench and reached for the robe when someone whistled.

"Nice butt," Kei said. "No wonder you always get flowers." He set a vase of irises on the bench. "There's a card this time." He held out a small envelope.

Dai took the envelope and read the few words on the card inside.
How do I find you?
How do I get back to you?
Please tell me the way.

The words swam in Dai's vision as his eyes filled with tears. Angrily, he blinked them away and crushed the card in his fist. *Not fair, Will.* Dai was not moved by the flowers Will had sent every day, but the poem was a shot straight to the heart.

"Whoa," Kei said. "Bad news?"

"No. It's nothing. Is Mr. Watanabe here yet?"

"Yeah, he's giving the busboys a pep talk."

"Thanks." Dai left the locker room without another word.

Kei raised his eyebrows at Harlow.

"Forget it," Harlow said. "Man trouble."

Kei nodded sagely and left to take a shower. Harlow picked the crumpled card up off the floor and smoothed it out. He read the poem and then got dressed and waited for Dai to come back.

"Well, it's done," Dai said.

"I wish you'd thought about it longer, but I'm sure they'll take you back in a second if you need a job later."

"I just need to make a change."

"I know." Harlow took the card out of his breast pocket. "Want to talk about this?"

"Not even remotely."

"Sounds like he's suffering."

"Cats can sound like crying babies. What's your point?"

"I'm not sure I have one, but I can see there's something wrong, and it's driving me crazy that you won't tell me."

"We've had this discussion. I'm fine. Breaking up with Will threw me a little, but I'm really fine now."

"You're making all these changes."

"I should have made them a long time ago. I'm actually grateful to Will for showing me I was stuck in a rut."

"I don't believe you."

"Okay." Dai snatched the crinkled card from Harlow's hand and tossed it in the trash. "How'd the audition go?"

Harlow immediately brightened. "I'm one of three who got asked back. The director will be there tomorrow morning to make a final decision on the casting."

"What time?"

"I need to be there at eight, so I should leave around seven."

"You'll get the part."

"I have a really good feeling about it. The choreographer likes my body type."

"Who wouldn't?" Dai put an arm around Harlow's shoulders. "You're perfect."

"Whatever."

"How's your Russian? Any progress?"

"Are you going to ask me that four times a day every day?"

"Every six hours," Dai said. "Or until I get an answer I like."

"I might have news for you tomorrow."

"What? Are you seeing him tonight?"

"After work, we're going for an early breakfast. He's working as night manager at the Frisco Disco."

"That must be torture for a classically trained dancer."

"Actually, he gets a kick out of it, or so he says. I presume I'll learn more tonight."

"I want to hear all about it later." Dai finished combing his hair and turned to Harlow for inspection. "My last night as a naked sushi boy," he said. "How do I look?"

"Open the robe, and give me a spin."

Dai untied the belt and turned in a circle.

Harlow eyed Dai's sleek, sculpted muscles. "Sublime," he said. "I bet Watanabe cried when you told him you were quitting immediately."

"He wasn't happy." Dai sighed. "If I didn't know Kei had a couple of friends dying to work here, I'd probably feel worse about not giving notice. The knowledge made Mr. Watanabe feel better too."

"You should give him two weeks. In two weeks, with me pimping you, you could walk away with some serious bank."

"I have savings. My mom had to be both parents, since my dad was gone so much for work, and she was very practical. I kind of hated her a little growing up because she was so strict, but she gave me a lot of good habits."

"Don't I know it, dog," Harlow said. "You're the first American I could stand rooming with."

"I'll take that as a compliment."

"You should." Harlow patted Dai's shoulder. "If I can't talk you out of leaving, I'm going up front to get the table ready. See you in ten."

Dai picked up the blow-dryer off the counter and took most of the dampness out of his thick, silky hair. He still had seven minutes before he had to be in place on the platform. He let the robe slide off his shoulders and appraised his appearance critically. He wasn't vain, but he was self-aware, and he knew he was physically attractive. It had to be something else he lacked that explained his inability to find a man who both wanted and *respected* him. Will sure as hell hadn't respected him.

Dai tilted his head back and blinked until the extra moisture left his eyes. He focused on his reflection again. "Don't cry over him," he told his doppelgänger. "He isn't crying over you. Be grateful you walked away before it turned into something ugly."

"Who are you talking to?" Kei said from the shower room door.

"Myself."

"Hey, look, if you need, you know, a shoulder to cry on...."

"I'm fine, thank you."

"I'm here for you, precious."

"I appreciate that. Gotta go. Harlow's waiting."

CHAPTER EIGHT

COPE IGNORED the first knock, but the second one jarred him from the flow of imagery. He put down his pen and got to his feet. He was a little surprised by how stiff he was, but the shadows in the room said a few hours had gone by since he sat down.

"Who's there?" he called out as he put his eye to the peephole.

"It's Lukas Janonis, Mr. Copeland Shore," said the tall, dark, and handsome man with the Slavic accent. He reached behind him and drew a diminutive woman around to stand at his side. "And Miss Amy Waxwing. We got your name from the super."

"What can I do for you?"

"Amy used to live here, and—would it be possible to speak face-to-face?"

"I don't make it a habit to open the door to strangers."

"You have a phone? Look up Amy Waxwing."

Curious, Cope retrieved his phone from the coffee table and googled the name. He looked at the images for a few seconds and then unlocked the door. "Come in," he said. "Your photos are very impressive, Ms. Waxwing."

"Call me Amy, please. Sorry to barge in like this, but Lukas—"

"Lukas is rash and headstrong," Lukas said. "But he gets what he wants." He smiled at Cope. "If we could have a few minutes of your time to explain?"

"Sure. Would either of you like coffee? Some tea? Water?"

"If it's no trouble, coffee would be nice," Amy said. "May I go out on the terrace?"

"Of course." Cope went to the kitchenette and started the coffee machine. A short while later, he carried a tray out to the terrace and set it on the glass-topped table. "It's pretty out here at this time of day," he said. "I haven't been here long, but long enough to appreciate the lack of tall buildings around me."

"This apartment is a real jewel," Amy said.

"Did you say you used to live here?"

Amy nodded, chestnut curls bouncing around her ears. "I had an opportunity to go to Prague, so I had to let the place go." She glanced at Lukas before she spoke again. "The thing is… the light here is perfect early in the morning and just at sunset. I took a lot of photos here. With your permission, I'd like to take a few more."

"I'm not sure I want a lot of traffic through my house."

"It would just be me, my equipment, and one subject at a time, starting with Lukas."

"Is it a project of some kind?"

"I hope to turn the shots into a calendar. I'll donate half the money to the School of American Ballet."

"How long will this take?"

"Conservative estimate? Three days to a week."

"And you'd be here at specific times so I could clear out if I wanted to?"

"Absolutely."

Cope gave Lukas an appraising look. "So you're a danseur?"

Lukas made a little bow. "I'm told I have some talent in that area."

"And he's gorgeous," Amy said. She took a sip of her coffee. "Don't you think?"

"What makes you think I'm any judge of beauty?" Cope asked.

"You chose this apartment. Your clothes are casual but chic." Amy paused. "And I saw your poetry while you were making coffee." She saw the frown forming on his face and spoke quickly. "Just a couple of lines. I wasn't trying to pry. The notebook was open and I—"

"It's all right," Cope said rather unconvincingly.

"*The lines of your upper lip. Like the wings of birds. In a child's drawing of the sky*," Amy said softly.

Lukas stared at Cope. "You wrote this?"

"This is really embarrassing," Cope said.

"Don't be embarrassed," Amy said. "You have talent."

"I just write things sometimes when I feel too much."

Amy smiled. "I have a friend who plays blues guitar. She says the same thing. Are you a sad man, Copeland Shore?"

"We're getting a little personal for people who didn't know each other fifteen minutes ago."

"I am Lithuanian," Lukas said as though offering a rationale.

"Yeah? What's her excuse?" Cope replied.

"I'm a meddling busybody," Amy said. "Everybody says so."

"And she's clueless," Lukas said.

"It's true." Amy shrugged. "Until my first lawsuit, it never occurred to me that some people might not want me to photograph them."

"You're making that up," Cope said. "No one's that naïve."

"In my defense, I was eleven."

"Who sues an eleven-year-old girl?"

"Well, the neighbors actually sued my parents—who were not happy that their little girl had nudie pics of the neighbors. But I ask you, even with an eight-foot fence, why would you do naked yoga in front of a plateglass window when you knew perfectly well the neighbor girl had a camera and a trampoline?"

Cope snickered.

"He doesn't look so sad now, *Saulėkaita*," Lukas said.

"Lukas calls me Sunshine because I light up his life." Amy shrugged.

"He may have a point," Cope said. "When would you want to start your project?"

"As soon as humanly possible."

"Can I call you?"

Amy's smile slipped sideways, but her disappointment didn't color her voice when she answered. "Of course. You'd be doing us a great favor, after all. Let me know when it's convenient for you." She handed Cope a business card.

Cope looked at the card for the length of time it took to read the information. "Okay. You can use the terrace."

"Really? But I thought—"

"I made a snap decision," Cope said. "Hang on." He snagged his business card case from the bookshelf and gave Amy a card.

"Thank you so much!" Amy said. "We'll get out before you change your mind."

Lukas took Cope's hand in a firm grip. "You will not regret it," he said. He winked as he relinquished Cope's hand.

"I'll call you later about shooting this evening," Amy said as she and Lukas left the apartment.

Cope stood in the middle of the floor for a few minutes like a man getting his bearings after being caught in a whirlwind. "What have I got myself into?" he wondered aloud. However, he was looking forward to observing the photo shoot. He needed a distraction to keep him from brooding over his ignorance of Will's true character or why he was too cowardly to sign his name to the poems he sent to Dai. Having a troupe of dancers and a high-energy photographer hanging around might be the perfect alternative to skydiving lessons. It would certainly be better than sliding further into depression over a quixotic obsession. No way he wanted to go through that again. Yet… he couldn't stop wondering what it would be like to love Dai.

Cope's phone chimed, and he picked it up off the end table. He had a text from Amy. He opened the picture message and gazed at the image for several moments. On the screen, the sun was setting behind storm clouds over a field of barley glowing like molten gold. Above it flew a gull, its wings arched in the shape of Dai's upper lip. Longing gripped him so hard that he couldn't draw breath for a few seconds.

"Snap out of it," he told himself. "What the hell are you doing? You're sending dreary poems to a guy you have a passing acquaintance with. It's not like you had some epic love of a lifetime. Plus he probably thinks you're as sleazy as your friend Will."

Cope knew he could find Dai's phone number, just as he knew he could find Dai at either his apartment or at work. He also knew he would not call Dai or drop in on him. The fear that he was right—that Dai knew about the sex film and assumed Cope had seen it—kept him from making contact. His cowardice knew no bounds. Apparently he'd rather live alone and miserable than take the risk of Dai confirming his hunch. No, it was best to keep his distance.

Half an hour later, Cope had used a program on his computer to superimpose the words of his poem on Amy's photo. Having sought Amy's permission, he printed the image. He slipped on his shoes, put his phone wallet in his pocket, and walked to the FedEx around the corner. He purchased an envelope and had it sent to Dai. The clerk didn't give him any hassle about not having a return address. He paid and went back home feeling a little lighter.

A WEEK after breaking it off with Will, Dai was making breakfast when Harlow returned from a date. "Omelet?" Dai offered.

"Split one?"

"Sure. Coffee's hot."

"Bless you, my son." Harlow poured a cup and sat on a stool at the breakfast bar. "I really needed this," he said after a few sips. "I don't want to fall asleep. I have a class in two hours."

"Yeah, you need to be in your best shape."

"Too early for sarcasm, my man."

"I'll make a note of that." Dai folded the omelet and transferred it to a plate before cutting it in half. He put half the omelet in front of Harlow and gave him a fork. He pulled the other barstool under the counter and sat down opposite Harlow. He had a direct view of the top of Harlow's drooping head. "Time to touch up those roots," he said archly.

"My boyfriend likes it this way." Harlow ran a hand through his platinum hair. Where it grew out of his scalp, it was jet-black for about a quarter of an inch.

"It's eye-catching."

"That's what he said. So do you want to hear about my date, or can we just sit here in blessed silence?"

"As you wish."

Harlow smiled. "I love you, man. For reals."

"Ditto." Dai smirked as he forked a bite of eggs into his mouth.

"Bang. Bang. *Princess Bride* and *Ghost*."

"I thought you wanted to be quiet."

"So did I. Get any lines on interesting jobs?"

"Now that you mention it, I couldn't wait to tell you." Dai ate the last bite of his half of the omelet and then sprang to his feet. "I'll be right back."

"What the fuck?" Harlow said under his breath as Dai dashed into the bedroom. He finished his eggs and poured another cup of coffee before Dai returned. Harlow was glad he was sitting down again. Nothing could have prepared him for the sight of Dai in Spider-Man's full-body, red-and-blue leotard. "What the fuck?"

"I'm Spider-Man." Dai struck a superhero pose.

"Clearly. But why?"

"This is my new job."

"Level with me. Are you doing porn?"

"That would be creepy, since I'm working for Toys"R"Us."

"Where are you hiding your junk?"

"The costume comes with something like a dance belt. I shouldn't have to tell you that."

"Right. Right. I'm still a little stunned."

"It pays well, and the work is light. I just have to hang around and let kids take pictures with me."

"I'm proud of you, of course, but just one question. You couldn't try for FAO Schwarz?"

"My Japanese Jewish mother." Dai rolled his eyes, forgetting Harlow couldn't see his face. "Sadly, FAO is gone."

"Seriously, though, if you're happy, I'm happy."

"I'm happi*er*. Will that do for now?"

"That'll do, pig."

Dai laughed. "You win. I won't come up with a better quote than that. I'd better go take this off now. I wouldn't want to get anything on it."

"Hey, Dai?" Harlow called out as Dai crossed to the bedroom again. "You think I could borrow that costume sometime?"

"Didn't you hear me say I don't want to get anything on it, Monica?"

"Stingy."

"Pervert."

Harlow shrugged. "You've got me there," he said as Dai disappeared into his room. He put his cup and plate in the sink and went to the futon. He opened the chest that served as a coffee table and took out clean clothes. After a quick shower and changing into fresh clothes, he felt refreshed. When he came into the living room, Dai was flipping through channels on the TV.

"What are you doing today?" Harlow said after he flopped down next to Dai.

"I don't start work until tomorrow. Today was a kind of orientation. Four hours of learning to move like Spider-Man. I had it down in four minutes. The rest was a great big snoozeburger listening to a self-important dickweed intimidate the betas in the group."

"Have I mentioned that your outlook is less sunny of late?"

"No, and I'd advise you not to."

"I'm hip." Abruptly, Harlow sat up straight. "Wait! Go back!"

"Why?"

"Why? Are you fucking kidding me? That was *Ladyhawke*."

"Oh come on," Dai scoffed. "I saw a bird too. Doesn't mean it's *Ladyhawke*."

"It is! Go back!"

"Keep your tits on." Dai clicked back until Harlow yelled at him to stop. "You're right. It's *Ladyhawke*," he said.

"I'm amazed you'd doubt me… and a little hurt." Harlow snuggled up to Dai. "But I forgive you because Matthew Broderick is so frickin' awesome in this movie."

"You ever wonder why we like movies made before we were born?"

"Never."

"Neither do I." Dai put the remote down and settled back against the cushions with Harlow's warm weight against his side. For at least an hour, he was assured life would be good. He was beginning to wonder if anyone could ask for more.

COPE'S PHONE rang, and he answered it without hesitation. Almost two weeks now, and Will had yet to sniff him out. Of course, that had necessitated breaking all ties with anyone they knew in common, but it was worth it to have the time to think without Will plying his almost subliminal seduction techniques on him. Since they'd known each other, Will had always been able to coax Cope back to his side after an argument. However, Will had never done anything this slimy before. Up until now, the worst was probably Will hiring the male stripper for his twenty-first birthday party after Cope had explicitly forbidden it. Cope was pretty sure his visiting aunt had been scarred for life. He'd never received another card from her, anyway.

"Hi, Amy," he said into the phone.

"Are you home?"

"Almost. I went out for some cold cuts and cheese."

"Have you got a few minutes to talk?"

"Well, it's a little awkward with the bag and the six-pack."

"Call me back?"

"You always sound excited, but right now, you sound like you're holding in a squeal."

"Because I am."

"Hang on." Cope opened his front door, picked up the six-pack, and carried his groceries to the kitchenette. "Okay, tell me."

"Well, the press that was going to do the calendar—"

"What?" Cope paused in the act of opening the fridge. "*Was* going to?"

"They're still going to, but the chief editor liked the photos so much, she wants to do a book also." Amy paused. "If they can use your poems."

"What!" Cope almost dropped a jar of blue-cheese-stuffed olives.

"Don't say no right away. Please. Wait until you see your words with the pictures."

"You looked through my notebook?"

"Well… I kind of thought if you left it open, you must not mind if people read it."

"Hm."

"Please don't be too angry. Say you'll look at the images before you make up your mind."

"When can I see them?"

"I can email them. I can bring them by. Or you can come to the office."

"How much trouble would it be to bring them here? I can promise you snacks and beer from Barcelona."

"I'm on my way."

Cope hung up and made a platter with the Iberian ham, chorizo, manchego cheese, and a couple of handfuls of oily, garlicky olives. He put the platter on the coffee table and sliced a few pieces from a crusty, skinny loaf of bread. Two bottles went into the freezer along with two mugs, and then he sat to munch olives and wait for Amy. Less than ten minutes passed before she knocked on his door.

"Can you believe it?" she said as she bounced into the apartment.

"Nope," Cope said succinctly. "Sit. I'll get you a plate and a beer."

"That would be fantastic. I didn't have time for lunch, and I need to keep my girlish curves."

Cope set a plate and a full mug in front of Amy and went back for his. "Tell me more," he said as he sat down.

"Edith, the chief editor, absolutely adores the photos, and she was blown away by your poetry. She couldn't believe she'd never heard of you, but I told her that's because you're a hermit."

"I'm not, though."

"Okay." Amy took a long drink of her Estrella Damm. "Good beer."

"I like it. It goes really well with the manchego and chorizo. I wish I had some goat cheese and honey, but I didn't feel like walking all the way to the Catalan place."

"You're so sophisticated," she said. "You told me you used to sell clothes, but I get the feeling you didn't work behind the counter at Urban Outfitters."

"No, I didn't." Cope put some manchego on a bread round and bit into it, leaving Amy without a clue as to his attitude. He liked her and genuinely found the project intriguing, but he wasn't quite ready to let her off the hook for snooping.

"Sorry for changing the subject. Anyway, Edith is really eager to meet you and discuss possible future books. She thinks the combination of images and words will appeal to a broad spectrum of people."

"Let's see them," Cope said. "Or would you rather wait until after we eat?"

"They're in transparent sleeves," Amy said. She picked up the large portfolio next to the couch and unfastened the latches. The leather satchel unfolded to reveal a stack of eleven-by-fourteen prints. Amy picked up the one on top and passed it to Cope.

It was a picture of a young dancer from Sierra Leone named Victoria Koroma. She had the body and the doe eyes of a saluki. Her dark skin contrasted sharply with her classic Swan Lake tutu. Her hair was covered by a cap of white feathers that curled against her forehead, neck, and cheekbones. She was poised on one foot, every part of her yearning upward. The rosy-bronze light of the setting sun highlighted the sleek, elegant contours of her face and body—a statue of a wild goddess come to life and about to take to the sky. Over the stones of the terrace's back wall were printed the words of Cope's poem about Dai's mouth.

"What do you think?" Amy asked.

"Epic."

"Really?"

"Really. You can't see the tears because I'm crying on the inside."

"Are you messing with me?"

"No. I'm serious. Your Edith is right. The words with the picture work like a charm."

"So we can go ahead with the book?"

"Not so fast. What would that involve?"

"More poems and more pictures."

"I have more poems, and you could take more photos here, so that's not a problem."

"What is the problem?"

"I can't think of any. I just don't like being rushed."

"So…?"

"Okay, I'll do it. God knows, I need to do something." Cope looked at the next image. "Lukas really is gorgeous," he said.

"He makes a wonderful Hermes." Amy passed over another photo, and then another, until Cope had seen all twelve.

"You memorized all of those?" Cope asked.

"No, I took pictures with my phone, silly goose."

"Right. I guess I've lost my edge after being a hermit for so long."

Amy laughed at his melodramatic tone. "So, how long ago did you decide to turn your back on the world?"

"About… three weeks."

"That long?" Amy laughed again. "So what was it? Business? Family? A woman? A man?"

"A man."

"Is he the one who made you so sad?"

"There were two."

"Two men?"

"That's right."

"Don't want to talk about it, huh?"

"No… and yes." Cope sounded surprised.

"I won't judge you. Scout's honor." Amy paused. "Can I have another beer?"

"Of course. I'll join you." Cope poured two more Estrellas and sat back down. "I'm not going into detail, no matter how drunk you get me," he said.

"But I was right. You're gay."

"Exclusively since my teenage years."

"You gave heterosexuality a go, did you?"

"I was confused."

Amy smiled slightly. "When did you know for sure?"

"The summer between twelve and thirteen. I was packed off to my mom's grandparents in Orlando, Florida. Kind of the pits for someone that age because it's Florida but not on the beach."

"What about the theme parks?"

"Too expensive. Too crowded. Too dangerous."

"I see."

"Yeah, they weren't much fun. They were nice and they loved me, but they didn't 'cater to kids.' Anyway, there was another kid in the condo sentenced to four weeks with his grandparents. We met at the dinky pool and became friends by default. One day when we were elevating the blood pressure of several residents who were waiting to play shuffleboard, Brett asked me if I ever yanked it. Then he told me to close my mouth because I looked like a fish. I'm sure I did. My jaw dropped to my shoelaces."

"So you masturbated together?"

"Yeah. How'd you know?"

"It's pretty common."

"Not for me, it wasn't. Brett showed me his secret place—the shed where the shuffleboard equipment was stored. He shoved his trunks down and grabbed himself, and at that moment I knew something with absolute clarity. I wanted it to be my hand stroking him. And that was it; I knew what I was."

"Mine was a babysitter, but we won't talk about that right now. Tell me who broke your heart… most recently."

"My best friend and a guy I suspect was *The One*."

"Did they cheat on you with each other?"

"It's actually worse."

"How is that possible?"

"He was my best friend's boyfriend."

"You cheated with him?"

"No. We all met at the same time, and I was attracted, but I had to go on a business trip, so my friend asked him out first. When I got back, it was a done deal."

"Ouch."

"So I'm eating my heart out and being a good sport, but then my friend does something incredibly sleazy to his boyfriend."

"And they broke up?"

"I assume."

"You don't know?"

Cope shook his head. "I went on radio silence. I haven't talked to anyone for weeks."

"All or nothing with you, huh?"

"I guess. Is that bad?"

"Since I'm already armchair psychoanalyzing you, I have to tell you that you don't give a person a lot of clues. Have you always played it so close to the chest?"

"Yeah, I guess. I've always thought it was a good habit."

"It's not the worst, as long as you remember that people can't read your mind. When someone is self-contained the way you are, it's kind of a pain in the ass."

"Damn, don't sugarcoat it."

"Don't worry. I won't."

"It's okay. This is actually… refreshing."

"I warned you I was a meddler. Now tell me about this man who got away. He must be something special."

"Yeah. Don't laugh, but honestly, he made me believe in love at first sight."

"I would never laugh at that, but do you really believe you fell for him the moment you saw him?"

"Yeah… I guess I do."

"So why don't you call him? See if he's free?"

"I should, but all I seem capable of is sending anonymous notes."

"You're kidding." Amy shook her head. "That's awful. You're not in fourth grade anymore."

"I know, and believe me, I'm not normally shy about asking a guy out, but this guy…."

"What? What's so different about him?"

"I can't explain it, but when I saw him, I just felt like, *yeah, that's him.*"

"Okay, if that's how you feel, why don't you stop screwing around and talk to him?"

"I'm afraid he thinks I'm as sleazy as my friend."

Amy shook her head, bedazzled barrettes catching the light. "Why are men so afraid of someone else's feelings? Accept that he feels the way he feels and that you can't change it. Go from there. Surely you can survive his disapproval. It'll be painful, true, but you'll be free of the doubts and regrets. Those are worse, believe me."

"I can't. Not yet, anyway."

"Don't wait too long. The special ones tend to get snapped up fast."

"I hear you. If I haven't said it, I'm glad you and Lukas knocked on my door that day."

"So am I, and not just because of your fascinating personality. I think our partnership is going to take me from a regionally known photographer to a nationally known photographer."

"You deserve it."

"Thanks for not judging me. I'm all for art for art's sake, but I want lots of people to see my work. I admit it; I want the recognition." She grinned. "If I get rich along the way, well, I won't bitch."

"May I assume you'll be here around five tomorrow morning?"

"You may."

"I'll have coffee ready. You bring the doughnuts."

"Deal." Amy held out her tangerine-nailed hand, and Cope took it. They shook solemnly.

"Why do I suddenly have this ominous feeling?" Cope wondered aloud.

"Shut up and ignore it. From now on, everything is going to be great."

"Is this what it's like to have a woman friend?"

"Shut up!" Amy repeated more vehemently. "Are you telling me you've never had a female friend?"

"Never. I've had female acquaintances, wives and girlfriends of friends, colleagues, but no one I'd call a friend. No one I'd get together with to see a movie or have a drink. No one I'd confide in."

"You need balance in your life."

"Is that what I need?"

"In my opinion. For what it's worth." Amy finished her beer and set the mug down. She stood and tucked the portfolio under her arm. "I don't want to leave, but if I don't go now, I'll be up until four in the morning getting the shoot organized."

Cope was pretty sure she had everything organized before she called him, but he let it go. He assumed she was feeling the need for distance after their frank discussion; he certainly was. After seeing Amy to the door, he took his half-full mug and iPad out to the terrace. He intended to look for a show that might tempt him to actually book a ticket and go farther than ten blocks from his new apartment. Instead, he watched the light fade on the stone walls, in the crescent of grass, and in the neatly trimmed miniature shrubs and hedges. The small backyard area had an elegant simplicity that reminded him of Asian gardens. He visualized Dai in this setting and was struck by a sense of absolute rightness. Dai belonged here… with him.

He remembered the moment in Hong Kong when he'd decided he was going to pursue Dai. And he remembered faltering at the last moment. He'd sent a gift and a poem, but he hadn't identified himself. Why *was* he behaving like a teenager in a romantic comedy? What was his plan anyway? Was he really going to wait for Dai to mention the poems and then dramatically announce that he'd written them? Did he think Dai would swoon and fall into his arms?

"I'm not very good at this," he admitted to the pawn-shaped potted topiary on his right.

Cope sighed. He was thirty, and he'd never had a serious relationship. The longest had lasted just short of three months. He hadn't initiated a single one of them. Was that normal? He'd always assumed it was. When he and Will went to bars, they never hit on anyone. According to Will, you had to have the quiet cool. Let them come to you like deer to the watering hole. Why had he never found that analogy disturbing before? Was he getting wiser, or just older and slower, which is no doubt what Will would say? Will would make a crushing joke about testosterone levels, but Cope found he didn't care anymore what Will would say.

For a little over a decade, Cope had walked and talked to the rhythm Will had established on the day they met. Cope was ambitious, but he recognized in Will a relentless drive that would keep them both on task when Cope had one of his blue periods. Will was an essential element of Cope's universe, like gravity. He'd never imagined a world where Will didn't take the lead.

Abruptly, Cope took out his phone and made a call. He was a little surprised when Will answered an unfamiliar number, and he spoke quickly before he lost his nerve. "Hi, Will, it's Cope. I thought I should at least call and let you know I'm still alive."

"I'm glad you did. I've been going crazy looking for you. Where are you?"

"Not yet," Cope said. "I haven't forgiven you, but I wanted you to know I don't hate you."

"That's a relief. When are you coming back?"

"I don't know."

"How can I plan a party around 'I don't know'?"

"I don't know."

"How 'bout a little help here, bro?"

"I'm still very upset about what happened."

"Oh. So… you're going to sulk for a while longer?"

"If that's what you want to call it."

"Okay, bad choice of words. Don't worry about work. I sent Wells to Hong Kong."

"The Chongs will eat him alive."

"Call it his baptism by fire."

"He could lose the deal."

"If he does, I won't open a vein. Seriously, I don't even care about that right now. I'm worried about you."

"Are you?"

"What a thing to say. Especially now when everyone is deserting me."

"Are you really trying to play the victim?"

"You were right. Somehow Dai knew. I don't know how he knew, but I know he did."

"What happened?" Cope asked despite himself.

"I called him the next day and he cut me dead. No explanation, just a quick chorus of 'Hit the Road, Jack.'"

"So you're just assuming," Cope chided, though he'd done the same.

"You didn't hear the tone of his voice. Gave me the chills. Believe me, he *knows*."

"Poor Dai."

"Poor Dai? He left me flat. Let me get used to the fantastic sex and then just dropped me."

"You deserve it."

"Thanks, that really helps."

"I didn't call to help you. I just wanted to let you know I was alive and somewhat well."

Will tried the one line that always worked with Cope. "I miss you, man."

"I miss you too," Cope said. "But I can stand it."

Shaken, Will hesitated before speaking again. "Are you going to forgive me?"

"Probably, but not yet."

"Are you coming back to work?"

"That's looking less and less likely."

"Why?"

"Aside from the obvious awkwardness of working with you, I've realized I'm tired of it. I used to love the pace, but I want to step off for a while."

"What will you do with yourself?"

"I thought I might become a high-priced gigolo."

"Let me know when you open for business."

"Negative." Cope almost hung up, but he couldn't resist the opportunity to put a bee in Will's bonnet. "Actually, I'm publishing a book."

"What?"

"So I don't think I'll be bored. Good night." Cope ended the call and immediately blocked Will's number. It was a cheesy, high school kind of thing to do, but he knew Will. Now that Will had his number, he'd start his campaign of persuasion. Even if Cope had informed on him to Dai, it was a move Will could admire, and he wanted Cope back in his life.

Cope opened his iPad and looked through the scans Amy had emailed to him. He had the urge to send Dai another anonymous gift. If only he wasn't tainted by association with Will, he might even dare to sign his name. Or he could give up this sad and futile obsession. Almost idly, he opened a window, and his fingers moved on the keyboard.

I cannot touch you.
You're no longer in my world.
Still I reach for you.

CHAPTER NINE

THE DELIVERYMAN was surprised but unfazed when Spider-Man answered the door; he'd been making deliveries in New York for thirty years. Spidey signed for the envelope, said thanks, and shut the door.

Dai set the envelope on the counter and peeled off his head covering. He'd just walked in the door when the deliveryman knocked. Quickly, he changed into a T-shirt and track pants and got a bottle of sparkling water out of the fridge. After he took several long swallows, he set the bottle down and picked up the envelope.

Another photograph taken in the same location as the last one. Dai recognized the stone wall and the shallow granite bowl. The bowl was filled with seed, and a sparrow perched on the rim. The poem was printed in the shadow of the bowl. *I cannot touch you. You're no longer in my world. Still I reach for you.*

Once again, Dai felt the twinge of doubt. How could the man who wrote these poems be the same man who betrayed his trust? Maybe he should call Will. *No.* Dai ruthlessly squashed that thought. There was nothing Will could say to excuse what he'd done. No. It was better to not entertain thoughts of giving Will a second chance. Even if the poems made Dai melt inside.

After dropping the photo on the counter, Dai went back to the fridge to forage. Five hours of leaping about had left him with an appetite. He found a takeout box from Hadaka and gleefully ate Harlow's leftovers. He was just finishing when Harlow showed up.

"Is that my food?" Harlow asked.

"You can have it back." Dai opened his mouth wide.

"You're lucky I don't come over there and fill that hole."

"I don't know. I'm pretty horny."

"So fuck somebody. It's not like they wouldn't come running if you winked at them."

"Who are *they*?"

"Every top in the city."

"Where do they hang out?"

"Not at Toys"R"Us."

"Yeah, I knew that."

"Seriously, man, you need to shake this off."

"Am I still moping?"

"You've never been this negative."

"Sorry. I'm starting to hate my job already."

"So find something else. Meanwhile, quit the job that makes you unhappy."

"My savings won't last forever. More like a couple of months."

"Don't worry about the rent." Harlow touched the back of Dai's hand. "With my savings and earnings from the dance company, my bank account is solid. But if you want a job, I have an idea. Let me make a call." He took out his phone and walked out the back. When he returned, he was grinning. "Congratulations! You're a model."

"I am?"

"Well, you don't mind being naked, right?"

"You know I don't."

"Perfect. This photographer I know needs beautiful people to take pictures of. You can go with me tomorrow morning."

"I'm supposed to go to work."

"You *are* going to work… with me. Call in drunk to the toy store. That should get you fired."

"I don't want to get fired, but I can get one of the other guys to cover for me."

"Awesome. This is going to be out of control."

"I could use some fun. How's your Russian?"

"I think we'll see action soon. At lunch, he actually kissed me first when I had to leave."

"Whoa, slow down, Slutty McSlutterson."

Harlow laughed. "We're slow, right?"

"For two gay men who are attracted to each other? Yeah. You're kind of slow."

"Stop profiling me!" Harlow said with mock-indignation. "Not all gay men are promiscuous."

"You are."

Harlow gasped. "Take that back, right now!"

"Okay."

"I'm a good Japanese boy."

"That's what it says on the men's room wall next to your phone number."

Harlow laughed. "That's better," he said. "I've missed your disparaging banter."

"Let me put on something else and I'll take you to dinner. Unless you have plans?"

"I'm taking a break tonight so I can get plenty of sleep. I want to look my best tomorrow."

"So... dinner?"

"Cosmo's Pasta Factory?"

"You got it. I'll go change."

The hostess at Cosmo's sat Dai and Harlow at a table for two in the coveted outdoor seating area. They were among her favorite regulars, and she chatted for a moment until the server arrived. Harlow ordered his favorite all'arrabbiata pasta dish, and Dai asked for whatever the chef felt like throwing together. They decided to split a bottle of wine and drank the first two glasses with the complimentary bread. Their main courses arrived, and Harlow tucked right in to his pasta topped with spicy marinara. Dai waited while the server explained that his pasta was tossed with a creamy tuna-lemon sauce, caperberries, and strips of carpaccio. Harlow and Dai were mopping their empty dishes with the last of the bread when Harlow glanced up and froze.

"What?" Dai turned to look over his shoulder. "No way."

Will saw Dai see him and raised a hand in greeting. Dai didn't acknowledge him. Dai pointedly turned to face Harlow again. Deliberately, he picked up his glass of wine and took a sip.

"Dai," Will said as he stopped beside the iron railing that defined the seating area. "Can we talk for a few minutes?" He glanced at Harlow. "If you don't mind?"

"*I* mind," Dai said.

"All I'm asking for is five minutes."

"No."

"*Five* minutes, Dai."

"Go away, and let me enjoy my dinner in peace."

"Tell me one thing, and I'll go."

Dai sighed. "What?"

"You saw, didn't you? That's why you broke up with me."

Dai met Will's intense blue gaze. "Yes. I saw." He paused to steady his voice. "You broke me, and that's why I broke up with you."

"It was just—"

"Go," Dai interrupted. "Just leave."

Harlow stood up. "You should go," he said to Will. "Unless you enjoy scenes, because I'm about to get loud on your ass."

Will gave Harlow a calculating look. "Okay. I found out what I needed to know." He turned his attention back to Dai. "I'd take you back in a second," he said. "Let me know if you ever get over yourself."

"Asshole," Harlow said as Will strode away.

"It's okay," Dai said. "Honestly, I'm glad that's over with."

The hostess came over. "Is everything all right?" she asked. "The gentleman said he was a friend of yours. He seemed to know you well, and he'd been in with you before, so I didn't think anything of—"

"It's okay, Vanessa," Dai said. "No harm done."

"Bull," Harlow said. "You're upset. I can tell."

"Well, no need to upset Vanessa too."

"But it's my fault," she said. "He asked me to let him know when you came in again. I should have known it was the wrong thing to do. Is he a stalker?"

"Not exactly," Dai said. "And please don't worry about it."

"Fine, as long as you agree not to worry about your bill for tonight. It's on the house."

Harlow raised an eyebrow. "Another bottle?"

"You got it," Vanessa said. "Dessert?"

"More bread," Harlow said. "Please. And maybe some of that fig jam. And some brie?"

"No problem. Francis will bring it right out."

"Sorry," Dai said.

"Don't be," Vanessa said. "It's a crappy way to get a free meal. Try and enjoy."

"She's nice," Harlow said when Vanessa was gone.

"You're a pig."

"Oink oink."

Dai smiled. "Drink your wine."

The walk home was a meandering affair, with Dai and Harlow supporting each other. The effects of two bottles of strong red wine imbued random, everyday objects with the power of locomotion. Sudden swerves to avoid the street signs and garbage cans that leapt into their path led to staggering, desperate attempts to maintain equilibrium.

"Is our apartment farther away now?" Harlow asked as he peered down the street.

"Possibly. Are we on the right street?"

"Don't say that." Harlow looked wildly around. "Okay, there's the Greek deli. We're good."

"That's a florist shop."

"The hell you say." Harlow leaned on Dai. "This is our street. Unless we turned the wrong way coming out of Cosmo's. If we did that and made a right turn, we'd be on...." He walked to the nearest cross street and looked at the sign. "This is our street. Definitely." He swayed on his feet and grabbed at the pole. "Come on, Dai."

Arms around each other's shoulders, they set off again.

"What did you see?" Harlow asked.

"When?"

"Will asked you if you saw something that made you break up with him."

"I'm not telling you."

"Why not? I'm your best bud."

"Because it's just too embarrassing. I can't believe I let myself get taken advantage of again."

"Are you blaming yourself?" Harlow came to a dead stop.

Dai hung onto Harlow and stayed on his feet. "I knew what kind of guy he was, and I played along... most of the time. He wanted a sweet and submissive freak, and I gave him that."

"Tell me what happened."

"No. I won't. Not drunk in the street, I won't."

"Let's go home and make coffee."

"What a great idea."

"You told me you caught him with someone else."

"Yes, I did. The answer isn't going to change." Dai glanced up. "Yay, I can see our light."

"I've thought about it a lot," Harlow said. "And I still can't believe you'd toss aside a rich, gorgeous stud the first time he steps out on you."

Dai opened the gate and guided Harlow down the three brick steps to the alleyway that led to their door. "He did something without my permission, okay?"

"He date-raped you?"

"Could you not shout? And no, he didn't rape me. He's dominant but not like that."

"Then what?"

"He filmed us having sex, okay?"

"Okay." Harlow went in as soon as Dai got the door open. "So he had a hidden camera."

"Yeah."

"That's pretty damn sleazy."

"He also showed the film to his buddy."

"Son of a bitch!" Harlow dropped onto the futon like he'd been shot. "You're kidding!"

Dai shook his head. "I saw them watching it when I went back for my keys. They didn't even know I was there."

"I can't believe he had the nerve to approach you after that." Harlow sounded completely sober now.

"Yeah, well, you know how alpha males are."

"Right. Right. They can never understand why you're so upset, and they're sure they can win you back."

"Exactly. Now I'm going to brush my teeth and go to bed."

"But I'm not done being outraged."

"I'm too tired. Sleep well."

"It was a low-down dirty thing for him to do."

"No argument. Good night."

"Dammit," Harlow said to Dai's back. "How am I going to get to sleep?"

"One more glass of wine and you'll pass out. I think there's a bottle of burgundy open. Look on the counter by the stove."

Dai went into the bathroom, and Harlow changed into the XL T-shirt he slept in. Harlow passed on the wine in favor of the sedative of late-night television. Sprawled on the futon, he channel-surfed until the flickering light put him under. Dai lay awake for a little while, his brain furiously manufacturing clever comebacks for each thing Will had said. It was a futile exercise; there were no do-overs. It was simply over. He hoped Will would accept that now.

It was no use. Logic couldn't douse his anger at Will. He admitted it. He was mad as hell that Will had charmed Vanessa into informing on him. He was furious that Will's question had led to Harlow knowing his secret. Will hadn't cared what effect the confrontation might have on Dai. Will only cared about what Will wanted. Dai needed to remember that when he started to think Will might deserve a second chance.

"The next poem that shows up here is going to burn," Dai told his pillow. He punched the unoffending pillow into a new shape and burrowed his face into it. Feeling somewhat more at peace, he drifted into sleep.

CHAPTER TEN

DAI GOT out of the cab and waited for Harlow to pay. He liked the looks of this neighborhood. You could see the skyscrapers from here, but most of the buildings were old brick and none more than ten stories high. Harlow got out and waved at a tall man who stood under a green-and-white awning. The man smiled, waved, and blew a kiss before taking the box he carried into the door that opened behind him.

"I told you that you'd get to meet him," Harlow said to Dai.

"That's your Russian? He's even more gorgeous than the pictures you've shown me."

"You're so right. Come on. If we're late, we miss the light."

"So that's why we're here so early." Dai waited while Harlow knocked on the door.

The tall handsome man opened the door, and Harlow leaped into his arms while wrapping his legs around the man's waist. The man swayed, regained his balance, and put his arms around Harlow. "Are we a monkey today?" he asked in a rich baritone. "Sorry I didn't wait for you, but I had the ice cream cake."

"Dai, this is Luk!" Harlow said brightly. "Luk, this is my best friend in the whole world."

"I'm pleased to meet you. I've heard much about you from this one. If I had a hand free, I would shake with you."

Dai smiled. "Maybe when Harlow is done using you as a jungle gym."

Harlow slid down until his feet were on the floor. "I can't help it," he said. "When I'm around Luk, I want to touch him."

"I have no trouble understanding that," Dai said.

Luk returned Dai's smile. "I will take that as a compliment. It's good of you to come along with Harlow to the shoot. I think Amy will like you very much."

"What will I like?" Amy came in through the open french doors and set a camera down on the kitchen counter. "Lukas, love, would you put this baby back in her case for me?" She focused on Dai. "And who is this gorgeous hunk of man?"

"This is my friend Dai I told you about."

"You didn't exaggerate," Amy said. She walked a circle around Dai. "No problem with nudity?"

"The opposite," Harlow said.

"Come on now," Dai protested. "It's not like I'm an exhibitionist or something."

Harlow leaned to whisper loudly in Amy's direction. "He used to lie around naked while people ate sushi off him."

"And *you* still do," Dai retorted.

"Why does no one tell me about these restaurants?" Amy wondered aloud.

"The nantaimori places?" Lukas said.

"Oh, so the Russian émigré knows about it, but I, a lifelong New Yorker, don't have a clue."

A whippet-thin man with waist-length dreadlocks called in through the doors. "Light's going, people."

"My bad, Christophe." Amy grabbed another camera from the pile of cases on the couch. "Come on out if you want. It doesn't bother me if people watch me work."

"That's Madina Feng," Harlow said as they walked outside. He pointed to a young, vaguely Asian-looking woman dressed in a piece of cloth the approximate size of a tea towel. The hot-orange rectangle of silk hung from a thin gold chain that looped around her delicate neck and under her arms. As she rose en pointe, she extended one leg parallel to the ground in a classic arabesque. The feather-light fabric floated on the air, revealing her martini-glass breasts and the taut plane of her abdomen. Her thick clay-red hair was pulled up into a banana clip on top of her head like the crest of a Roman centurion's helmet. Amy walked slowly around Madina, taking photos. In what seemed like a short time, Amy told Madina her shoot was over.

"Harlow," Christophe beckoned. "You're up, my man." He patted one of the lawn chairs. The table beside it was covered with makeup kits and hairstyling implements.

"Excuse me," Lukas said to Dai. He slipped out of his shoes, jacket, jeans, and T-shirt and piled them on a chair. Naked except for the loincloth he tied around his hips, he did a few lunges until Amy called him.

Dai alternated watching Lukas pose and Harlow being made up as a faun and tried to stay out of everyone's way. He jumped when someone spoke at his elbow.

"I just made fresh coffee if anyone is interested."

Dai knew that rich baritone—would know it anywhere. Shocked, he spun around to face Cope. "What are you doing here?" he exclaimed.

"This is my house."

"No it isn't. You live in Manhattan… like Will."

"Not anymore."

"I don't understand."

"I moved."

"Yes, but—"

"I'll take a cup if you're pouring and don't mind bringing it to me," Christophe called out.

"No problem," Cope said. He nodded to Dai and then turned to go inside. His heart was pounding so hard his ribs felt bruised. With shaking hands, he managed to pour a cup of coffee without spilling too much. *What is Dai doing here?* The person Cope had been longing to see had appeared, and now he was a mess, praying he'd be able to deliver the coffee without a humiliating mishap.

"Thank you, my brother," Christophe said when Cope set the cup down. "Sit still, Harlow. These horns be a bitch to get right. Don't blame me if they come out crooked."

"Coffee?" Cope said to Dai. Maybe if he spoke in short interrogatives, he could keep from babbling.

"Sure." Dai went inside with Cope and helped himself to a cup. He moved around to lean on the opposite side of the counter. Watching Cope over the rim of the cup, he took a sip. "Good coffee," he acknowledged, despite the fact he didn't want to talk to Cope.

Cope turned to get a cup for himself and to escape Dai's scrutiny. "Coming from you, that's a real compliment," he said. "I have croque monsieur and assorted pastries too, if you—"

"No, thanks."

Cope took a bite of a croque monsieur to give him time to think of something to say. He was usually pretty good with the banter when he wanted to be, but Dai's presence had robbed his tongue of any facility with words. "It's good to see you again," he said. "The last time I saw you, I—"

"The last time you saw me? Was it in real life or in the movies?"

Cope's mouth dried up, his spit evaporating as it did when he faced imminent danger.

"So you know about Will's little porn experiment," Dai said. "Don't bother to lie. I can see it on your face."

Cope gulped his coffee and grimaced when he burned his tongue. He held up a hand like a cop directing traffic as he blinked moisture from his eyes. "Yes," he said. "I know Will filmed you."

"Did you enjoy my performance?"

Dai's sarcasm was not lost on Cope. The next words he said to Dai would be among the most important he spoke in his life. It wouldn't be an exaggeration to say that his world hinged on this moment. "Look, I didn't—"

Dai interrupted, his voice rising sharply. "Didn't what? Didn't think I was convincing? Didn't like the lighting? What?"

"Hey," Harlow said from the doorway. "What's going on in here?"

"We're out of cream," Cope said without hesitation, desperate to escape. He wanted to explain to Dai, but he wanted to do it in the right setting. "I'll be right back." He scooped up his phone wallet from the bookcase and hurried out.

Harlow turned to look at Dai. Dai glared at Harlow. "What?" Harlow said.

"Seriously," Dai said. "You didn't recognize him?"

"Who?"

"The guy who just left."

"Is he famous or something?"

"He's Will's best friend. He was there that night. The dinner was a birthday party for him."

Harlow's brow furrowed and then smoothed out again. "Hey, you're right. He had his hair in a ponytail that night. Looks different with it down." He paused. "Oh shit! Was he giving you shit?"

Dai shook his head. "The opposite."

"Good for you. Was he in on it?"

"He's Will's wingman. What do you think?"

"Aw, hell no." Harlow groaned. "What a shame. He's so sexy. And I was kind of thinking you two might hit it off, you know?"

"It's almost funny."

"Yo, Harlow," Christophe called out. "It's your time, boy."

"Be right there," Harlow said quickly. "Dai, are you all right?"

"I'm fine. Go be gorgeous."

"Come watch."

"I think I'll head home."

"What? Why?"

"There are some things I want to do. And you know you'll end up going out with Luk anyway."

"What about the job?"

"I'll find something else. Thanks, though."

"Don't go. Amy will be disappointed."

"I'm sorry. I really am, but I can't stay."

"Okay, I understand."

"Harlow!" Christophe said loudly.

"See you at home," Dai said as he turned away from Harlow.

Harlow hovered for a second and then dashed out to the terrace.

Out on the sidewalk, Dai looked around to make sure Cope wasn't in sight before he started walking. At some point he'd catch a cab or a train, but right now, he wanted to walk. He was wound up and needed to work it off. A few blocks away, he found himself in a crowd of strangers waiting to cross at the light.

"Hey, Dai! Daimaru Tanaka! Look over here."

Dai turned to his left. Sitting at the red light on the cross street was a black Escalade. Sitting in the passenger seat with the window rolled down was Kei.

"Yeah, over here. Hey, man, what are you doing?" Kei called out.

"I was hanging out with Harlow. Now I'm headed home."

"Get in. We'll take you." Kei turned from Dai to the driver. "Shut up. Yes, we will. You just drive, bitch. No one wants your opinion." He turned back to Dai. "Get in, bro."

"Are you sure?"

"Yeah, he's sure," the driver called out. "Come on, man. We're just messin' with you."

Dai opened the back door and got in. The seat was a black leather captain's chair. "Nice ride," he said.

The driver glanced back and smiled. Sunlight backlit the edges of his fair hair, but his face was in shadow. "Thanks, man. She's comfortable," he said in a dry twang that was somewhere between Texas and California.

The light turned green, but the driver waited for a few stragglers to make it to the sidewalk before he pulled out. "Which way?" he asked.

"Take a left," Kei said. "Dai, this is my new friend Brad. Brad hangs with my cousins." He waved toward the back of the big vehicle.

Dai nodded to Kei's three cousins. He'd seen one of them before when the kid came in for a job interview, but they looked enough alike that he wasn't sure which one it was. "What's up?"

"Usual, man," said the one in the middle.

"Yeah, same old same old," said the one on the right.

The one on the left nodded, a short, sharp chop of his chin.

"I'm up here visiting the fam," Kei said. "These little gangsters introduced me to Magic Man here."

"That's my stage name, you might say," Brad said. "I'm a pyrotechnician."

"So you do something with fire?" Dai guessed.

"So close!" Kei said. "Fireworks."

"Cool," Dai said at the same time Kei told Brad to turn right.

"I design fireworks displays, and I also make my own shells. I was always good in chemistry."

"Hey, we're going to a site to watch Brad set off a few," Kei said to Dai. "Want to come?"

"Why not?" Dai said.

"Cool," Brad said. He made a U-turn. "Fourth of July is right around the corner, and I need to try out a couple of things."

Many blocks later, Brad pulled in at a large, fenced-off lot. A security guard came out of his hut, money changed hands, and the gate was rolled back. Inside was a vacant lot scoured almost clean of the rubble of a demolition job.

"One more week before construction starts," Brad said. "Then I'll have to move to an alternate site. But for now, I have this luxurious laboratory."

As soon as the SUV stopped, Kei's cousins swarmed out and unpacked boxes from the cargo area. With intense efficiency, Brad and the cousins assembled tubes, spheres, wiring, black match fuses, and other arcane items. They carried the assemblage to the middle of the block-sized lot. Dai and Kei brought over a long folding table and set it up. The fireworks went onto the table, and Kei beckoned to Dai to join him standing behind Brad.

Brad had donned a chocolate-brown cowboy hat to shield his eyes from the sun as he checked fuses and adjusted angles. In his worn jeans, white T-shirt, and West Coast tan, he looked like a cowboy to Dai. The kind of cowboy you see in bars that feature male strippers. Dai liked the way the light made golden splinters of the whiskers on Brad's chin and upper lip. He could imagine what that scruff would feel like on his inner thighs.

"What a hottie, right?" Kei said in Dai's ear. "His name isn't really Brad, by the way. The boys call him that because they think he looks like Brad Pitt."

Dai squinted. "Aside from being blond and having a *Fight Club* bod, I don't see it."

"Me neither. More like that other guy, you know?"

"You'll have to give me more than that."

"He's blond. He does a lot of movies."

"That's half of Hollywood."

"Come on. He was in that movie about cars. Swift and Seething?"

Dai laughed. "*Fast & Furious*?"

"Whatever. That guy."

"We're all set here," Brad called out. "Who wants to see some magic?" He looked over at Dai and gave him a dimpled smile. "I use that Heart song 'Magic Man' when I do private shows, but this is just practice. Of course, the display is gonna be smaller too."

"I'll let it go this once," Dai said and smiled back to show he was joking.

"Won't happen again, boss." Brad chuckled. "Okay, everybody. Hang on to whatever makes you feel good." He leaned forward and used a barbecue lighter to ignite a black match fuse. A shell went up thirty feet and exploded into two fans of twinkling purple light. The cousins applauded, so Dai and Kei followed suit. "That was called a butterfly," Brad said. "This next one is a series of Roman candles. In a show, I'd set them off electronically, but no point in doing all the wiring until I get the design worked out."

Dai was fascinated by the process, and time passed quickly. He looked at his phone and saw it was two in the afternoon. His stomach reminded him he hadn't eaten since seven that morning, and he was glad and sorry to see Brad and the cousins packing up the equipment.

"Hey, Kei," Dai said. "You know anywhere around here to get a bite?"

"Sure, no problem."

"Where to?" Brad asked as he got into the driver's seat.

"There's a Pret A Manger around the corner. Stop and let homeboy grab a sandwich."

"Will do," Brad said. He waved at the guard as he drove off the lot.

Dai wolfed down a chicken avocado wrap on the way home and listened to Kei and his cousins talk in Japanese, which Brad also seemed fluent in. Dai understood most but not all of it; however, he felt comforted hearing Nihongo spoken around him. It took him right back to his childhood, when he had someone who protected him and made all the hard decisions.

"Hey, Dai, this is your street, right?" Kei said.

Dai looked out the window. "Sorry, I zoned out for a minute."

"Want to change and go clubbing? My cousins have been bragging about some place they hang out."

"Not tonight." Dai opened the car door and got out. "Thanks," he said into the open window. "See you later."

"Hey," Brad called out. He got out of the SUV and caught up with Dai. "You think I could call you sometime?"

"Sure." Dai exchanged numbers with Brad. "Have fun tonight."

"No way, man. I'm not going clubbing with those little maniacs. I don't have the energy or the amphetamines to keep up with them."

Kei blew the Escalade's horn. Dai and Brad laughed.

"Hey, why don't you be my guest at the May the Fourth Be with You festival? There's going to be street food, buskers, a Gay Pride parade, and my fireworks display."

"That actually sounds like fun."

"I'll text you the details." Brad grinned. "Good night, Dai. Sure am glad we ran into you."

"I'll see you soon." Dai waved as Brad got into the vehicle. "What a nice guy," he said to the ivy-covered fence. Even though Kei had volunteered Brad to drive a ridiculous number of blocks out of his way, Brad hadn't once acted put out about it. Maybe he'd ask Harlow and Lukas to come with him to the festival. Yeah. That sounded like a great idea.

COPE LOOKED at his phone, saw Will's name, and almost ignored the call. It was only the second time Will had called since Cope had unblocked him, so Cope rewarded him for his restraint. "Hi, Will," he said. "How are you?"

"Dandy. Yourself?"

"Slightly less mopish, thank you. I saw the proofs of the book this morning. It looks good."

"That's fantastic," Will said less than convincingly. "Are you giving any thought to coming back to work?"

"Not at all. I'm enjoying what I'm doing right now. What more can any of us ask?"

"A great piece of ass."

"I think that falls under the category of things I'm doing right now."

"Oh?"

Cope could visualize the arch of Will's eyebrows. "Not right this moment, you randy bastard."

"Who is it?"

"We're not going to talk about my love life. Why did you call?"

"Because it's Thursday and you haven't called me."

Cope looked at the date on his watch. "I wasn't paying attention to the date," he said. "Do you know what a luxury that is?"

"Hippie." Will juggled the phone to his other ear. "So are you coming to my folks' for fireworks like always?"

"No."

"Come on. They'll want to know why you aren't there. I know my mom thinks we've been secretly married since college. Don't break her heart."

"Fuck you, fucker."

"Too far?"

"Jesus, Will. You use your mom as emotional blackmail and ask if you've gone too far? You've got my answer, okay? Have fun at the cabin. Give Grammie Osbourne a hug for me."

"She'll miss you, and who knows how many more Fourth of Julys she's got in her."

"Fuck you. I'm hanging up."

"No! Please don't." Will lowered his voice. "I really, really miss you, man." As much as Will loved being a successful executive, Cope was his link to the wild, carefree days of college. Will missed those heady years of being best friends with benefits and the right of first refusal. In those days, Cope had always been his first choice. There was even a time when Will might have convinced himself he was in love. Those days were gone, but as long as Cope was around, Will could relive them for hours at a time. To let go of Cope was to let go of some of the glory.

"I miss you too," Cope said.

"Then what are we doing? Come to Connecticut with me. It'll be the perfect chance to reconnect. We can take the boat out and scout the yacht club."

"No."

"Why not?"

"Because I haven't forgiven you yet. Because you've never said you were sorry. Because I don't hear the faintest hint of remorse in your voice."

"I talked to Dai."

"When?"

"I don't know. Maybe a week and a half ago. I staked out that pseudo-Italian place he likes. You were right. He knew about the video."

"Did you apologize?"

"That's between him and me."

"So you didn't. Bye, Will." Cope disconnected and turned his phone off. "Bow down to the King of Passive-Aggressive," he announced to the hedges.

"Hɪ!" Brad came around the small platform to greet Dai. "Hope you didn't have any trouble finding me."

"None at all. Your directions were good, and security had my name on a list."

"I'm all wired up here. Nothing else to do until showtime. Want to walk around?"

"Love to. I told my friend we'd meet him at the end of the street."

Brad finished cleaning his hands and tossed the wipe in a trash bin. "Shall we?" He gestured toward the blocked-off street lined with vendors' carts and festivalgoers.

"I love street fairs," Dai said as he stopped at a truck selling waffle cake fries. "And I love powdered sugar. Please don't judge me."

"I'm chill." Brad took one of the sticks of deep-fried dough. "Sweet," he said after he chewed and swallowed. "Could benefit from some cinnamon."

"Yum!"

"So… is this a first date?" Brad asked casually.

"I don't think we could call it anything else, do you?"

"Good. Can I hold your hand?"

Dai held out his free hand and Brad took it. "I haven't held hands with anyone in forever," Dai said.

"Do you like it?"

"I do, but it makes it hard to eat my million-calorie snack."

Brad took a waffle cake fry and fed it to Dai. "Problem solved. I'm gonna grab a coffee. Want one?"

Dai shook his head and moved to stand at the corner of the cart while Brad waited in line. Several times, Brad looked over and smiled.

"I don't want to embarrass you," Brad said when he joined Dai. "And I don't want to sound shallow, but I have to tell you, you're the most beautiful man I ever saw."

"You haven't met Harlow. Put him in a dress and heels, and a straight man would hit on him."

"You don't look like a girl," Brad said. "You're obviously a dude. Only women bodybuilders have shoulders like that." He paused. "I don't know why I try to talk. I'm not good at it."

"You're doing fine." Dai smiled.

"Good. I want to make a good impression. This'll probably sound all kinds of stupid to you, but you're way out of my league."

"I don't recognize leagues. I'm a free agent."

Brad grinned in relief. "I know you're a gorgeous, glamorous New Yorker, and I'm a scruffy firecracker wrangler, but I have to take a shot at you. I'd regret it the rest of my life if I didn't try to get next to you."

"That was some real good talking there, Magic Man," Dai said. He spotted Harlow and Lukas at a handmade-jewelry booth and waved. Lukas saw him and touched Harlow on the shoulder. Harlow saw Dai and waved like a drowning semaphore signalman.

"I'm guessing those are your friends," Brad said.

"Harlow is colorful, and he's my best friend. I don't know Luk well yet, but I like what I know of him."

"Good enough. Let's go meet 'em."

The two couples strolled the street, sampling food and drinks from the carts, making jokes, admiring the work in artisan booths, and generally getting a little better acquainted. Harlow slowed to look at a silk batik vest, and Dai stopped with him. Brad and Lukas continued to the next food truck for beer.

"Brad's cute," Harlow said as he stroked the material.

"That's not the word I'd use. He's sexy, though."

"No kidding. He's like Brad Pitt in *Thelma & Louise*."

"Exactly, so how about just letting me have this one without making a big deal about it."

"Excuse me?"

"I just need to be physically close to somebody."

"Fine."

"You tend to invent romances where they don't exist."

"And that annoys you, I guess."

"I didn't say that. I just want to have some fun with Brad. I don't need you ringing a wedding bell."

"I wouldn't worry about that if I was you," Harlow said stiffly. "I'll try really hard to stop bothering you with my romantic shit."

"Please don't take it that way."

"How else should I take it?" Harlow's eyes gleamed like pools of ink. "Look, Dai, I know I'm ridiculous with my American slang and my insistence on sprinkling glitter on everything, but that's what makes me happy. In case you haven't noticed as you sail through life, I'm not exactly a raging success in the world of dance, and very soon, I'll be past my prime. If I want pink balloons and candy hearts, that's none of your business."

Dai grabbed Harlow's hand as Harlow turned from him. "I'm sorry. I really didn't mean it that way." He squeezed Harlow's fingers. "I'm sorry I'm so self-involved."

"It's okay," Harlow said. "You're horny and don't know what you're saying."

"I got used to a steady diet of spectacular sex."

"Shut up. You're making me glad you broke up with him so I don't have to hear what great sex you're having."

"What about you? Is Lukas still holding out?"

"I might have to put a ring on it."

Dai hugged Harlow. "I really am sorry I hurt your feelings."

"You should be. It's not easy keeping up my image *and* making you look good at the same time."

Dai laughed as he let Harlow go. "I can only imagine," he said as Brad and Lukas joined them.

"It'll be dark soon," Brad said. "I should get to the platform."

"Are you really going to set off fireworks in the city?" Harlow asked.

"The festival has a permit from Safety and Health, so yeah, I'm going to light it up." Brad grinned. "Come on."

Dai, Harlow, and Lukas went with Brad to the platform where he had series of aerial shells ready to go. While his new friends leaned on his car, Brad filled the night sky overhead with sparkling fire flowers, cascades of glittering light, and fiery streamers that exploded into balls of shooting stars. With the click of a small electronic device, he unleashed the finale—a rainbow that dissolved into silver drops. The mostly LGBTQ crowd cheered and applauded until it was obvious the show was over. They drifted down the street to the next marvel.

"Impressive," Lukas said as he shook Brad's hand.

"Aw, that was just a little display," Brad said. "But thank you just the same."

"It was fantastic!" Harlow said. "So is this, like, your job?"

"Yeah, I travel and do shows. I've worked a couple of parks, but I like designing my own displays, you know?"

Harlow nodded and ignored the look Dai was giving him. "It must pay pretty good." He patted the Escalade.

Brad laughed. "No, man, I could never afford that car. I borrowed it from Mr. Katz, the guy who owns the fireworks company."

"That's enough, Harlow," Dai said. "The interview is over, and Brad is officially date material."

"No argument," Harlow said. "Me and Lukas are going. I assume you're hanging out?"

"I can take you home, Dai," Brad said quickly.

"Good night, then," Harlow said. He held up his hand in the Vulcan salute. "I have been, and always shall be, your friend. Live long and prosper."

Dai started to reply, but Brad cut him off. "Every now and then, say 'What the fuck! What the fuck gives you freedom. Freedom brings opportunity. Opportunity makes your future.'"

Harlow laughed. "Now I know Dai's going to have a good time. See you later." He and Lukas walked away down the side street.

"So I take it that was a good thing—pulling that *Risky Business* quote out of my ass," Brad said.

"It's never a bad idea to be on Harlow's good side."

"What about you? Am I on your good side?" Brad leaned close.

"So far, so good. Can I help you pack up?"

"Nope. Everything that isn't disposable belongs to the organizers. All we have to do is drive away."

Brad unlocked the SUV, and they got in. He turned the key, and cool air rushed from the vents. The radio came to life on a salsa station. Dai tilted his seat back and looked up through the sunroof.

"I've got half a doob if you feel like smokin'," Brad said. "Righteous herb."

"I haven't smoked weed since high school."

"So… last week?" Brad chuckled.

Dai laughed with him. "Sure, I'll take a hit. I'm feeling goofy tonight."

"Feeling goofy?" Brad grinned. "Does Disney know about this?"

"Boo," Dai said. "Lame."

Brad struck a flame and lit the end of a hand-rolled smoke. A pungent smell filled the interior of the vehicle, and Dai was instantly transported to his school parking lot at lunchtime. He took the joint when Brad passed it and inhaled cautiously. The smoke seized his lungs, and it took all his willpower to keep from coughing. Eyes watering, he passed it back. Even as he breathed out, he felt the familiar, warm, creeping euphoria spreading through him.

"Nice," Dai drawled. "You weren't lying."

"Another swat?"

Dai shook his head. When he answered, he had no sense of how long ago Brad had asked his question. *Damn, this was some powerful ganja.* "I'm good," he said, and the words echoed in his head, sounding stranger with each repetition until they might as well have been Klingon for all the sense they made.

"How you doing?" Brad leaned over the seat. "You okay?"

"I'm pretty wasted."

"Want to go get something to eat?"

"Why go anywhere?" Dai reached down for the seat controls. "How far does this recline?"

"The back bench seat folds down."

"Thank you, Cadillac! Now how long before you kiss me?"

Brad didn't wait for more encouragement. He dipped his head and covered Dai's mouth with his. Lips moving gently, he strayed to Dai's cheek, his ear, and down to his neck. Dai put his arms around Brad and pulled him down. Brad stretched out on top of Dai and looked down into his eyes.

"I want you so much," Brad whispered hoarsely.

"I love it when a plan comes together," Dai said.

"That's *A-Team*. I loved that show." Brad took Dai's mouth again, flirting his tongue along the seam of Dai's lips until Dai opened to him. For several breathless seconds, Brad demonstrated the suppleness of his tongue.

"Let's move into the back," Dai said when their lips parted.

"You sure? We can go to a—"

"I want you now."

"You got it. I couldn't be more ready." Brad slipped into the back and released the seat latches. The unfolded seat was large enough for two people to lie on if they were fond of each other.

"Did you come prepared?" Dai asked as he followed Brad. "If not, I did."

"I've got condoms. Lubricated."

"Fantastic." Dai pulled his T-shirt over his head and draped it over one of the front seats.

Brad whistled. "How did I get so lucky?" he asked the ceiling. Quickly, he unsnapped his shirt and tossed it toward the driver's seat.

Dai sat and beckoned to Brad. Brad dropped onto the makeshift bed and took Dai in his arms. Dai hugged Brad tightly and sought his mouth. As the kiss went on, they learned the topography of each other's bodies with their hands. Dai moaned when Brad slipped a hand down the back of his jeans and stroked his crack.

Dai broke the kiss. "Wait," he said breathlessly. He unzipped his jeans and pushed them down.

Brad looked down. "Nice," he said as he reached for Dai's cock.

Dai moaned as Brad's fingers closed around his shaft. Unwilling to wait, he unzipped Brad's jeans and shoved a hand in. "Well, *hel*lo!" he said.

Brad sucked in a breath as Dai's fingers moved on him. Greedy for more, he eased Dai onto his back and lay on his side next to him. His tongue teased Dai's mouth as his saliva-slick fingertip teased Dai's hole. Dai pulled Brad's cock through his fly and shuttled his hand up and down as he fondled Brad's balls with the other. Brad moved to straddle Dai and sank down until his cock rested on Dai's. Slowly, he dragged his hard-on up, down, and across Dai's dick. Dai groaned and bit his lower lip.

"Feels good, don't it?" Brad growled. "Want more?"

"Yeah," Dai managed to say. The weed had heightened his perception considerably. Each stroke of Brad's hand, tongue, and cock reverberated through his entire body. It was like all his skin was as sensitive as the head of his penis. He was connected to Brad through his nerve endings, and each caress set off a wave of overwhelming pleasure. He could barely breathe, much less make conversation. "More."

Dai had forgotten he was in a vehicle on a public street packed with holiday crowds. All he cared about was how good he felt. He didn't protest when Brad pulled his jeans all the way down and off along with his shoes. Brad moved between Dai's thighs, realigning their cocks. He leaned in until he could reach Dai's lips. The torrid kiss drove Dai to squirming, desperate heights of desire as Brad thrust his tongue in time with his hips. Dai planted his feet against the ceiling and pushed back against Brad's stroke.

"Fuck yeah," Brad breathed into Dai's mouth. "Get hot, baby."

Brad reached down and took hold of his shaft. The head bumped against Dai's opening, and Brad suppressed a cry of victory. He snugged the tip against the small hole and applied pressure. Dai continued to pump his hips and on his next thrust, Brad leaned forward.

Dai froze as the head of Brad's dick pushed into him. "Wait!"

"Almost in."

"Not without a condom." Dai's voice sounded weak in his ears. "In my pocket."

"Aw come on. I'm halfway there already." Brad rocked his hips.

Dai gasped. "Lube."

"It's fine. I got plenty of spit in there with my finger." Brad wrapped his hand around Dai's wilting shaft and stroked it. He bent at the waist and nibbled at Dai's left nipple. "You aren't hurting, are you?"

Dai shook his head. "Feels good."

"Yeah, it does." Brad pulled back and thrust shallowly, taking his time, gentling Dai along. He tongued Dai's nipples, stroked his cock, and massaged his balls.

Dai slipped back into the sensual rhythm, yearning with single-minded devotion toward release. He thrilled to the feel of Brad's hands and mouth on his body. Eagerly he accepted Brad's cock, rising to meet each thrust, breath catching when the knob bumped over his prostate. And it was good—so good.

"Am I treatin' you right?" Brad asked.

"Don't stop."

Brad sped up, and Dai peaked abruptly with a sharp little cry. Dai's seed spilled over Brad's knuckles as Dai's orgasm shook him from head to toe. Brad closed his eyes for a moment as Dai's interior muscles clamped down on his shaft. When Dai eased up, Brad pulled out and smeared his cock with Dai's cum. He eased the tip back in and moaned when Dai promptly squeezed it. With a roll of his hips, he buried his full length, grasping Dai's flanks when Dai recoiled. He held on until Dai relaxed again.

"Damn, that's good," Brad said as he pulled back and thrust deep. "So good." In five strokes, he shuddered and shot his seed. He panted a little as he rested on his hands. "Didn't mean to rush through it like that."

"It was good," Dai said drowsily. He could barely keep his eyes open.

"I'm movin'," Brad warned before he eased out of Dai.

Dai got his underwear on but had a harder time with the jeans. Brad helped him get the pants over his butt and zipped. Dai flopped into the passenger seat and did his best not to melt into the leather. "Phew! That was some hot down and dirty action."

"I don't remember the last time I came like that." Brad turned the fan up on the AC and stuck his face near a vent. "Hot, hot, hot!"

"I needed it."

"Me too." Brad gave Dai a sideways look. "Hey, sorry about the… you know."

"What?"

"I forgot the condom. By the time I thought about it, we were goin' like a freight train."

"I don't want to talk about that now. Let's get a snack. Something crunchy and salty."

Brad opened the console and tossed a bag of Doritos to Dai. "Here. Just until we find real food."

Dai tore open the bag and stuffed several orange-powdered triangles into his mouth. He was aware of Brad stealing looks at him as they navigated the streets, but it didn't make him uncomfortable. He'd just had spontaneous, sweaty sex with the guy in his car on the street on their first date; what was there to be embarrassed about? Maybe getting carried away wasn't the smartest thing he could have done, but he was so horny, and Brad was so sexy. He felt so good right now that almost nothing could ruin it.

"IT'S HERE!" Harlow danced into the apartment holding a package in his arms. "It's here!"

"What's here?" Dai looked up from the pot of stew he was stirring. "We're having gumbo tonight. With shrimp. And sticky rice."

"Sweet! This continues to be an amazing day."

"Pinot grigio in the fridge. Pour us both a glass?" Dai made puppy eyes at Harlow. "And then show me what's in the box."

Harlow poured wine and set a glass on the counter near Dai. He found scissors in the utility drawer and cut the tape on the box. After wiping his hands on his jeans, he lifted out an eleven-by-fourteen book. The cover was a black-and-white photo of small hedges and miniature shrubs against a stone wall. The title was *The Terrace*—images by Amy Waxwing, words by Copeland Shore. Harlow held it up in front of his chest. "Isn't it beautiful? Let's find the page I'm on!"

Dai smiled indulgently as Harlow slapped the book down on the counter. He added a few more herbs to the stew before he picked up his glass and came to look over Harlow's shoulder.

"That's beautiful," he said sincerely as he gazed at the photo of Harlow. He read the short poem. *Are you beautiful? Are clouds painted gold and red by sunset beautiful? Are daisies hung with dew at dawn beautiful? You tell me.* "Hey." The word came out on a soft puff of air. He reached out and turned the page, and there was the poem about his lips. "Why are Will's poems in this book?"

Harlow held it up so Dai could see the front again. He traced a finger under Cope's name. "You look so precious right now," he said. "Really. You should see your face."

"Cope wrote the poems?" Dai said slowly.

"I don't know about *the* poems, but he wrote these poems."

"You saw the first one he wrote me."

"Yeah, but we thought that was Will."

"And when you saw these poems, it didn't occur to you that they were similar?"

"They're poems." Harlow shrugged.

"All that time, I was giving Will the benefit of the doubt because I thought he wrote the poems."

"Why didn't Cope sign them, though? That's kind of weird." Harlow gasped. "Unless…."

"Unless what?"

"He pined for you in secret but you belonged to his best friend, his sworn brother. What could he do but write romantic, anonymous poetry?"

"Wasn't that the plot of *Secret Admirer*?"

"No. What do you think of my theory?"

"I think you're not wrong, but there's probably more to it. Damn."

"What's the matter?"

"I've been thinking of him as Will's sleazeball-in-arms, but what if I'm wrong?"

"He seems like a really cool guy," Harlow said. "For what it's worth."

"He's funny too." Dai smiled.

"And he plays the movie quote game."

"Yeah."

"Why don't you come to the party with me?"

"What party?"

"The book-release party. Where have you been?"

"Right. When and where is it?"

"Tomorrow night on the terrace at Cope's place. Seemed appropriate since all the art was created there." Harlow reacted to Dai's change of expression. "Come on. You know it's the right thing to do. Clear the air with the guy. For fuck's sake, he wrote those poems."

"I was going to meet Brad for Western night at the Forge, but I can talk him into going to the party."

"Not exactly what I had in mind, but I'm glad you're going."

"Don't try to set me up with Cope, okay? Promise me."

"Why? He's perfect for you, and you're not serious about Brad. You're fuck buddies, and you know it."

"Yeah." Dai sighed.

"Glad you can admit it. At the risk of losing your friendship, I have to tell you…."

"What?" Dai sighed again. "Just say it."

"I don't like him."

"What did he ever do to you?"

"I'll sound like a whiner, but when you're not around, he treats me different."

"Like what does he do that's different?"

"It's hard to explain, but I get the definite feeling he'd be happier if I wasn't around."

Dai smiled. "Probably because he wants to get busy."

"No. It's more than that. I don't think he likes the fact that I'm Nihonjin."

"That doesn't make sense. I'm half-Japanese."

"Yeah, well, he's fucking you."

Dai changed the subject. "What makes you think Copeland Shore is perfect for me?"

"Everything?"

"So this is just your gut we're talking about?"

"When is it ever wrong?"

"That time you answered a personal ad for me?"

"I think you and She-Hulk could have been good together."

"Yeah, it's funny now, but at the time…." Dai sighed. "Seriously, though, don't do any matchmaking."

"What am I? A Jewish mother?"

"Sometimes I think you *are* a Jewish mother disguised as a tragically hip gaysian boy."

"Tragically?"

"I'm just thinking of the future of the New York City Ballet with you in the corps."

"Why would you say that?"

"Oh, come on. A hip-hop danseur?"

"Oh, I see. You're trying to be funny. Well, you can't distract me."

"From what?"

"Shut up," Harlow suggested. He opened the book again. "I'm proud to be part of this."

"You should be." Dai looked over Harlow's shoulder again. "No kidding."

"So you'll be nice at the party?"

"I'm nice… until it's time to not be nice."

"If you're going to quote *Road House* at me…."

"Nope, I'm going to feed you, and then I'm going to call Brad."

DAI TOOK extra pains getting ready for the book-release party, even though Brad didn't care what he wore. Brad wore the same thing every day: T-shirt under pearl-snap shirt, jeans, and boots. And it worked well for Brad, but Dai liked to show a little more style when he went out. It had nothing to do with the fact that Cope would be there. Dai certainly didn't care what Cope thought about how he looked.

"Are you ready yet?" Harlow asked for the hundredth time. "Luk will be here any second."

Dai came out of the bathroom and held his arms out to his sides. "Ta-da!"

Harlow took in the tight cream-colored trousers and the berry-red T-shirt that hugged the contours of Dai's torso. "You look delicious," he said.

"Eat me."

"If we don't get to the hors d'oeuvres soon, I might start noshing on you."

"Promises, promises." Dai looked over at the door at the sound of a knock.

"That's Lukas," Harlow said. "Are you ready?"

"No, but I'm committed."

They got in the car door Lukas held open for them, and the cab pulled into traffic. Fifteen minutes later, they got out at Cope's house. Brad's Escalade was conspicuous among the late-model Volvos and new BMWs. A giddy Amy answered the door and swept each of them into a welcoming hug.

"Your host is out procuring more ice. Drinks are set up on the counter, beer in the fridge, let's see, what else, oh yeah, nibbles are everywhere, so you can graze while you mingle, and mingle you shall." Amy giggled. "We were crazy to have the party in such a small space, but somehow it works."

"Because we all like getting close." Harlow kissed her cheek. "Come on, Luk. I'm starving."

"He's so good for Lukas," Amy said as Harlow dragged Lukas out to the terrace.

"It's mutually beneficial," Dai said.

"Symbiosis." Amy's expression underwent a swift change. "That's it," she said. "That's my next photo collection. I'll take photos of all kinds of couples… starting with Harlow and Lukas."

"I like it." Dai spotted Brad in the kitchenette and waved to him.

Amy turned and smiled when she saw Brad. "Maybe I can talk you into posing for this one."

"Can't make any promises right now." Dai smiled as he accepted the bottle of beer Brad held out to him.

"That's him all over," Brad said. "*No promises* is his middle name."

"That's because I'm honest." Dai took a long swallow of the beer. "Brad, have you and Amy met?"

"Yep. She made me feel right at home."

"You're adorable," Amy said. "Would you two excuse me? My glass is empty."

"She's a firecracker," Brad said when Amy was gone.

"I like her too. She's the main reason I wanted to come to this party. We can go whenever you want."

"I'd still like to hit Western night, but I wouldn't mind havin' a couple of beers and some eats before we go."

"As long as you're not uncomfortable."

"Nope."

"Cool. Is most of the food outside?"

"Yep. Come on." Brad took Dai's hand and led him out to the terrace. Tables had been set up with plates, silverware, and platters of substantial hors d'oeuvres. Brad helped Dai fill a plate and held his beer while he ate. "This is a real nice place," he said. "Kind of small, but nice."

"It's okay for one person."

"Exactly what I was tryin' to say." Brad raised the bottle to his lips and drank. "I need another beer. How you doin'?"

"I'm good." Dai smiled as he saw Christophe approaching.

"I might mingle a little," Brad said. "Meet some more of your friends."

"Go ahead. I'll be right here."

Brad went back inside and emerged with a fresh beer. He raised the bottle in a salute to Dai before he drifted over to a bevy of ballerinas.

"He's mighty cute, my man," Christophe said to Dai.

Dai smiled. "He does have his charms."

"Are you two exclusive?"

Dai met Christophe's eyes. "Are you interested in me or him?"

Christophe smiled gently. "I don't want a man as pretty as you. I would always be worrying about who was trying to steal you away."

Dai made a snorting noise. "To answer the question, Brad and I don't have any kind of understanding. We like each other, and we have a good time together. But he'll most likely be gone soon, so...."

Christophe nodded. "No attachments. I understand."

"I won't make a scene if you hit on him. If he wants to go with you, then I guess me and him weren't meant to be."

"You are wise, child."

Dai snorted again. "Not so far. This is a new thing I'm trying out. I call it *thinking*."

"Yeah? Well, I think you're going to be good at it." Christophe laughed. "Excuse me while I flirt with your man?"

"Have at it."

Harlow came over as Christophe walked away. He hand-fed Dai a crab puff and took a drink of Dai's beer. "Can you believe Amy doesn't have her camera out?"

"I don't know her as well as you do. Is that unusual?"

"Believe me, it's a miracle she's not taking pictures."

"I wouldn't blame her. Here, life is beautiful. The girls are beautiful. Even the orchestra is beautiful."

Harlow laughed. "*Cabaret*. That one was easy, and it's not even eighties."

"I'm expanding my horizons."

"Spider-Man gig not working out?"

"I'm starting to hate it. Who knew kids could be so mean? I'm righteously tired of getting kicked in my spider-butt." Dai gave a heavy sigh. "I'm just so tired all the time."

"I'll help you find something else. Would you ever consider acting?"

"We've already talked about that. I'd feel weird being filmed doing stuff."

"I'm not talking porn."

"Neither am I. Maybe I should go back to—"

"What's going on over there?" Harlow interrupted.

Dai turned to see what he was looking at. He heard raised voices and saw Brad confronting Christophe.

"Back off," Brad said loudly.

Christophe held up his hands and backed away as Dai hurried over with Harlow tripping on his shadow. The three dancers looked shocked, frozen with their glasses halfway to their mouths.

"What happened?" Dai asked.

"That black fella hit on me," Brad said.

"No big deal. It's a party," Dai said. "And he thinks you're cute."

"You're okay with this?"

"Why wouldn't I be? You can date whoever you want."

"I sure as hell am not dating a… black guy."

Dai heard the ballerinas murmuring as they edged away. He was aware of a new tension in the air. He was also reeling from Brad's last statement. "Actually you are."

"Say what?"

"I'm one-quarter black."

"The hell you are. You—"

Dai held up a hand. "You know what? Let's not have this conversation here."

"Good idea," Harlow said from behind him.

"Okay, I get it," Brad said. "I'll go."

"Thanks," Dai said. "I'll call you tomorrow."

"Yeah, do that. We'll talk."

There was a hint of a sneer in Brad's voice, but Dai ignored it. "Yes, we will." As soon as Brad was gone, he left the garden to escape the stares and whispers. Behind him, he heard Harlow begin an explanation/apology. To his relief, the kitchen area was deserted except for Amy.

"Yes, I heard it all through the doors," she said. "And I don't think any less of you." She gave Dai a warm hug.

"That's really nice of you." Dai smiled wryly. "So much for a couple portrait."

"Come on now. You'll have someone new by the time I start the project."

"You sound so confident."

"Look at you. You're cute and you're kind and you're fun. Harlow says so. So who wouldn't want you?"

"Well… when you put it that way…."

"I'm not kidding. Just be yourself and be open to opportunity. I guarantee you'll have a lover by the time I call you for a shoot."

"I'm going to hold you to that."

"I'll stand by my prediction. Want a drink? I'm making something fruity." She held up a bottle of limoncello.

"Thanks, but I'm on my way out."

"You don't have to leave."

"I *want* to leave."

Amy stood aside. "I hope I'll see you again."

"Me too. Now, I have some important drinking to do. I'll leave you amateurs alone."

On his way to the corner, Dai texted Harlow to let him know what was happening. Harlow sent a flurry of texts denouncing Brad, swearing his loyalty to Dai, and mentioning that Christophe didn't hold Brad's behavior against Dai. Dai texted back that Harlow was not to worry; he was going home to bed.

The next day, Dai and Brad broke up over the phone. It was over in less than thirty seconds. Dai explained that he didn't date racists, and Brad accepted the ultimatum without argument. It was as though he'd been expecting it. Ten minutes later, Brad texted that he was leaving New York headed for a carnival in Pennsylvania. Feeling more relieved than anything, Dai wished him the best of luck and deleted him from his contacts list. He decided to take Amy's advice. He was just going to be himself and try to be open to opportunity. If he had to force something to work by modifying his behavior, he was probably doing it wrong. If it was right to begin with, he wouldn't feel the need to be anything but himself.

Then he started noticing that he felt tired all the time no matter how much sleep he got. His chest felt heavy and his head was in a perpetual fog. One day, he couldn't find the energy to make it to work. He barely made it to the toilet before he threw up the contents of his stomach. Then he threw up some more. Weak and feverish, he collapsed on the futon with his arms around an empty plastic wastebasket.

HARLOW LOOKED at the thermometer, and his expression turned grave. "Come on," he said. "You're going to the emergency room."

Dai stared pitifully up from the futon where he'd been ensconced for the past three days. He had a fluffy blanket, a remote control, and a puke bucket near at hand, and he was too weak to go much farther than the bathroom. Still, he protested. "My insurance went away with the job and anyway, this is just a cold."

"No, it isn't."

"I don't want to go."

"Why not?"

"They can't do anything for me."

"Bullshit. At the least, they can hook you up to an IV and get some fluids back into you."

"Just go get me some more Gatorade."

Harlow glared. "Dammit, Daimaru! Why are you being so stubborn?"

"Why don't you just respect my wishes?"

"I just moved out two weeks ago. How did you manage to fall apart so fast?"

"Don't flatter yourself." Dai kicked the blanket off his legs. "Seriously, if you want to help, go to the Duane Reade around the corner and get me some Gatorade, some ibuprofen, and some Afrin. And some ice cream. Strawberry."

"Dairy is the last thing you need." Harlow stalked into Dai's bedroom, made a noise of disgust, and then opened the tiny closet. He came back with a pair of sweatpants and a long-sleeved T-shirt. "Put these on."

"I'm not going."

Harlow dropped into the chair opposite the futon. "Please?" When Dai didn't answer, Harlow spoke again. "At least tell me why you won't go. Because if it's about the money, I have money."

Dai shook his head. "It's not the money."

Harlow watched a tear slide down Dai's cheek. "Dai? You'd better tell me what the hell is going on."

Dai met Harlow's eyes. "What if it's not just a cold?"

"What are you saying?"

Dai looked down again. "I've been feeling run-down for a while. It occurred to me that I've been feeling like this since Brad left."

"Brad?"

"The fireworks cowboy?"

"Right. Brad. He was a jerk."

"Yeah, well... the first time we had sex—" Dai swallowed. "—we didn't use a rubber."

"No, no, no. You're not telling me this. You're not telling me you think you have HIV."

"But what if I do? I can't help thinking about it."

Harlow was quiet for a minute and then sprang to his feet. "Put on those clean clothes and then you're coming with me. No arguments, bro."

"Where are we going?" Dai asked as he struggled into the sweatpants.

"A gay-friendly clinic. We're going to settle this. You're getting tested."

"What if I don't want to?"

"I get it," Harlow said. "I really do. It's fucking scary. It really is. But believe me, it's better to know. It just is."

"I know I'm probably being a real idiot and scaring myself for no good reason, but I can't get it out of my head, you know? What if Brad had something and gave it to me?"

"It's possible," Harlow said carefully. "He was a sleaze, an exceptionally attractive sleaze but a sleaze nonetheless. Now come on. I'm taking you to the clinic, and I'll wait with you, okay?"

"Okay." Dai slipped his feet into his Uggs and then shuffled to the door with Harlow's help.

SIX HOURS later, Dai was sitting on a gurney in a recovery room because the waiting room was full. Harlow sat on a molded plastic chair that he'd pulled over next to the gurney. Both had their phones out. Harlow was stalking wild Pokémon. Dai was obsessively checking the time. They looked toward the door as it opened.

"Hi," said the young woman who swept into the room. She had a white coat and carried a clipboard, the symbols of authority and acumen in the halls of healing. Her dark hair was pulled back and restrained by an overworked purple scrunchy. She looked and sounded exhausted. "I'm sorry you had to wait so long, Mr. Tanaka, I'm Physician's Assistant Fielding. I have the results of your tests."

"I'm ready," Dai said.

"You have a particularly virulent strain of flu, but you'll be fine if you follow instructions and take your meds. You can pick up your prescriptions at the receptionist's desk. She'll call them in to the drugstore down the street for you. The pharmacist can answer any questions you have about dosages and interactions. Stay in bed. Replace your fluids. This thing will run its course."

"That's it?"

"You're free to go."

"Okay… thanks."

Harlow stood up and offered Dai his arm. Dai took the help gratefully. He felt much better after the IV, but he was still shaky. PA Fielding held the door for them.

As Fielding walked briskly away down the hall, Dai turned to look at Harlow. "I have the flu," he said. "And I feel like a real idiot."

"Don't," Harlow said. "And if you're ever this sick again, you'd better call me."

"I promise." Dai leaned on Harlow until they reached the receptionist. He collected his prescriptions, paid the bill, and took Harlow's arm again for the walk out of the building. "Thanks for taking care of me."

"You're my friend," Harlow said. "Now, you sit here on this bench while I go get your drugs. Then we'll get a cab back to your place."

Dai sat down and watched Harlow hustle down the sidewalk. He was too weak to walk without help, but he was buoyed up by an immense sense of relief. He felt foolish as well for overreacting and turning an illness into a soap opera subplot. But the fear he'd felt had been very real. What if the rapid test hadn't come back negative for HIV?

"That's it," Dai murmured. "No more taking chances."

As though to reward him for his new resolve, the universe responded with a new job courtesy of Lukas's friends at the Lithuanian embassy. Dai settled into the work of maintaining the ornamental plants in and around the building and tried not to think about how lonely he was. The way he saw it, he was lucky to be alive.

CHAPTER ELEVEN

HARLOW PACED in the living room of the little garden apartment. He had moved in with Lukas, but now and then he had a sleepover with Dai. Tonight Lukas was in Waterbury with some cousins recently arrived from Lithuania. Harlow already had plans to spend Halloween with Dai. Now here he was dressed as Pikachu, once more waiting for Dai to finish getting dressed.

"Come on, bro. Give me a break. Ash Ketchum is a pair of jeans and a red baseball cap. What could possibly be taking so long?"

"I told you," Dai yelled from the bathroom. "I got here just before you, and I had to take a shower. I'll be right out."

"You still liking the gig?"

"I really am," Dai said as he came into the living room. "Being a groundskeeper keeps me grounded."

Harlow groaned. "That was lame, and you're not even a groundskeeper. You take care of the plants inside the consulate."

"You're ludicrously cute," Dai said. He stroked one of Harlow's long, pointed ears. "Give Lukas an extragood blow job for me. The Lithuanian Consulate General is a very nice place to work."

"Poke me, mon."

Dai groaned. "So, are you ready to go?"

"Just a second." Harlow opened a book lying on the coffee table and looked inside the front cover. "Just checking," he said. "I can't find my copy."

"Get another one."

"Mine is signed."

"Get it signed."

Harlow sighed loudly. "Barbarian. Come on. Let's see if a cab will pick us up."

"Of course they will. It's Halloween. I guarantee we aren't the worst they've seen."

"You have a point." Harlow waited while Dai locked the door.

They walked to the larger cross street while Dai called for a cab.

"Do you keep that book out, or were you looking at it recently?" Harlow asked.

"I look at it sometimes, and I read the poems. It's a very good book."

"Amy says word is spreading and sales are going up."

"I'm happy for her."

"Yeah, me too. And I can't wait to see what she's wearing tonight."

"Doesn't matter. We're going to win that costume contest."

"We do look amazing," Harlow said. "My tail is on point."

"How do you sit in that costume?"

"The tail is flexible." Harlow batted at his tail.

"Here's our cab." Dai got into the back seat.

Harlow wedged himself in and gave the driver directions. The guy set his GPS and cruised off into the night streets. Harlow was just beginning to bitch about how uncomfortable he was when they arrived at Amy's. Dai got out and pulled Harlow from the back seat like a cork from a bottle. A doorman greeted them, asked which party they were attending, and sent them up in an ancient elevator.

Amy, dressed as Alice in Wonderland, answered her door. After hugs, she showed them into a loft apartment that took up half the top floor of the building. Most of the space was open except for a few partitioned areas. The thirty or so guests were gathered on or around the long balcony.

"I'm so sorry Lukas couldn't make it," Amy said as she led Harlow and Dai across the floor. "You two are beyond cute, though! Best so far." She paused. "Though it's so hard to judge. I tend to like each costume for a different reason. Anyway, you won't know everyone here yet, but by the end of the evening, I'm sure you'll have some new friends. Come on over here and get a drink first."

Amy left them at the bar, where a man dressed as a mad scientist was mixing drinks. Hovering near the bar, Dracula chatted with a Ghostbuster while Bigfoot looked on. An Imperial Stormtrooper took two drinks from the bartender and handed one to Xena.

"These are my people," Harlow said reverently as a man strolled by dressed as Jessica Rabbit.

"If you want to talk to him, I don't need a babysitter."

"Well… I'd love to talk to him about cross-dressing."

"Go. Scamper." Dai shooed Harlow with a swat on the bottom.

Someone spoke from behind Dai. "I never thought I'd see you again."

Dai knew that dark chocolate baritone. He knew who was standing behind him before he turned back to the bar. Sure enough, it was Cope, dressed in a very sharp suit with his shoulder-length hair slicked back from his forehead. Dai shrugged. "It seems we have friends in common."

"Can I get you a drink?"

"I don't know. Can you?" Dai said more sharply than he intended.

Cope sighed as he turned away. "I wish you didn't hate me."

"What?"

"Nothing. I'll leave now. I can't imagine how uncomfortable I make you."

"No you don't." Dai took hold of Cope's wrist and pulled him to a deserted corner. "I want to know what you said."

"Fine. If you really want to know what's on my mind, I'll tell you. I've had a lot of time to think about it, and I still don't have the right words, but if I don't say something, I'm going to explode. If you think I'm pathetic, then so be it. Maybe you'll feel sorry for me."

"That would be an improvement?"

"Believe it or not, yes, I'd rather have your pity than—"

"Than what?"

Cope sighed. "If I could have one wish, I'd wish that you didn't hate me. I'd take back everything that happened all the way to the night of my birthday dinner. I'd call you the next morning instead of going to Hong Kong. Somehow, I'd make you understand that I wanted to know you better as well as jump your bones. But that's not what happened, and that's what I have to live with."

"Wow."

"Wow as in 'I'm impressed this guy bared his soul to me'? Or, 'wow, this guy is not only pathetic but also embarrassing'?"

"Uh… not really sure."

"Story of my life. I'm either too distant or too insistent. Or so I've been told." Cope smoothed his hair. "It's possible I'm manic-depressive." He paused. "Please say something so I can stop babbling. Something about you turns me into a pimply seventh-grader with a crush."

Figuring he had nothing to lose, Dai plunged in. "I thought Will wrote those poems to me." He shook his head. "Looking back on it, I should have known he didn't have those words in him, much less the feelings." After a few moments of silence, he spoke again. "Why didn't you just sign them?"

"I wish I had, but—"

"Let me guess: it's complicated?"

Cope groaned. "Along with 'It's not you, it's me,' 'I just need some space,' and 'We can still be friends,' that's one of the most fatuous phrases in the English language."

"If fatuous means stupid and pointless, I agree. So why didn't you sign your name? It would've saved a lot of trouble."

"You think I don't know that?" Cope ran a hand through his gelled hair again, leaving it in disarray. "If I hadn't run out that day you confronted me, I might have got you to listen to me. You might have believed me when I told you I never saw more than a few seconds of that video before I made Will turn it off. I haven't seen him since that night."

Dai blinked. "Seriously?"

"How could I be friends with someone who could do something like that?"

"It happens."

"I don't have a lot of friends. Just Will. He said he's never done this before, but I don't believe him. He thinks I'm being unfair."

"Of course he does. You're not giving him what he wants."

Cope leaned against the wood paneling and crossed his arms over his chest. "It occurs to me that we rejected Will at the same time."

"We've got that much in common," Dai acknowledged.

"It would be so sweet if we could just start over." When Dai didn't answer, Cope went on. "Listen, Dai, it's important to me that you believe I had nothing to do with Will's movie-making activities. None of it. I had no idea. When I found out, I flipped out."

"Harlow said you quit your job. Is that true?"

"Technically, I'm taking personal time, but I can't see me going back there. I want something else now, and I'm not sure CdG or Will is going to be part of it." Cope shrugged.

Dai pursed his lips in thought. He had no reason to trust Cope, but he *felt* that Cope was telling the truth. "That's pretty amazing."

"What's amazing?"

"You stood by your principles to the point of quitting your job. That's extreme, but I admire you for it."

"I guess that's what I did, but I wouldn't want to repeat the experience. It cost me my best friend and a lot of sleep."

"But still… you did the right thing."

"I think I did. Some people think I'm overreacting and being too harsh. Maybe I am."

"That's just Will working on you. He's a master manipulator. And when he can't manipulate you, he bulldozes you."

"I've never been able to stay mad at him… until now. If he'd just admit he did something wrong, I think I could start forgiving him."

"I'd rather forget him. I don't need any more Wills in my life."

"Well… I'm glad you're okay."

"Let's say I'm better. Sometimes I'm okay, sometimes not. When I think about Will showing that video—" Dai's voice broke, and he swallowed before he went on. "When I think there might be people I don't know who've seen it… someone could be talking to me, and I'd be wondering if they'd seen it. I'm starting to feel paranoid."

Cope squirmed until Dai stopped speaking and then blurted out, "Will's an idiot."

"Yeah."

Cope chuckled.

"What?" Dai's eyebrows drew together. "What's funny?"

"You know that saying 'hoist on your own petard'? Will is a perfect example."

"How's that?"

"When I thought about it, and I *did* think about it, I realized Will intended to acquire you even before the dinner. He told me that when he'd made the reservations, he looked at a picture book of available tables and chose you. I forgot about that until I did some serious brooding. Dinner was all about Will showing off the trophy he would shortly put on his shelf. He wanted to give me a party, but he also wanted the rest of us to see you so we'd envy him later when he bragged about sleeping with you. I guess it didn't occur to him that I'd be attracted to you. Or maybe it did. Maybe he was never who I thought he was. Maybe that was the problem. He was always a jerk, but I thought he was cool."

"I thought he was cool too."

"He told me he made the video because he was so proud of bagging you. You were the pinnacle of his cocksman career."

"Are you saying I was his Moby Dick?"

Cope wasn't sure if he should laugh or not. "I just meant that it was Will's own pride that fucked things up for him." He tried a smile. "Anyway, if anyone is the Captain Ahab of the piece, it's me."

"Do you want to harpoon me?" Dai could not resist saying.

Before Cope could recover and cobble together a reply, they were interrupted.

"What are you two doing in the corner?" Amy exclaimed. "It's time for the parade of costumes!"

"We're coming," Cope said. He turned back to Dai. "Can I see you again?" he asked. "Just to talk?"

"I think we probably should, but I don't know."

"Harlow has my number. Call me when you're ready."

"No promises, but I'll think about it."

"Then I guess we should join the parade." Cope glanced at Dai as they walked to the small crowd. "Who are you dressed as anyway?"

"I'm Ash Ketchum." Dai struck a pose. "From Pokémon?"

"Okay, I know what Pokémon is."

"Who are you supposed to be?" Dai asked.

"It's not obvious?" Cope leered in classic evil villain fashion. "I'm Loki. From the *Avengers*? In civvies."

"Lame."

"I'll have to try harder, then." Cope reached into his jacket and deployed a telescoping metal staff. He pushed a button, and blue lightning crackled in a globe at the end of the tall scepter.

"Now I see the resemblance. Just let me—" Dai reached up and smoothed Cope's hair back behind his ears. He resolutely ignored the fluttering in his belly. It was much too soon for that. "That's better." He saw Harlow waving frantically at him. "Gotta go."

"What the hell, dog?" Harlow said. "Where have you been?"

"Am I late for something?"

"You're going to be the late Daimaru Tanaka if you don't start taking this seriously."

"Calm your sphincter."

"Did you really just tell me to calm my sphincter, or is that a quote from *Blazing Saddles*?"

"You're kidding, right?"

"You've gone all seventies on me tonight. What's next? Olivia Newton-John?"

"Well, if you want to get physical, physical."

"There's something different about you tonight."

"I'm dressed as a ten-year-old Pokémon Master."

"That's not it. *Shiz*! Amy's waving to us. Okay, do it just like we rehearsed."

"Relax."

Harlow scampered out ahead of Dai, and Dai chased him. Dai threw his arms around Harlow, and Harlow hit the switch that activated the flashing lights embedded in his costume. Dai pretended to be electrocuted until the lights went out. He and Harlow bowed to a round of applause.

"Okay," Harlow said after accepting compliments. "I need something to drink, and I need to figure out what's different about you."

Dai handed Harlow a ginger ale. "I'm having a good time. Let's not analyze it."

"Are you trying to be funny? You know I live to analyze your personal life." Harlow stared into Dai's eyes until Dai glanced away. Harlow followed the line of Dai's gaze and found Cope. "Are you interested in him, after all?"

"I think we have things to talk about. Don't send out wedding invitations just yet."

"But when it's time?"

"You can help me pick a china pattern."

"That's all I've ever wanted, Dai-chan," Harlow said in a voice that dripped sincerity.

Dai laughed, and when he looked around the room again, he caught Cope watching him. He tossed Cope one of his friendly smiles—the one that said "I like you but you're fine where you are for now." At least, that's what he hoped it said. At any rate, Cope appeared to understand, and Dai appreciated him for that.

"I saw that! You like him!" Harlow pointed a finger at Dai.

"One more time," Dai said. "I don't think they heard you on Long Island."

"Eat me. Why be coy? Let the boy know you like him."

"I don't know yet if I like him."

"That's a lie." Harlow put a hand over Dai's heart. "But it's your business, my brother."

"Thanks." Dai looked over Harlow's head. "Don't look now, but I think we're about to be declared winners."

Harlow was thrilled with the tiaras Amy bestowed on him and Dai. Dai spilled his glass of champagne on Harlow, and there was a momentary panic before Harlow assured everyone his wiring was water—*and* sparkling wine—proof. When Dai looked around, Cope was nowhere to be found. It was probably just as well, given his propensity for falling into bed on the first date. Then again, what did he have to feel guilty about? "Screw that. I like sex," he muttered.

"That's not exactly news," Harlow remarked. "Are you still good with me staying overnight? Lukas is still planning on staying in Connecticut."

"Of course. It'll always be your home."

"Ugh, I sure hope not."

"Fuck you, shorty."

"How dare you!"

"Not my fault you're vertically challenged."

"I'm within the parameters of average height."

"Sure you are… in Oz."

Harlow snickered and then sobered. "I miss hanging out with you all the time, but I love living with Luk."

"As long as you're happy," Dai said, and he meant it. He and Harlow shut down the party and went home. They made popcorn and sat on the futon watching *Scream*. When Dai got up for water, he made sure to say, "I'll be right back," and Harlow said it along with him. They fell asleep in the middle of *Fright Night* with Harlow's head on Dai's shoulder.

WHILE MAINTAINING the greenery at the Lithuanian consulate, Dai met the man who owned Stone Gardens, the nursery and plant delivery business that serviced the building and grounds. After a look at the foliage and a few minutes' conversation, Mr. Stone gave Dai his card and said to call him if Dai wanted to change jobs. Dai called and spoke with Mr. Stone and soon after gave notice at the consulate. He started delivering and installing indoor plants. He was encouraged to create his own designs, and Stone Gardens was soon getting calls requesting Dai's touch. Within six weeks, he stopped driving the van and moved into an office with a drafting table. Mr. Stone assured him he didn't have to know how to make a shrub look like a shrub. He could use circles and squares and triangles and whatever shapes he wanted. Excited about this heretofore unsuspected gift for arranging plants in a pleasing manner, Dai forgot all about calling Cope.

However, Harlow was not going to let him forget. "You're coming to my thing, right?" Harlow faced Dai across an inadequately sized table at a medium-pretentious café in Hell's Kitchen.

"Is that why you invited me to brunch? You could have called."

"I wanted to see you. I'm still annoyed you didn't come for Thanksgiving."

"I was going to, but Luk told me you were serving pineapple turkey."

"It was delicious."

"If you say so."

"Hey! You know who you should invite?"

"No, I don't know—oh, wait, how about Cope?" Dai said sarcastically.

Harlow stuck out his lower lip. "You're mean. Maybe I was going to say someone else."

"No, you weren't."

"Well, he asks about you, you know? He has this look in his eyes. What's that word? Wistful, maybe. Anyway, it's pitiful the way he tries so hard not to mention you whenever he sees me, but he just can't help himself."

"I've actually been meaning to call him," Dai said less than truthfully. "You have his number, right?"

Harlow whipped his phone out. "Sending it to you now. Done." He tilted his head to the side. "You look good. You've gained back the weight you lost when you had the flu. Just don't cut your hair."

"I wasn't planning on it. I haven't had it cut in about three months. The plants don't seem to mind. They haven't offered any opinions, at least."

"I like it. You look cute—like that guy from Tokio Hotel. Remember Tokio Hotel?"

"How could I forget? Anyway, they aren't gone."

"You're kidding. They're still around?"

"And touring."

"Who would have guessed a German electropop boy band would last… what is it, like, fifteen years now?"

"Something like that. Google it if you're interested."

"No, thanks. Are you going to eat that scone?"

Dai shoved the plate of miniscones over to Harlow; they had too much glazing on them anyway. He sipped his coffee while critically eyeing the dry, boxed yew hedge outside the window of the café. It reminded him of the last place he'd seen Will. Over three months after the breakup and Dai still couldn't stop picking at the scab, no matter how many times he resolved to let it go. He kept thinking he could find some clue as to why his relationships always ended this way—in rank betrayal of some kind.

"Are you okay?" Harlow asked.

"Am I too nice?"

"What?" Harlow made a face. "No! What gave you such an erroneous idea?"

"Am I a doormat?"

"I wouldn't characterize you as such, but on the other hand, you *are* very chill." Harlow fastidiously dusted crumbs from his fingertips. "What I mean is, you don't get your panties in a wad over every little thing. You're low-maintenance."

"That's a good thing, right?"

"Oh hell yeah."

"But do you think that's why the guys I like end up walking all over me?"

"No." Harlow leaned forward. "Read my lips, Dai-chan. It's… not… you. It's them."

Dai sighed. "I have the worst luck with men."

Harlow quoted Eric Draven from *The Crow*. "It can't rain all the time."

"I know. I'm just being a drama llama."

"No, you aren't, and you can always talk to me. So other than that, how's your life?"

"Other than that, I'm great. I love my job, and I'm putting money back into savings. I might even consider moving out of the old apartment."

"I miss our beach-chair conversations in the morning."

"I miss the smell of napalm in the morning."

"Yeah, I miss that too. Lukas is woefully ignorant of American pop culture."

"I know. Please don't ruin him."

"Bitch."

"You can count on it." Dai leaned back in his chair. "I like your hair too. The blond was awesome, but I like your natural color."

"I think it's too short, but it'll grow." Harlow finished his coffee. "I've got to run. Rehearsals all day."

"See you tomorrow night."

"Yeah." Harlow stood. "Hey, I should give you these." He handed Dai two tickets. "VIP, baby."

"Thanks. I would gladly pay, though."

"This is one of the perks, so just lump it."

"Consider it lumped." Dai smiled at Harlow's back as his friend walked away. He truly was happy for Harlow, who appeared to finally be receiving all the good luck he deserved. The waiter filled Dai's cup again. Dai thanked him and then picked up his phone. Before he could think too long about it, he found Harlow's message and called Cope's number.

Cope answered on the second ring. "Copeland Shore speaking."

"That's pretty formal, isn't it?"

"Dai?"

"Hi. You busy?"

"I'm—no, I'm not. Not busy at all."

"How about tomorrow night? Are you busy then?"

"If you want to see me tomorrow night, I'm sure I don't have other plans."

"Smooth," Dai commented. "Here's the deal. I have two tickets to a ballet. Would you like to go with me?"

"Is it Harlow and Lukas's ballet?"

"It is."

"I'd love to go. I was planning to go anyway, but this is much nicer."

"Good. I'm glad."

"Since you're taking me to a show, can I take you to dinner first?"

"Well… I got the tickets free."

"I promise to take you somewhere they won't charge me."

"Where would that be?"

"I have connections."

"Connections? Should I be worried a rival gang will put a hit on you while we're at dinner?"

"If that's what you want."

As Cope's sable voice stroked his ear, Dai realized they were flirting. And it didn't feel forced or phony. It had happened naturally while they were talking. "I should go. Um, what time?"

"The ballet starts at eight, so I'll make reservations for seven, pick you up at six thirty?"

"I can meet you at the restaurant."

"Okay." Cope didn't try to sweet-talk Dai or argue with him. "I'll text you the address."

"Groovy." Dai grimaced. "I can't believe I just said 'groovy.'"

"Far out," Cope responded. "Listen, before you go, I'm really glad you called."

"Okay. Bye." Dai hung up quickly. Did he really want to do this? Sure, he was attracted to Cope, but maybe that wasn't a good sign. The men he was attracted to generally turned out to have massive flaws. He had a knack for digging up the imperfect diamonds. "It's done now," he said under his breath. "No point in stressing over it."

"Sir?"

Dai looked up at the waiter. "Check, please?"

Dai paid and took a walk to eat up some time before he went to the gym. He was glad it was cold. It felt good to be striding briskly along with his fellow New Yorkers for a while. After his workout, he did some grocery shopping, stopping at several small shops for bread, sliced meat, liquor, and fruit. He spent his day off watching movies in between switching clothes from washer to dryer and folding them on the futon. He missed Harlow most at times like these.

He made dinner at six and thought about going out to a movie or a bar, but he couldn't think of anything he wanted to see, and he wasn't in the mood to drink. Nor was he in the mood to sit in a bar drinking a soda... ever. He was inventorying the contents of his fridge when the thought he could call Cope strayed through his head. *And say what? "I'm pathetically lonely"?*

Nothing in the fridge disagreed with his assessment of his situation. Dai took out a beer and then put it back. "Am I really thinking about drinking out of sheer boredom?" He looked around the kitchen. "Goddammit. I'm talking to myself."

Dai's gaze skipped over the book on the counter and then came back to it. He sat down and opened Amy and Cope's book. He looked at each page and read each poem. He remembered how his heart had fluttered when he read the first poem Cope had sent him. If not for a stupid circumstance, things might have been far different.

Dai looked at his phone and once more thought about calling Cope. Instead, he called Kei and caught up on gossip. When Kei tired of talking, it was late enough for Dai to justify a snack. He made a plate of cheese, crackers, and salami and opened a beer. One of the cable channels was showing all of the Indiana Jones movies, and he settled in to watch until he got sleepy.

COPE WOKE up and remembered he had a date with Dai that evening. He smiled as he brushed his teeth and got dressed. His plan was to stay busy and not give himself time to worry about screwing up his second chance with Dai. Or maybe it was a first chance. Either way, he didn't want to obsess over it and make a self-fulfilling prophecy.

After breakfast and email, he called Amy on Skype. They talked for about two hours about the proofs for the calendar they were collaborating on, and then he went out to do some errands. As he was talking himself out of doing something stupid like buying Dai a present, he thought about Will. He was looking at an elegant pen in the Mont Blanc window, and it reminded him of the man who'd been his best friend for so long. Though he'd found ways to fill the hours that were once dedicated to Will, it was taking time to adjust. He kept getting ambushed by memories.

Cope took out his phone. There was something he should do before he saw Dai.

Will answered in the middle of the first ring. "Cope!"

"Are you busy at the moment?"

"Not galactically busy."

"Could you get away to meet me?"

"When and where?"

"You like O'Brien's. I can be there in twenty minutes."

"Okay."

Cope hung up and called for a cab. When he was dropped off at O'Brien's, he found Will had arrived before him and secured a table. On a whim, Cope ordered the pub breakfast—fried potatoes, bangers, poached egg, black *and* white pudding, baked beans, sliced tomato, and toasted soda bread—with a Murphy's Irish stout. Will ordered a club sandwich and a draft Bass.

"You're looking... casual." Will took in Cope's jeans and long-sleeved T-shirt.

"Eat your heart out."

"Me? I like looking sharp."

"If only you knew how."

"Bazinga," Will said brightly.

"Bazinga?"

"Yeah, they say that on that TV show you like."

"You don't watch TV, except the Super Bowl and porn."

"Well, I tried watching it because you liked it so much, and it's really funny. The jokes aren't stupid, and all the actors have really developed their characters."

Cope sat back as his stout was set in front of him. "How many episodes have you seen?" he asked when the server was gone.

"I'm almost through season three."

"Jesus!"

"Really, Cope, you have to stop mistaking me for your lord and savior."

Cope was silent for a few moments before he replied. "You're right."

"Easy now. Don't go all deep and meaningful on me." Will sipped his ale.

"Sorry, but that's why I'm here. I need to have it all laid out so I can draw a line and walk away… or not. Depends on you."

"What do you need from me?"

"Whoa. Don't you want to hear my proposal first?"

"If you're making noises about letting me back in your life, all I need to know is what you need from me to make that happen."

"Do you want to eat first?"

"Yeah, good idea."

"So… you've really watched three seasons of *The Big Bang Theory*?"

"I have."

"Why?"

"I told you. Because you like it so much. It made me feel better when I was missing you."

"I can't tell anymore when you're being sincere."

"Take my word for it?"

Cope shook his head. "I've seen you in action too many times."

"What's that mean?"

"I'm talking about the nights we'd go clubbing with the express intention of bringing home some hot stud to share. It was an education to watch you operate."

"I don't recall any objections from you at the—" Will broke off as the waiter arrived with their food. "Damn," he said as a heavy platter thumped onto the table in front of Cope. "It looks like you ordered the kitchen sink, son."

"I'm planning on skipping lunch."

"This *is* lunch, space cadet."

"Maybe for you. I'm out of the corporate sector."

Will chewed and swallowed. "I googled your name and recent publications and ordered the book. It's lush."

"Thanks."

"I can't believe you're writing poems again."

"I can't believe I let you convince me writing poetry was useless."

"It kind of is."

"I guess it depends."

"On what?"

"On whether you have a soul or not."

Will put down his sandwich. "Are you getting religious on me?"

"No, but I do believe living things have souls. Don't you?"

"What use would it be?"

"Not an answer I had anticipated." Cope took a drink of the stout. "We agreed we'd save the talk until after breakfast."

"Lunch."

"Whatever." Cope dunked a forkful of black pudding in the egg yolk and put it in his mouth.

"So this is all going to be on your terms?"

"Eat." Cope gestured with his fork.

"Just as I thought." Will tucked in to his club sandwich and polished it off. He nursed his ale while Cope soldiered on through his massive meal.

"God, I can't eat another bite." Cope groaned as he pushed his plate away.

"Finally," Will said. "I've got the check."

"I invited you. Ergo, I pay."

"Not gonna happen."

Cope sat back. When the waiter returned, he asked for a cup of coffee. Will ordered one too and asked for the check.

"You ready?" Cope asked when their server had gone.

"Hit me," Will said.

"I don't want to cut you out of my life."

"Well, there's good news."

"But I will if I have to. I know you think I'm being too sensitive, and that's not okay. Since when is standing up for basic human decency called being too sensitive? I think you're being too *in*sensitive if you can't see why I object to what you did to Dai."

"This again?"

"This is the central issue, Will."

"Why can't you let it go?"

"Because it isn't the kind of thing you brush aside like taking an extra newspaper from the machine."

"Who gets newspapers from machines these days?"

"Dodging the question?"

"I don't see why this has to be on your terms exclusively."

"Because *you* want *me* back, not vice versa."

"So... you *don't* want me back?"

"I didn't say that."

"Yes, you did."

"I hate that I have to make conditions, but I'm not the one who fucked up."

"And the fuckup didn't even involve you, I might add."

"Add whatever you like, but it does involve me."

"I don't see how. I filmed me having sex with Dai. I couldn't resist showing it to a couple of my best buds. How is that grounds for divorcing me?"

"We're talking about your character, Will."

"Yeah? Why do you or anyone else get a say in my character?"

"Because I love you." In the sudden silence, Cope realized he'd raised his voice. He drank some coffee, praying someone would drop a tray, until the buzz of conversation started again. "I want to keep loving you," Cope said. "But I can't love a sleazy jerk. For my sake, will you destroy the video and apologize to Dai?"

"And then what? We'll be friends again?"

"It would be a start."

Will shook his head. "I'm sorry, but I won't negotiate friendship."

"Think about it."

"I don't have to. If you think you have the right to put conditions on our friendship, have at it, but I'm not playing ball." Will frowned. "I still can't believe you cut me out of your life like someone you met once at an office party. I'm your best friend. I know you better than anyone."

"Probably true. So?"

"Are you really ready to toss it all away?"

"I don't have a choice."

"Bullshit."

"You think it doesn't hurt me as much as it hurts you? Because it does. It hurts worse than losing my parents. You—" Cope's voice choked off. "You were my everything."

Will didn't say anything for several moments. When he spoke, his voice sounded strained. "I'm… honored. And I've never loved anyone the way I love you." He glanced around the restaurant. "Please just come home. I swear in a couple of months, you'll forget all about this. I'll make sure of it."

"I wish it was that easy."

"It is. Just make the decision and forget about the rest of it."

"I can't."

"Why not? I do it all the time. If a deal tanks, I put it behind me and start on the next one."

"Dai is a person, not a deal."

"He'll get over it. It's not like he's a Catholic schoolgirl."

"So it's okay to hurt him because he's a big, strong man?" Cope shook his head. "I can't figure out if you became an ass overnight, or if you were always like this and I just didn't see it."

"I don't think I've changed."

"I guess I must have got a lot more sensitive or something." Cope glanced up when the waiter brought the check. "I've got this," he said firmly.

"Fine," Will said unconvincingly. "Does that mean we're done here?"

"It means I can't take any more of this."

"I don't feel like we really settled anything," Will said as Cope gave his card to the server. "What's the upshot?"

"I'm not coming back to CdG. I won't rule out the possibility of us being friends again, but not right now." Cope signed the bill and put it on the corner of the table. "Look, I realize I have no right to ask you to change for me, but that's what I'm doing. If you can't or won't, there's not much else to talk about."

"You're too much, man. You change your phone. You leave your job. You get a new apartment."

"I knew if I didn't, you'd hound me. I had to act fast to head you off."

"Probably true."

Will got to his feet and waited for Cope to walk down the stairs ahead of him. At the bottom, they collected their coats and went outside.

"Are you headed back to work?" Cope asked as he dug gloves out of the pocket of his down jacket.

"Yeah. Wells got back from HK last night, so we have lots to talk about this afternoon." Will smiled. "He's working out really well for a heterosexual."

Cope almost laughed. "He seemed ambitious and reasonably intelligent."

"Yeah, he's a great exec assistant, but he's never going to let me forget I took him to eat sushi off a naked guy."

Cope didn't comment. They had reached Avenue of the Americas, and Cope stopped in the throat of the plaza. Overhead, the flags snapped loudly in the winter wind.

"Was that insensitive?" Will asked. "Maybe I shouldn't mention anything concerning Dai."

"Yeah, maybe."

Will cocked his head to the side. "You want him," he said softly. "You want him for yourself."

"Since I first laid eyes on him. So?"

"It's just that I finally get why you're so torqued about the video."

Cope took a deep breath and let it out slowly in a plume of white mist. "So that's it," he said.

"What?"

"The end of any hope for our friendship."

Will's fair eyebrows drew together. "Why?"

"Because you just came up with a rationale that lets you keep your worldview intact. I've seen you do this before, just never with me. Before long, you'll convince yourself that the whole thing was my fault or Dai's or anyone but you. You'll decide I'm mad because I was jealous of you, even though it makes no sense. You'll find a way to put the blame somewhere else, and you'll go on with your life like you hadn't ruined someone else's."

"That's a little strong, don't you think?"

"And so it begins." Cope turned away from Will.

"So... this is goodbye?" Will called after him.

Cope kept walking.

"Fine. If this is the last time I'll see you, what about the dream box?"

Cope stopped in his tracks and turned back to stare at Will.

"Well," Will said. "What about it?"

"You brought it up."

"It means a lot to me."

"If you want it, just say so. I'm not going to have some kind of absurd custody battle with you, so you can forget that ploy."

"Ploy? Listen to yourself." Will shook his head. "You know what? Keep it. It doesn't mean anything anymore."

WILL COULD tell by Cope's change of expression that he'd wounded him, and he was glad. Will had come to this meeting prepared to remind Cope of what he was throwing away. He had even watched that cartoonish television show so he could talk about it. He'd made an effort, but apparently Cope wasn't interested. If their friendship meant so little to Cope that he'd toss it away over a random piece of ass, then let him go. Will could wait for the day Cope came crawling back, and he'd welcome him with open arms because *he* didn't hold grudges.

"If you ever change your mind…." Cope's voice trailed off. He looked at Will for another few seconds and then walked away.

Will watched Cope move away from him between the short banks of snow on either side of the walkway. He remembered the skiing trip to Tuxedo Ridge where Cope had bought that bright orange, thigh-length down coat. They'd done a sixty-nine on it in front of the fireplace in their lodge. The next day, the binding on Will's ski failed and he twisted his ankle badly. Cope had climbed back up the ridge to get cell reception and shared his flask with Will until the ski patrol arrived. He had laughed until he cried at something Cope had said… something he couldn't remember now.

Will turned his collar up against a sudden gust of chill wind. It appeared to blow Cope around the corner at the cross street, and then he and the orange coat were gone from sight. Will blinked and trained his mind on his afternoon meeting with the head buyer from Milan. First things first.

DAI GOT out of the cab at Stella's in Manhattan, just a few blocks from the theater district. The interior was old-school classy Italian with high ceilings, lots of carved plaster, and a piano bar. He was fifteen minutes early, and the hostess took him to the bar, where Cope was waiting.

"I'm early too," Cope said as he rose to take Dai's hand. "I'm having a drink. Want one?"

Dai sat on the barstool next to Cope's. "At one of her parties, Amy was making something with limoncello. Any idea what that might be?"

"Let's ask an expert." Cope caught the bartender's eye. "Do you know any drinks made with limoncello?" he asked.

"Dozens. A lot of people drink it on the rocks, but you can make anything from a martini to a frozen daiquiri with it. It's basically a sweet lemon liqueur."

"What do you recommend?" Dai asked.

"Let me make you one and you can see what you think." The bartender poured limoncello into a glass and topped it with club soda. He added a sprig of mint and a lemon curl before setting it in front of Dai.

Dai sipped. "That's really fresh," he said. "Thanks." He held his glass out to Cope. "Want a taste?"

"Of course I do." Cope took the glass and sipped. "Yep, that's fresh. Not very interesting, though."

"Yeah? What are you drinking?"

"A Sazerac. It's—"

"I know what it is. I've been to New Orleans. I didn't like the Sazerac. I guess it's a matter of taste."

"It's all about taste," Cope said. "From the minute we're born. Our mouths are our first point of contact with the world. Babies don't see well at first. After our vision sharpens, sight becomes the primary sense for most of us. But before that, we tasted everything, and our subconscious remembers that."

"Did you rehearse that? Or are you prone to talk like that out of the blue?"

"The latter. When I warm up to someone, I tend to expound. Just trying to impress, I guess."

"I'm not dissing you. Just asking."

"Sorry if I apologize too much. I'm nervous."

"Relax. It's not as if we're total strangers."

"No, but I sure wish we were."

"One of the reasons I wanted to see you was to clear the air completely. I just feel like I don't have closure or something."

"I feel the same."

"I feel like you got screwed as much as I did, and then I treated you shittily because I assumed you were in on it. I feel bad about that."

"Not your fault." Cope looked up. "The hostess is ready for us."

Cope and Dai were seated at a table against the left-hand wall. The veal scaloppini was recommended, and Dai ordered it. Cope ordered shrimp diavolo and a bottle of prosecco.

"What else would you like to clear up?" Cope asked before he bit into a breadstick.

"Now that I'm here, eating warm bread and drinking wine, I'm not sure."

"I'll start. I saw Will today."

"By accident?"

"No, I called and had him meet me somewhere. I guess I had some air to clear too."

"What happened?"

"I told him I'd be willing to forgive him if he promised me he'd destroy the video."

"And?"

"I was hoping he was going to be a man about it, but the gist of his speech was that I should mind my own fucking business."

Dai sat back as the waiter arrived with plates, grateful for the distraction. He sipped from his water glass until the man had gone and then changed the subject. "This looks good," he said. "Ugh, that was lame."

"Not if you were sincere. And you're right; it looks good. I almost wish I'd ordered it." Cope was a little surprised Dai hadn't made a remark about Will, but on the other hand, he didn't want to talk about him either.

For a few minutes, they ate in silence, each taking surreptitious glances at the other. The waiter returned and refilled their glasses. Dai picked his up.

"Would it be corny to make a toast?"

"Go right ahead." Cope picked up his glass.

"To new friendships," Dai said.

Cope touched his flute to Dai's and then drank. When he set the glass down, he felt inexplicably lighter. The pain of his meeting with Will was still a heavy weight in his heart, but it wasn't consuming him anymore. He started a conversation that wasn't about Will and held his own in movie quote banter. By the time they had to leave for the theater, he was almost buoyant.

At the venerable venue, Dai and Cope were shown to balcony seats by an usher who helpfully pointed out the location of the men's room and the fact that there was a bar on this level as well as in the lobby. At 7:59, the lights dimmed and the curtain rose. For an hour and a half, Lukas and his troupe enchanted their audience, using every inch of the small stage to tell their story in a dance both athletic and ethereal. If anyone was surprised or upset by the lack of female dancers, they kept their feelings to themselves. When the ballet was over and the dancers returned for a curtain call, Lukas and Harlow were singled out for their unconventional pas de deux. They took several bows as the audience applauded.

"There were a lot more people here than I expected," Cope said as he and Dai descended to the ground floor.

"Yeah, at least three-quarters of the seats were filled."

"Maybe it's the new trend: gay ballet."

"New?"

"Okay, there have always been gay dancers, but how many ballets have pas de deux for two men?"

"I have no idea." At the bottom of the stairs, Dai pulled Cope to the right. "I have instructions to bring you backstage. I should warn you. When Harlow is amped up, he's very demonstrative."

"I don't know what that means."

"He might hug you."

"He's hugged me lots of times. I think he feels sorry for me."

"I forget that you're all friends, you, Amy, Lukas, Harlow."

"And you."

Dai smiled over his shoulder as they reached the end of the hall. After a brief conversation with the man at the door, they were allowed backstage. Eight or so dancers were sitting, standing, or walking around in various stages of costume removal. Several had peeled the tops of their leotards down to their hips. The clinging fabric highlighted their sleek musculature as they removed makeup or made their way to the shower room.

"This is almost enough to make me believe in heaven, because if God made anything better, he kept it up there." Cope paused. "Not to objectify these artists or anything like that."

Dai grinned. "Let's go congratulate Harlow and Lukas. Try not to grab an excellent dancer butt on the way."

"I'll do my best."

Harlow radiated joy. Dai had the feeling that if Harlow hadn't been anchored by all the people hugging him, he would have floated up and bobbed around the ceiling. He patiently waited his turn and braced himself for Harlow's full-frontal assault. Sure enough, when Harlow saw Dai, he let out a high-pitched whoop of laughter and leapt into Dai's arms. Harlow jumped up and down, grinning and laughing until Dai jumped with him.

"Can you believe it?" Harlow said breathlessly.

"It was awesome. Can we stop now?"

Harlow laughed as he let go of Dai. "I'm just so excited."

"And I'm so happy for you. You were brilliant." Dai raised his voice. "You were all brilliant."

"Thank you," Lukas said. "Nice to see you again, Dai. Cope, thanks again for your generous gift."

Dai glanced at Cope. "What's all this about a generous gift?"

"The company needed help securing the deposit on the theater, so I stepped in. No big deal."

"You didn't mention it when I invited you."

"Why would I? It was between me and Lukas."

"You and Dai make such a cute couple," Harlow said.

"Don't start," Dai said. "This is your night. You were fantastic."

"Are you going to celebrate?" Cope asked.

Lukas and Harlow laughed. "No party for us," Harlow said. "We'll be going to bed early. Tomorrow we have class, rehearsals, and a performance."

Dai hugged Harlow. "I love you, you divine maniac."

"I don't know what that means but I love it," Harlow said. "Enjoy the rest of your evening." He winked broadly.

"Cheeky monkey," Dai said.

"I know that one," Cope said. "*Saturday Night Live*, right?"

"I'm telling you, Dai-chan, he's a keeper."

"We're going." Dai led Cope out of the theater and down the sidewalk toward Forty-Second. After a couple of minutes, he slowed his pace.

"Where are we going?" Cope asked. "It doesn't matter much to me; I'm just making small talk."

Dai stopped. "It's barely ten. I don't feel like going home just yet."

"I hesitate to ask, but… I got proofs for the new book I'm doing with Amy. Would you like to see them? Oh God, that really sounds like a pickup line."

Dai didn't notice. "A new book?" He was a little annoyed by how hurt he was that Amy hadn't called him, even though he wasn't part of a couple. "The one with pictures of couples."

"No, that's a much bigger project. It's still in the planning stage. And I should have said calendar, not book. She and I went through her portfolio of unused images and matched them with some of my poetry. Papyrus is using it as their promotional calendar this Christmas."

"Nice."

"And it paid much better than I would have expected. One of the things I wanted to tell Will in person was that I wasn't going back to CdG."

"Actually, I would like to see the calendar, and I'd like to continue the conversation somewhere besides the sidewalk."

"Walk or cab?"

"I like walking when it's cold, and if I remember right, your place is about twelve blocks away?"

"More like fifteen."

"Let's go."

CHAPTER TWELVE

"COME ON in and have a seat," Cope said. "I'll get us both some water."

While Cope was busy in the kitchen, Dai walked around the living area. It was the first time he'd been in here alone and had a chance to see what was on the bookshelves. He tapped the spines of books by Stephen Fry, Chuck Palahniuk, and Carl Hiaasen. He gazed at the photo of a happy young couple standing in front of a Beechcraft Bonanza aircraft; he was dark and dashing, she had Cope's eyes and lips. When Cope returned, Dai was stroking a finger along the top of an old cigar box.

"You found a real treasure," Cope said as he handed Dai a glass of water. "The dream box."

"I'm intrigued."

"Go ahead and open it if you want to." Cope sat and watched Dai lift the box down from the bookcase. "I could watch you all day," he said.

Dai looked up. "What?"

"Just, you know, you look nice. I can see why you got hired at the restaurant."

"Yeah, well, I work out a few times a week." Dai lifted something from the box. "Looks like a magazine photo of somewhere like the Bahamas."

"That's Bora Bora. One of our dreams was to buy a tropical island."

"Our?"

"Me and Will. We were roommates for four years in college. The first Christmas, he took me home with him. His parents are standard WASP poster people. Gracious, hospitable, attractive in a white teeth and tennis tan kind of way." Cope paused. "I shouldn't be so sarcastic. They were always good to me. Anyway, we were out on their boat despite the cold, and I said I'd like to have a boat someday. That night, Will emptied one of his dad's cigar boxes and gave it to me with a brochure for yachts. And that was the beginning of the tradition." He smiled. "You used to be in there."

"Excuse me?" Dai looked up with a picture forgotten in his hand.

"Well, not you precisely, but a picture of a *nantaimori* restaurant. Will clipped it from a *GQ* article about yakuza crime lords."

"So it's like a bucket list."

"Yeah, but I like the sound of 'dream box' better. The idea is when the dream or wish is fulfilled, you take the picture out and put it in the scrapbook."

"Where's the scrapbook?"

Cope smiled. "I'm afraid that's privileged information." He opened the attaché case on the coffee table. "Here are the prints we've chosen," he said.

Dai looked at soft-black-and-white photos of stormy skies with poignant bird silhouettes, melancholy rocky beaches that seemed to stretch to infinity, people caught in the act of living unobserved, and tender blossoms soon to wither. A dozen in all, and each matched to a poem.

"It's amazing," Dai said. "I doubt writing poems will make you rich, but you're really good at it."

"I feel pretty pretentious calling myself a poet, but it's something to do, and I enjoy it." Cope deflected the conversation away from himself. "Harlow tells me you're designing plants? Can that be right?"

"I do arrangements of large potted plants in and around commercial buildings. To my surprise, I love it."

"I'm really happy for you."

Dai sipped his ice water, and for a few minutes neither he nor Cope spoke. Abruptly, both started to talk at the same time.

"Go ahead," Cope said.

"No, you."

"I was going to ask if we could go out again, but no pressure."

"Can you handle it if I'm slow to trust?"

"Can I handle it? I invented it."

Dai chuckled. "I like you," he said. "I did from the second I heard your voice. When I saw you, I couldn't believe you looked as good as you sounded."

"That's nice, but I'm a fairly ordinary-looking man."

"You're not handsome in the same way Will is, but you're definitely attractive."

"Okay, let's change the subject. When can we go out again?"

"Are you free tomorrow night?"

"I am."

"Do you like dim sum?" Dai asked.

"I grew up on it."

"You're joking, right?"

"Nope. Chinese is the food of my people."

"Bullshit, you don't look—"

"Jewish?" Cope laughed. "I know I don't quite fit the stereotype."

"Okay, dim sum tomorrow." Dai returned the cigar box to the bookcase. "I'm gonna take off."

"Let me call a cab for you."

"My phone isn't broken." Dai softened the statement with a smile. "I appreciate that you care, but I got this." He made a call and then put his phone back in his jacket pocket. "Thanks for a great evening," he said. "And relax, okay? I'm not looking for someone to take care of me. I'm done with that."

"Got it." Cope walked to the door with Dai. "I had a great time. I'm looking forward to tomorrow night."

"Me too." Dai shifted his weight from one foot to the other. "Awkward," he said. He cleared his throat. "There's just one more thing."

"What's that?"

"Harlow's litmus test. Are you ready?"

"How should I know? What are you going to do?"

"I'm going to kiss you."

"Then I'm ready."

"You sure? I know this is a little… unromantic, but I've found it's best to get it out of the way and not make a big deal out of it. Besides, Harlow says it's the only way to know for sure if you should have that second date."

"It does sound like something he'd say." Cope smiled. "He's a wise man."

Dai leaned forward until his lips touched Cope's. Cope put his hands on Dai's shoulders and returned the gentle pressure. Dai responded, moving his lips on Cope's and slipping an arm around Cope's back. Cope moved a hand up to cradle the back of Dai's head, fingers sliding through Dai's silky hair. Dai licked at Cope's full lower lip and pressed harder against him.

Cope broke the kiss and took a deep, shaky breath as he let go of Dai. Dai stared at Cope in disbelief; never in his experience had he been pushed away like this—especially by someone who professed to be smitten with him. He opened his mouth to speak, when the taxi driver blew his horn.

Cope opened the door. "See you tomorrow night."

At a loss for words, Dai walked to the cab doing his best to conceal his hard-on. It was true it didn't take much to get his motor running, but it usually took a little more than a simple kiss. When Cope's mouth had moved on his, he got hard so fast he became light-headed.

"At least I didn't sleep with him on the first date," Dai muttered.

"Sir?" the cabbie said.

Dai gave his address and sat back to look out the side window. Maybe he was making a mistake with Cope. He'd planned on taking a break from dating after Brad, but here he was already looking forward to a second date. And he really *was* looking forward to it.

CHAPTER THIRTEEN

"Excuse me, Dai."

Dai looked up from the drawing table and smiled at Mr. Stone. "Hey, Frank. What's up?"

"Got a minute to talk?"

"Sure." Dai put his pencil down and swiveled his chair to face Mr. Stone.

"I hate to do this to you, but I need you tonight. Can you work?"

Dai almost mentioned his date but changed his mind. "What do you need?"

"I wouldn't ask, but it could be a big contract for us if we ace it. I'd love to have something installed when the head manager arrives for work tomorrow morning."

"What are we talking about?"

"The Cartier store in Manhattan. They want a temporary Christmas display just inside the front door. Can you do it?"

"What's the area?"

"The floor plan has been emailed to you, but you'll have fourteen feet front to back, six feet side to side, and a twelve-foot clearance overhead."

"Does that include clear space?"

"No, those are the actual dimensions."

Dai already saw the arrangement in his head. He paused, calculating. "I'm thinking five to six hours including drive time."

"Need any help?"

"Nope. Can I have anything I want from inventory?"

"Knock yourself out. If something is earmarked for another project, make a note, and we'll order another one. I really appreciate this."

"I appreciate you giving me a chance to move up."

"When I saw how you took care of those plants at the consulate, I knew you belonged here. It's no secret around here that I love these plants like they were my kids. Our mission statement is to provide little pockets of green in the city. There are so many benefits to having plants in the workplace. It's not just the extra oxygen; plants remind people there's a world out there that has nothing to do with concrete, exhaust fumes, or fluorescent lights."

"That's beautiful, Frank."

"Fuck off."

"I'm not making fun of you."

"Sorry about the 'fuck off.' Sometimes I forget you bat for the other team."

Dai smiled. "Apology accepted, but what does that mean?"

"Well, you're, you know, gay. That's what you like to be called now, right?"

"You've known that since my first week on the job."

"Well, everyone knows gay guys are more sensitive."

Dai laughed. "There are only as many sensitive gay guys as there are sensitive straight guys."

"Are you sure?"

"We're just people, Frank. We don't have special powers."

"Yeah, but you…. Never mind. I should let you get to work."

"Go ahead and finish your thought first."

"I shouldn't talk about things I know nothing about. I just thought that because things are so tough for you guys, you're probably more sympathetic to other people who are having a rough time. Does that make any sense?"

"I think you're a very good man. I hope that's enough of an answer."

"I'm glad you think so. Use the big truck if you need it." Mr. Stone paused in the doorway. "You'll be pleased with your bonus, and of course, if the Cartier people like you, word will get around. Maybe that'll make up for missing a few hours off."

After Mr. Stone left, Dai checked his email and opened the file of the floor plan. His fingers itched to start sketching, but he took out his phone and made a call.

"Hi," Cope said.

"Hi. I'm calling because I have to cancel tonight."

"I'm sorry to hear that."

"My boss just asked me to work overtime. I would have said no, but it's a big opportunity."

"I understand. What will you be doing?"

"I'm going to do an installation at Cartier's."

"You're going to be in the store after hours?"

"Yeah."

"Like an international jewel thief."

"More like a gardener. I'll be hauling in plants and arranging them."

"Can I help? Or do you have a crew?"

"I don't have a crew, but I don't really…. Do you mean it, or are you being polite?"

"I think it would be interesting to watch you put together a display at night in Cartier's."

"It's going to take hours."

"I can run out and get food or whatever you need."

"You make it very tempting."

"People are always saying that to me. I don't know why."

"I'll just bet." Dai chuckled. "I'll text you later with a time to meet me."

WHEN DAI pulled the big green step van to the curb, he saw Cope in the recessed doorway. Cope had his shoulders hunched and his hands thrust deep in his jacket pockets. Dai tugged his cap down farther on his ears and stepped out into the cold. He waved to Cope and then went to the back of the truck and opened the doors. Cope appeared at the bumper as Dai climbed into the cargo area. Most of the floor space was taken up by dwarf boxwood shrubs that had been clipped into spheres and rectangles.

"What can I do to help?" Cope asked.

"Can I hand you plants and have you carry them to the door?"

"Absolutely." Cope reached up for the potted plant Dai held.

Dai picked up another and followed Cope to the store entrance. The security guard inside was already unlocking the door.

"Are you taking them out in a particular order, or can I just grab one?" Cope asked.

"No particular order. I have them numbered."

Cope jumped into the truck with Dai, and both moved plants until the truck was almost empty. Dai picked up one of the large boxes, and Cope grabbed the other one.

"That's it except for my toolbox," Dai said. "If you'll start carrying things in, I'll get my tools and be right back."

Under the guard's jaded gaze, Dai and Cope shifted the potted plants around until they were placed to Dai's satisfaction. When Cope moved away several feet, he saw the outline of a leaping panther formed with different levels of boxwood topiary. The representation of Cartier's logo rose from a mat of ivy that formed a shadow beneath it. After shifting a pot a few inches, Dai joined Cope.

"Not bad," Dai said.

"I'm impressed."

"No, you aren't, but you will be." Dai slapped Cope lightly on the shoulder. "Let's get the lights on it."

With Dai on a stepladder and Cope feeding him electrical cord, they covered the arrangement with a webbing of white fairy lights. When Dai turned on the power source, the giant cat was outlined in twinkling radiance.

"Okay, now I'm impressed," Cope said. "It's beautiful."

"Let me just conceal some of this wiring a little better and we're done."

"Where did you learn to wire things like this?"

"A guy I knew showed me a few things. He was into making things explode."

"I'm not."

"Me either. That's why he's not around anymore."

Cope pretended to shiver. "Ruthless."

"I wish."

"At the risk of—" Cope broke off as he remembered the cheerless presence of the security guard. "I'm starving. Let's go to Junior's."

"They close at midnight. We'll have to hustle."

"I can hustle."

"Okay, you're on."

Moving with a purpose, Dai and Cope cleaned up and put the tools and boxes in the van. Dai jumped behind the wheel and pulled into traffic. A cab horn blew, but Dai took no notice. He knew he hadn't cut the guy off by New York standards. The horn was obligatory, like saying, "how are you?" after someone says, "hello." He pulled onto Broadway at 11:40 and sailed into a parking spot being vacated by an SUV. He and Cope entered by the one-person revolving door and threw themselves on the hostess's mercy.

After rushing through a couple of open-face roast beef sandwiches, they ordered cheesecake to go. Dai drove them to Cope's place, and Cope made coffee.

"Sorry again for cancelling our date," Dai said. He put a forkful of creamy cheesecake in his mouth.

"You didn't. It just went in a different direction. Honestly, I had a great time. I still am."

"Me too. I like messing around with plants." Dai sipped his coffee before rash words could pass his lips. He'd almost said he liked messing around with Cope. How would that be interpreted?

"I like messing around with you," Cope said.

Dai sprayed coffee across the knees of his jeans.

"Too hot?" Cope asked.

"No. You just—you crack me up."

"I like hearing you laugh." Cope leaned back and sighed. "If I could turn back time, I'd sign that first poem. I intended to, but I was in a rush that morning. I used a piece of Will's stationery and left it up to Sophie to mail it. If I'd taken the time to take care of it myself—"

"But you didn't. Can we move forward now?"

"If you want to, I'm all for it."

"I'd like to see you again on a real date."

"I could take you out for a fancy-schmancy dinner."

"That might be fun."

"Or we could go to Five Napkins and see a movie."

"That sounds good too."

"We could have a picnic on the terrace and watch a movie on Netflix."

"Now you're talking. Tomorrow night?"

"It would actually be tonight." Cope turned to the french doors. "It's already today."

Dai walked out to the terrace, and Cope followed. The light of the low-wattage bulb beside the door cast the little garden in pewter powdered with crystal. Dai shivered, and Cope automatically put an arm around his shoulders. Dai turned slightly and took Cope into a warm embrace. Cope returned the hug, holding Dai tight, breathing in the scent of Dai's hair, wishing this moment would never end.

"Should have put my jacket on," Dai murmured.

Cope held Dai closer. "Is it cold? All I can feel is you."

Dai lifted his head from Cope's shoulder and found Cope's lips. He pressed his mouth to Cope's and kissed him so sweetly Cope felt tears gathering in his eyes. "That's for being such a good sport about tonight," Dai said when he drew back.

"Tell me more about this rewards system," Cope said. "But let's do it inside. It really is cold out here."

Cope and Dai sat on the couch side by side. Dai looked at Cope. Cope looked at Dai. Both smiled, and then they lunged at each other, lips meeting in a hungry kiss. Cope trailed kisses down Dai's neck as Dai slipped a hand down Cope's back to squeeze an asscheek. Cope pulled the hem of Dai's shirt up and tongued his nipples. Dai massaged Cope's ass with both hands, fingers creeping into his crack. Cope used his teeth, and Dai moaned in arousal. Cope sucked gently at the sensitive bud of flesh and pulled away with a last swipe of his tongue. He leaned in to kiss Dai again as he drew Dai's shirt back down.

"You don't have to stop," Dai said breathlessly.

"I know, but something in me says it's the right thing to do. I'll hate myself once you're gone, of course."

Dai kissed Cope gently. "Okay. I should go home and get some sleep."

"You could sleep here if you don't think you can drive."

"I'll be fine with all this coffee in me. And I don't think I should stay. I like the idea of waiting to sleep with you, and if I stay, I know I'll sleep with you. Well, not actually sleep...."

"No need to explain." Cope walked to the door with Dai. "See you tonight."

"I'll text you later." Dai leaned back in the door to kiss Cope.

Cope cupped Dai's cheek on his palm. "I'm going to be so good to you," he said. "Just so you know."

"Ditto." Dai smiled before he walked away to the step van.

CHAPTER FOURTEEN

DAI'S PHONE rang while he was in the patisserie a couple of blocks from home. He answered as he continued to eye the pastries in the glass case. Though it was six in the morning, he was fourth in line. He had plenty of time to chat.

"So tell me everything," Harlow said.

Though they were talking on the phone, Dai could clearly see Harlow's avid expression. "We've had a date and a half, or maybe both add up to one full date. Anyway, I like him. I'm seeing him this evening."

"You make me so happy, Dai-chan."

"Getting a boyfriend is a pretty nice Christmas present."

"So happy!" Harlow was almost squealing. "And there's more!"

"Go on."

"Amy's ready to start the Symbiosis Project. Isn't the timing perfect?"

"Sure seems like it. Before I forget, Kei says hi. He's headwaiter now. Thinks he wants to be a maître d' someday."

"Good for him. You're coming to my Christmas Eve party, right?"

"I wouldn't miss it." Dai looked up as the girl behind the counter nodded at him. "Gotta go. Call you later." He hung up and pointed to the items he wanted. As he was walking out of the store, his phone rang again. He juggled his shopping bags and got the phone to his ear. By the time he'd walked to his place, he'd agreed to pose for Amy's photo book project and to talk Cope into it.

DAI ARRIVED at Cope's house with two weighty, reusable shopping bags.

"You shouldn't have," Cope said. "I'm serious. I've got enough food here to feed an extremely hungry army."

"Shut up," Dai suggested as he set out two bottles of wine and a box of assorted pastries. "See, that's it. That's all I brought."

Cope put his arms around Dai's waist from behind, but he did it gingerly, as though he expected to be scolded. "You brought the most important thing right here," he said.

"God, I love your voice. It goes right into me and settles right here." Dai took one of Cope's hands and pressed it to his stomach over his pubic bone. "I can feel it rumbling around in there."

Cope kissed Dai's nape. "Fuck me, I'm so turned on just from standing close to you. Do you feel it, or is it just me?"

"I feel it. It's like the way the air feels right before lightning strikes. You can almost smell the ozone. I feel like I'm vibrating at the same frequency as—"

"As what?"

"I don't know. I ran out of—"

"Analogies?"

"Yeah." Dai squinted at Cope. "Are you making fun of me?"

"No way. Now, let's see this wine."

"Don't be a snob."

"I'll curb myself. Just don't be upset that I have a bottle open already."

"Why would an open bottle upset me?" Dai took a balloon from the wineglass rack and poured from the bottle on the counter. "Where's the grub?"

"You said picnic, so it's outside."

"Duh." Dai grinned. "How crazy is it having a picnic in this cold?"

"On a scale of one to ten?" Cope grinned back. "Come on. Let's be lunatics."

He led Dai to the patio table, which was flanked by two tall propane heaters. Cope had set out a feast of finger foods, and Dai descended on them like he hadn't eaten in a week. Cope nibbled and smiled indulgently as he watched Dai.

"Okay, I admit it," Dai said after he finished his wine. "It's too cold. Let's go in."

Between them, they carried stacked trays into the house and laid them out on every horizontal surface. "It's not like it'll all fit in the fridge," Cope said.

They finished the bottle of pinot noir, and Cope opened a bottle of red blend Dai had brought. "It's cheap, but it's inexpensive," Dai said.

Cope laughed and spilled wine on his shirt. Dai made him take it off and demanded lemon juice and salt. He rubbed the lemon Cope gave him over the stain and covered it with salt. He scrubbed the material vigorously before leaving it to soak in the sink.

"Well, what have we here?" Dai said as he turned from the sink to a shirtless Cope.

"Just your average skinny white boy."

"Those shoulders." Dai ran his hands across Cope's shoulders and down his arms. He brought his hands back up and stroked Cope's chest. He ruffled the puffs of hair that haloed Cope's tea-stain nipples and then tweaked them.

Cope jumped. "Hey!"

"Couldn't resist. The pouty little things were begging for a squeeze."

"Well, by that logic…." Cope reached down and gave Dai's crotch a gentle squeeze.

Dai sucked in a breath through his teeth. "We're not stopping this time if we start making out," he warned. "I'm not going home to jerk off in the shower again."

"As you wish."

Dai's eyes met Cope's and searched his gaze. "It's only fair you should know I'm falling for you."

"Shit." Cope's voice was tight with emotion. "I'm gonna cry."

"Go ahead. I'll lick the tears off your face."

"You make weeping sound so sexy instead of… pathetic."

"Well, I *am* trying to seduce you."

"Talk about the definition of wasted effort."

"Are you saying you're a sure thing?" Dai laughed.

"Well, I *am* a guy."

"That's racist," Dai joked.

Cope cracked up. "Male isn't a race. Now come here," he said as he pulled Dai into his arms.

Dai met Cope's passion with equal force and tenderness. Deliberately, he set aside his doubts and prejudices and enjoyed the feel of Cope's mouth and hands on his skin. The world was starting to blur around the edges when Cope excused himself to "suit up" as he put it.

While Cope was in the bathroom, Dai quickly undressed and got on the couch. He lay back and placed a slice of pepperoni on each nipple. He nestled an olive in his belly button, covered his abs with Havarti, and draped some prosciutto over the curve of his hard cock. When Cope returned, Dai grinned up at him. "Remind you of anything?"

Cope didn't answer. He crouched over Dai and sucked the olive from his navel. He chewed and swallowed and then dipped his tongue into Dai's belly button. "Sweet *and* salty," he murmured against Dai's quivering belly. "My favorite."

Dai held in his laughter as long as he could. A pepperoni slice slid off his chest, but Cope caught it before it hit the cushion. "This was a dumb idea," Dai said as he started to sit up.

"Whoa! Not so fast." Cope put a hand on Dai's stomach and eased him back down. "I'm still snacking."

Cope kissed his way down from Dai's navel. Delicately, he took an edge of the prosciutto in his teeth and dragged it slowly off Dai's cock. Dai moaned at the exquisite sensation and lifted his pelvis. Cope rubbed his cheek down the shaft of Dai's dick, stubble prickling deliciously against sensitive skin. He finished chewing and swallowed the prosciutto, but his mouth wasn't empty for long. Dai gasped when Cope closed his lips over the head of his cock and made a teasing circuit with his tongue.

"Come here," Dai said.

"Now?" Cope looked up and met Dai's liquid gaze. He stroked a finger up Dai's crack.

"Just—" Dai made a frustrated noise. "Just get up here so I can get my mouth on you."

"Oh." Cope got up on the couch and straddled Dai, head to feet. "Is this what you want?"

"Your pants," Dai said, stifling laughter.

"Right." Cope chuckled. "Could I be any more nervous?"

"I don't think so."

"Brat!"

Cope shucked his trousers and underwear and got back into position. "Now where the hell were we?"

"In my favorite position."

"Hang on while I make a note of that." Cope lowered his head and swiped his tongue the length of Dai's cock.

Dai wrapped his hands around Cope's lean flanks and pulled him down. Cope's balls dangled just above his mouth like some exotic fruit at the peak of ripeness. Dai raised his head and sucked at the velvety skin of Cope's sac, pulling one ball and then the other into his mouth. Cope groaned as he nipped his way up the fat vein on the underside of Dai's cock. When he reached the tip, Cope drew the head into his mouth and swirled his tongue around it. As Cope bobbed his head to engulf Dai's full length before pulling back, Dai licked, sucked, and nibbled from Cope's asshole to the end of his dick. When Cope settled into a rhythm, Dai slowed down a little. Cope hummed his pleasure around the hard flesh in his mouth as Dai shuttled his hand up and down Cope's cock. Dai glided his fingers in a slick of saliva, unconsciously increasing speed with each stroke. He licked his way from Cope's balls to his hole and thrust his tongue into the tightly clenched opening. Cope made a small, strangled noise and then relaxed again. He spat saliva mixed with precum onto his fingers and resumed sucking Dai's cock.

Dai's throat vibrated with a sound of pure need as Cope circled his slippery fingertip around Dai's hole. He thrust his tongue deeper into Cope as a hint. Cope eased his finger in to the second knuckle and rubbed the inner surfaces as if scratching a kitten's ears. Dai moaned and lifted his pelvis, driving his dick deeper down Cope's throat. Cope conquered the impulse to gag and dragged his fingertip over the spot that made Dai respond so ardently.

Intent on nothing beyond Dai's pleasure, Cope took Dai's cock to the root, breathing through his nose and maintaining strong suction. He slid his finger in and out of Dai in shallow strokes, dragging the tip over the springy swelling at the front of Dai's sheath. Dai pressed the soles of his feet against the cushions and tried to thrust. Cope pinned Dai's left thigh to the back of the couch with his free hand and bobbed his head faster. Dai crested with a small cry that was muffled between Cope's buttcheeks. As the head of Dai's cock swelled on Cope's tongue, Cope felt the sweet tension in his lower belly snap. Cope's orgasm rolled through him like a tidal wave while he swallowed Dai's seed.

Dai's hand shuddered on Cope's cock, and he let go to wrap his arms around Cope's hips and mash his face into Cope's crotch. Cope let Dai's dick slide from his mouth and rested his cheek against Dai's taut stomach. The tender rod of flesh was a breath away, and he could feel its heat on his lips. He let out his breath in a long sigh, blowing a stream of air onto Dai's shiny, sated cock.

"No," Dai said weakly.

Cope opened his eyes. "No what?"

"No more. I'm sexed out."

"I wasn't—" Cope levered himself up and turned to lie alongside Dai. "Are you a cuddler?"

"Are you going to ask permission for everything?"

Cope slipped his arms around Dai and pulled him to lie against his chest. "At least until we know each other better. I want you to feel like you can trust me."

"Hmm, I'm lying in your arms after a smokin' hot sixty-nine, so I must trust you a little."

"Good point." Cope shifted so his crotch nestled against Dai's ass. "So that's your favorite position, is it?"

"Mm-hmmm." After a few seconds of silence, Dai spoke. "I can feel you wanting to ask me a question. Just go ahead and ask."

"I don't want to ruin the moment."

"That would be impossible." Dai reached out and snagged a glass of water off the coffee table. He offered it to Cope before he drank.

"I'd have to mention our mutual ex-friend."

"You just did." Dai kissed Cope's knuckles. "Moment intact."

"I know Will, and he doesn't consider it sex unless he gets to dip his wick, as he says."

"Are you leading up to asking me to bottom for you? Because I'd be happy to."

"Actually, no, I wasn't. I wouldn't turn you down, but as it happens, *soixante-neuf* is my favorite position too."

"I don't know what that is."

"It's French for sixty-nine."

"I like French too." Dai snuggled his butt into Cope's crotch.

"Will and I took French for two years. We figured it was an easy grade and it would come in handy later when we went to Paris. And Will said it would impress clients someday."

"Get out of town! You can speak French?"

"Oui."

"You're so cool."

Cope's throat tightened so suddenly that it ached. "You're not uncool yourself," he said in a voice thick with emotion. "And I'd be happy to bottom for you too."

"I'm more of a blow-job man. Hand jobs are good too."

"Yes, they are." Cope trailed a hand down to Dai's crotch and cupped his cock and balls. He squeezed gently as he kissed Dai's nape. "Can you stay?"

"I think so. Let's give it a try, anyway."

"What?" Cope paused in his stroking of Dai's dick.

"Nothing." Dai turned onto his back and looked up into Cope's eyes. "You're doing great."

As though drawn by a magnet, Cope leaned until he could kiss Dai. He didn't know what god to thank for his good fortune, but his feeling of gratitude was immense. Not knowing what else to do with it, he poured it into Dai through his mouth, his fingertips, and his cock. It's doubtful there was anyone in the city better loved that night than Daimaru Tanaka.

He and Cope fell asleep tangled together and woke an hour later to forage from the forgotten platters. Cope poured more wine, which both ignored in favor of tasting each other again. Passion flared with a heat that couldn't be controlled. Cope pinned Dai to the carpet and stretched out atop him, aligned so their hard-ons were pressed together. Fused at mouth and hips, they writhed together, thrusting and bucking, until they came, breath mingling in ragged gasps for air.

"Goddamn," Cope said when he got his breath back.

"Best ever," Dai said faintly.

Cope's heart swelled until he feared for his rib cage. He didn't care if it was too soon. He was going to say it. "I love you," he whispered.

Dai answered with a soft snore.

DAI WOKE to the smell of coffee and warm bread. He had a half second of disorientation before he remembered where he was. He heard Cope moving around in the kitchen and smiled at the sunbeams coming through the glass of the french doors.

A moment later Cope came in with a tray. "You're awake. Good," he said. "I've got coffee and scones and raspberry jam."

Dai sat all the way up with the sheet pooled around his hips. He took the cup Cope handed him and sipped the strong, hot brew. He accepted a bite of scone from Cope's fingers and nodded his approval. "Aren't you going to eat?" he asked after he swallowed.

"Yeah, I was just enjoying the sight of you all sleep-rumpled."

"Do I have that well-laid look?"

Cope chuckled. "I don't want to sound conceited."

"You made me cum so hard, I forgot my damn name."

"Well then." Cope cleared his throat. "That's the nicest thing anyone's ever said to me."

"So far." Dai smiled. "I'm pretty sure I'll be saying even nicer things."

"That would make me very happy." Cope sipped his coffee. "I'm going to change the subject because it would be a shame to ruin this coffee with my tears. I was skyping with Amy, and she wanted to know how soon we could be ready to sit for her. I said anytime was good."

"I have the whole week off for Christmas, so anytime is good for me too."

"The whole week, huh? Could I talk you into spending it with me?"

"I'd say your chances were good. There's Harlow's Christmas shindig, but other than that, I'm all yours."

Cope put a hand over his heart. "You nearly killed me," he said.

"Can't have that. I have plans for you, mister."

"You have plans for me," Cope said in bemused delight.

"You and that monster swinging between your legs."

"You're delusional, but I love it. More coffee?"

"Yes, thanks. I gotta tell you, you made a lot of points with this breakfast-in-bed thing."

"Is this part of your rewards system?"

Dai laughed. "I know we're just joking, but damn it, this makes me feel so good."

"It feels right, doesn't it?"

"I don't want to jinx anything, but yeah, it feels right."

Cope poured coffee into Dai's cup. "I'm so glad you decided to give me a chance."

"I can't believe it took me so long. I already knew I liked you."

"You had the whole Will thing to get past before you could see me as myself…. That got garbled, but I think I said what I meant." Cope's voice was tinged with anxiety. He wondered if he'd ever be able to say Will's name again without feeling a twinge.

"You're adorable. That little frown is adorable. Dammit. You realize I love you, right?"

"No, I didn't, but I'm thrilled." Cope set the pot down on the side table and sat on the bed next to Dai. "When did you figure it out?"

"I don't know. Sometime in the last twelve hours, I guess. But just now when you were pouring coffee, I knew for sure how I felt."

Cope drew Dai into an embrace, and they held each other close for several long moments. "I love you too," he said in Dai's ear.

Neither would probably have been surprised to know they were thinking exactly the same thing at that moment. *Don't fuck this up.*

CHAPTER FIFTEEN

THE NEXT three days were a whirl of activity. Having no holiday plans for the first time in a decade, Cope did whatever Dai wanted to do. They went shopping. They went to brunch. They shopped more. They took packages to Cope's house and had daylight sex before going out for an early dinner. In the evenings, they snacked, curled together on the couch, pretending to watch a movie that was just an excuse for extended foreplay.

Cope was Dai's first lover who didn't want to go straight to the climax by the quickest route possible. Will had been sophisticated, had an impressive level of expertise, and was willing to make certain concessions to his partner, but when it came down to it, what Will really wanted was to plug it in and pound away. Cope seemed content to take his time and get to his destination by the scenic route. Not that they hadn't had pulse-pounding quickies fully clothed, like the hand job Dai gave Cope this morning in the dressing room at Armani Exchange. Cope had taken it in stride, muffling his sounds of pleasure against Dai's lips.

"That sales clerk *knew*," Dai said as he made two chicken salad sandwiches at the kitchen counter.

"Why don't you just move in with me?"

"What?" Dai turned with a butter knife in his hand.

"I want you around all the time. You don't have to give up your place, but consider moving in with me, okay?"

"Sure. I'm planning on living here this week anyway. I could bring over a few more things." Dai carried two plates to the small dining table. "Are you rested up for more shopping this afternoon?"

"I'd rather stay here in bed with you."

"Who wouldn't?" Dai teased. "I'm kidding. Shopping is mostly done. Tonight is Harlow's thing."

"Right." Cope frowned. "Did we buy something especially for him? In all that spending, I've forgotten a few details."

"Yes, *we* did." Dai laughed. "I love how you already think of us as *we*."

"Don't you?"

"Of course. I just love that you do too."

Cope finished his sandwich and potato salad and pushed the plate aside. "So is there a dress code for Harlow's party? Somehow I feel there might be."

"I'll make sure you don't embarrass yourself."

"I'm not worried. He loves me."

"Yeah," Dai said thoughtfully. "He really took to you. He's a friendly guy, but he was on your side from the beginning."

"Maybe you should pay more attention to him."

"Maybe you should take a shower so I can do something fun with your hair."

Cope bugged his eyes in a parody of terror. "That sounds dire." He got up from the table. "Okay, I'll shower, but you're not shaving my head."

"I'd rather die a slow, painful death than cut your hair. Go on. I'll pick out some clothes for you."

AS INSTRUCTED, Dai and Cope arrived a half hour before the party was scheduled to start. Cope was relieved that his party clothes were a black suit and a white dress shirt. Dai wore black jeans and a bright red cashmere sweater he'd appropriated from Cope's cedar closet.

"You can keep that sweater. It looks a thousand times better on you than it ever did on me," Cope said as they get out of the cab.

"Oh, I intend to keep the sweater." Dai gave Cope an impish smile. "And I look a *million* times better."

"Hilarious." Cope tucked the box wrapped in gold foil under his arm. "Shall we?"

Harlow opened the door before they could knock. "Come in. Come in." He hugged Dai tightly until Cope cleared his throat. "I know I'm mushy, but it's Christmas and I miss my bestie. Now come on in the living room. I have delicious food, drinks, and people." He winked at Dai. "It's a nasty little soiree."

Dai laughed as they entered the living room.

"Hey, boys," Amy greeted them. "How's day after tomorrow for you?"

"Hi, Amy, how are you?" Cope said wryly.

"Just answer the question, Shore."

Cope looked at Dai, who nodded. "It's fine," he told Amy. "Text me the place and time."

"Dress like you're dressed now," Amy said. "Like Cope is dressed, I mean. And coats, of course. Black coats. Boots. Okay?"

"Got it," Dai said. "I'm excited."

"It's actually kind of boring," Harlow said.

Dai laughed. "I'm still excited. It's the first time a professional has taken my picture, except for the guy who did the photo book for the restaurant."

"It'll be fun," Amy said. "I photographed Harlow and Luk in the dance studio this morning while they were practicing. I have the strong feeling I'm going to be happy with the shots."

"Hey, Copeland, my man," Christophe said as he stopped to shake Cope's hand. "Good to see you." He glanced at Dai. "Good to see you too."

"No hard feelings?" Dai asked.

"None at all. Wasn't your fault, baby boy." Christophe hugged Dai before he moved off.

Dai kissed Harlow's cheek. "You have a special glow about you tonight."

"The reviews of our ballet have been very kind," Lukas said. He kissed Harlow's other cheek. "It's all because of this ball of fire."

Harlow spotted the box under Cope's arm. "Is that for me?"

"It's for our hosts," Dai corrected. "Give it to him, Cope."

Harlow grabbed the box. "Can we open it now?"

"I insist," Dai said.

Harlow tore off the wrapping and lifted the top off the box. He reached into the tissue paper and pulled out a heavy object. "A hearth cricket!" he exclaimed. "I love it!"

Lukas reached for the brass cricket that was the size of a flip-flop. "What is the meaning?"

"It's for protection and good luck for our house," Harlow said. He went over and set the cricket in front of the fireplace. "Perfect."

Cope's phone rang. He looked at the number and ignored the call. A few minutes later, drink in hand, he felt the phone vibrate in his pocket. "Excuse me," he said to Dai and went out to the entry. "I'm at a party. What do you need?"

"Mr. Shore?"

"Yes. Who is this? Why do you have Will's phone?"

"This is Tom Wells, sir. Do you remember me?"

"Of course. Tom from Hotlanta. What can I help you with?"

"Will is really out of it. He keeps trying to leave, but he's in no shape to be seen in public. He claims you and he have a standing date for Christmas in Connecticut."

"He's not my problem anymore."

"Well, he ain't mine either. I'm not bein' paid to babysit his drunk butt."

"When you're upset, I can hear the South in your voice."

"Isn't there anything you can do? He's a real mess." Tom paused. "I understand you all used to be real good friends."

Cope sighed. He had to be strong. He couldn't let Will suck him back in.

Dai came to hover at the edge of Cope's vision. Cope turned, and Dai raised his eyebrows.

"It's Will," Cope mouthed. "We *were* friends," he said to Tom.

"Could you please just come and stay with him until he's sober? I need to get home to my family, but I'm afraid he'll hurt himself. Not suicide, you know, but like he might fall down or something. I know I sound—"

"Hang on." Cope held the phone down at his side. "I need to do something," he said to Dai.

"Okay, but I'm going with you."

Cope spoke into the phone again. "I'll be there as soon as I can."

"Thanks," Tom said. "I'll wait for you."

COPE AND Dai heard Will as soon as Tom let them into the apartment.

"You don't fucking tell me what to do!"

Cope raised an eyebrow at Tom.

"He's been like that all day," Tom said. "He came to the office drunk about three this afternoon. I had a hell of a time getting him out of there without anyone besides Sophie seeing us. I thought he'd gone to his folks for Christmas."

"I can't believe he showed up drunk at work."

"I've been smelling it on his breath for days," Tom said. "I'm gonna scoot, if that's okay. Sophie said you could call her if you don't want to deal with him, but I don't think she's eager to leave her family on Christmas Eve."

"Go on," Cope said. "I'll handle it from here."

"Thanks." Tom glanced at Dai, and his expression changed. "Don't I know you from somewhere?"

"We had dinner once."

"Yeah, that's right. I better hightail it or my wife will tan my hide and make a purse out of it."

"Who the *fuck* are you talking to?" Will bellowed.

Tom was already closing the door. Cope looked at Dai. Dai shrugged.

"I guess we might as well get it over with," Cope said.

Will looked surprised when Cope and Dai walked into the big living area. "How drunk am I?" he asked rhetorically.

"I don't know. Are you as drunk as you were the night we ran from the cops on the turnpike?"

"Much drunker. I was still able to control the car."

"That's because I was driving."

"You always say that when you tell the story. You're such a liar."

"Not anymore. I stopped lying when I quit working for CdG."

Will's gaze fell on Dai and his mouth fell open. "You."

"Yeah, it's me."

"Why?"

"Why me?"

"You broke my heart," Will slurred.

Dai shook his head. "I never saw any evidence that you have one."

"Whoa," Cope said. "Let's not go down this road."

"You're right," Dai said. "It won't help anything."

"God, you're beautiful," Will said. "I almost forgot."

Dai couldn't help himself. "At least you have a video to remind you."

"Not anymore." Will's bleary gaze fixed on Cope. "Mr. High Horse here made me get rid of it."

Dai's startled laugh was loud in the silence. "Sorry," he said to Cope. "It struck me funny. You know, like *Dances with Wolves*, only your name is High Horse."

Will chuckled and then dissolved in untidy laughter. "That's a good one. What's my Indian name?"

"Big Chief Ego Dick?" Cope said.

Dai laughed again.

"Still envying my penis after all these years?" Will said to Cope.

"Still believing I envy your penis after all these years?" Cope countered.

"It is an awfully nice penis," Dai said. "You have to give him that." He felt an odd sense of calm, as though nothing could hurt him, and words came easily to his tongue after bypassing his brain. He wondered if he was in some kind of shock.

"I need a drink." Will stood up and wobbled for a moment before he moved around the coffee table. "I know I have a drink here somewhere."

"Please sit," Cope said. "You're going to trip over something and bust your head wide open."

"Do you care?" Will shambled toward the bar in his socks.

"You're making it difficult, but yes, I care."

"Liar." Will stopped and swiveled his head from left to right. He focused on something and started toward it.

"Will, please," Cope pleaded. "Sit and I'll get you a drink. What do you want?"

Will turned to face Cope. "Are you still here? Go away. You aren't welcome." His gaze moved to Dai. "And take him with you. I don't want to see his face again."

"Now, Will, you know that's not true," Cope said.

Will's shoulders slumped. "No, it's not."

"Please sit down, and I'll bring you a drink."

"Put him to bed," Dai told Cope. "I'll get the drink."

"Is that what you came here for?" Will took a staggering step toward Dai. "I knew you'd have to come back even—ev—eventually, you cock-hungry whore."

"Whoa!" Cope moved between Will and Dai. "That's completely out of line."

"Is it?" Will's smile was an ugly thing. "You must know by now how much he loves dick."

"This is beneath you. Please shut up."

"You must have fucked him. He's too hot to wait for it."

"William." Cope's voice held a warning note that sent a shiver down Dai's spine.

"It's okay," Dai said quickly. "I'm not insulted. Everything Will says is true. I love cock, and I'm not shy about it. I don't think those are necessarily bad things."

"You're one great fuck, that's for sure," Will said. "It wasn't easy deleting that video of you."

"Well, I'm glad you did." Dai paused and then spoke again. "Aren't you tired?"

Will appeared to be thinking it over. "Yeah," he said at last. "I'm exhausted."

"Then why don't you sit down?"

Cope led Will back to the couch. Will watched Dai pour a half inch of vodka into a tumbler. When Will looked away, Dai filled another glass with grapefruit juice and carried it over. He set it in front of Will before taking the seat opposite him.

"So are you two a couple now?" Will's gaze swung between Dai and Cope.

Cope ignored the question. "I don't think I've ever seen you this drunk," he said. "You're completely without charm."

"What a burn," Will said. He was staring straight ahead at Dai. "I still don't get why you couldn't give me a chance to explain. How could you cut me off cold like that?"

"I doubt I could make you understand," Dai said. "You'd have to know how I felt, and I don't think you have it in you."

"Why not?"

"You're too caught up in being what you think is a man."

Will turned to look at Cope. "Do you understand what he's saying?"

Cope nodded. "I do, and he's right."

"So you're saying I'm too much man for you?"

Cope almost smiled. "You could look at it that way," he said. "In fact, you probably will."

Will picked up the glass and drank the juice in two gulps. "Here's my problem," he said when he set the glass down. "I thought you liked me the way I am."

"Me or him?" Cope nodded to Dai.

"Him." Will picked up the glass again and seemed surprised to find it empty. "I gave him exactly what he wanted, and he shit on me."

"What exactly did I want?" Dai asked.

"A man. You wanted someone to take charge, to protect you, to fuck you like a caveman."

"You got the last part right," Dai said. "But I don't need anyone to protect me. As for taking charge, I did find that part of your personality sexy, but it grates after a while."

"You should have said so."

"I didn't leave you because you're bossy. I left because you betrayed me."

"So you say. I still don't see the big deal."

"Then you never will." Dai made a frustrated noise. "If you'd slept with someone else, I would have forgiven you, but what you did made me feel like garbage, like I meant nothing to you."

"You know, we probably shouldn't be having this conversation while one of us is shitfaced," Cope pointed out.

"It's so weird," Will mumbled. "You're both right here, but I can't…."

"You should sleep," Cope said.

"I can't. For the first time in my life, I can't sleep."

Cope decided he needed to get tougher. "Well, Dai and I can't stay here forever, so how about getting your shit somewhat together?"

Will looked at Cope as though Cope had slapped him. "Right. I forgot you hate me now."

"I don't hate you. I just don't like you. Yet here I am, seeing you through whatever the hell this is."

"I'm not having a breakdown, goddammit!" Will said loudly. "Tom asked me that about twenty times today."

"Sure looks like a breakdown to me," Cope said. "And I'm just not willing to watch."

"Right. Don't do me any favors," Will said bitterly. "If it's such a hardship, why don't the two of you get the fuck out of my house?" He got to his feet. "Go home and fuck like—"

"Shut up!" Cope barked as he got up. "Just shut up."

Dai cringed away from the raw pain in his lover's voice. "Stop, please," he said softly.

"You just had to have him, didn't you?" Will said, his voice low. "You always want what I have."

"Stop talking," Cope warned again.

"No, we just should get this in the open finally. You've always been jealous of me. Just admit it."

"Will… I've envied you once or twice, but mostly I admired you and even wanted to be like you. You were always so cool, so confident. I thought you were what a man should be." Cope shook his head. "I don't think that anymore."

For the first time since Dai had met him, Will was genuinely still. He stood unblinking as his eyes slowly took on the shimmer of unshed tears. Abruptly he pivoted, intent on stalking away, but he banged his knee hard on the coffee table. The slab of agate stayed in place, though a few objects atop it fell over and rolled off. Will grunted in pain as he toppled sideways and threw out his left hand to catch himself. However, he was extremely impaired. His arm came around with nothing like the speed he imagined. Instead of breaking his fall with the table, he missed it completely and went all the way to the floor with his arm beneath him.

"Jesus!" Cope exclaimed as he lunged for Will.

Dai came around the table on the other side as Cope caught hold of Will's right hand.

"No one panic," Will said. "I just lost my balance." He gripped Cope's hand and tried to lever himself up. "I'm kind of wedged in here," he said.

"Can you get your other arm out?" Even as Dai asked, he was doing his best to budge the coffee table. "Fuck, this is heavy." He got it to move and pushed it up against the armchair.

Will sat up, and Cope gasped. "Jesus!" Cope said again.

Dai's gaze went to Will's left hand, which was awash in red. He tracked down to the broken glass on the carpet. A half second later, he was headed for the kitchen. "Hold his arm over his head," he said to Cope.

"Dumbass," Cope said to Will as he stretched Will's arm toward the ceiling.

"It was an accident."

"There are no accidents where you're concerned," Cope said.

"You think I planned to cut myself?"

"I think you planned to keep me around by any means necessary."

"Because you're my best friend. You're my brother. I love you."

Dai returned with some tea towels, a bowl of water, and a wooden spoon. He washed Will's hand and got a look at the cut before it was obscured by blood again. "Congratulations," he said. "You need lots of stitches."

"Well, fuck me."

"Hold still." Quickly, Dai made a tourniquet with one of the towels and the spoon. "Let's get you to the emergency room," he said.

"Why not call EMTs and let them take him off our hands?" Cope said.

"Because we can get him there just as quickly, and I doubt he'd want anyone else knowing about this," Dai answered.

"Why do him a favor?"

Dai sighed. "Because I feel sorry for him now. I know. I know. He's a predator and he doesn't deserve it, but I pity him anyway. We've got each other. Who does he have?"

"Us, apparently."

"Don't be bitter, okay?"

"I'll try." Cope put Will's arm around his neck and supported him with an arm around his back. "Let's go, killer," he said.

DAI AND Cope waited while Will's cut was stitched. Dai called Harlow and told him there was an emergency. After crossing his heart and promising to die if he didn't follow through, he said he'd give Harlow all the details later. He sat down next to Cope on a molded plastic chair and tried to ignore the hospital smell. After a couple of minutes, Cope took Dai's hand and held it.

"You're amazing," Cope said.

"Only in certain lights."

"I'm serious."

"I'm just an ordinary jerk. You think I'm amazing because you love me."

"No, I love you because you're amazing."

"I'm not, though. Will is absolutely right about me. Weird that he can see me more clearly than my best friend."

"What's he right about?"

"I throw myself at people I'm attracted to. It's like I'm trying to absorb them. I can't get enough of them until they do something that disappoints me. And then I cut them off completely." Dai turned his face from Cope. "The worst thing is I came between you two; I wrecked your friendship."

"That was definitely not your fault. That's all on him."

"But like you said, here we are."

"Suckers."

"I don't see it that way. The fact that we still care about him means there's something in him worth caring about. I'm not saying I forgive him, but I can't look away if he's in trouble."

Cope squeezed Dai's hand. "You were amazing, though. The way you, you know, sprang into action."

"I've worked in a few kitchens. People are always cutting themselves on a knife or the meat slicer. And seriously, everyone should know some first aid."

"So much more than a pretty face."

"Shut up," Dai said, but his dimples appeared in a pleased smile.

In an astonishingly short time, Will was released with a bandaged hand still numb from the local anesthetic, and prescriptions were called in for antibiotics and painkillers. Cope and Dai saw him home with a side trip to an all-night pharmacy for the drugs. Will was still woozy from the alcohol and didn't give Cope or Dai any trouble. Between them, they undressed Will and got him into bed.

"Thanks," Will said groggily as Dai and Cope left the bedroom.

"If housekeeping comes today, they're going to get a surprise," Cope said as he gazed at the blood-soaked carpet and the splattered couch.

"I'm not cleaning it up."

"You got that right," Cope said. "Do you think we need to stay?"

"Doctor said he'd be fine on his own."

"He never has been before."

"Stop it. He's not the epitome of evil."

Cope turned to look into Dai's eyes. "Really?"

"Come on. It's Christmas."

"That's true." Cope dropped the bantering tone. "I don't think he's evil." He paused. "Evil is…. Hitler, Darth Vader, Lucifer. Will is just very misguided."

"Misguided?"

"The things he wants don't make him happy. He thinks he's happy, but he's not. He needs different goals."

"But if he thinks he's happy—"

"I'm doing it again, aren't I? I'm making excuses for him. Giving him a toehold."

"You keep right on doing that." Dai put his hands on Cope's shoulders. "That you still think he's redeemable makes me love you even more." He kissed Cope. "Now, let's go home."

CHAPTER SIXTEEN

"WHAT IS it with us and daybreak?" Dai said as he looked out the french doors at the rising sun.

"I don't know, but I think it's nice." Cope put his arms around Dai's waist and leaned on his back. "Do you want your present now?"

Dai's eyes lit up. "Present?"

"I'll take that as a yes."

"But hold me for a few more minutes, okay?"

They stood looking out at the terrace until the sun rose above the buildings east of them. Cope kissed the side of Dai's neck and let him go. They separated to fetch their gifts and met back in the living room.

"For you." Cope held out a present the size of a large book wrapped in red and gold.

"And this is for you." Dai handed Cope a small red velvet bag. "It's really corny."

Dai sat on the couch and put the present on his knees to unwrap it. When he uncovered the cigar box, he looked up at Cope.

"Look inside," Cope said.

Dai lifted the lid. The dream box was empty. "There's nothing in it."

"That's because you made all my dreams come true when you said you loved me."

Dai jumped up to throw his arms around Cope. Cope returned the hug, leaning into Dai's warm, strong embrace.

"You're my heart," Cope said as he drew back a little to look into Dai's face. "I love everything about you. I love your spirit. I love your kindness to everyone from friends to complete strangers. I love your style, your laugh, the way you eat ice cream, that funny little snore, your utter fearlessness… everything. There's not a single thing about you I don't love."

"Oh come on. There must be at least one thing."

Cope shook his head.

"Bullshit."

"I can make something up, if you want."

"No, that's all right." Dai squeezed Cope tightly. "I love everything about you too." He sighed. "Harlow's always telling me I should hold back a little. But I just can't help it."

Cope cupped Dai's cheek on his palm. "I love the way you don't hold back no matter what you're doing. Don't hit me, but it's one of the things you have in common with Will." Cope stroked his thumb over Dai's soft lips. "And to think I almost didn't accept Will's invitation to dinner. What if I'd never met you?"

"What if I hadn't been naked?"

Cope laughed. "There's no one else quite like you."

"You know this can't last forever, right? Eventually, we'll find a way to annoy each other."

"Then let's enjoy it while it lasts."

A little shiver ran up Dai's spine. The moment had taken on such gravity that he could feel it settling on his skin with the weight of inevitability. His emotions were so large that he was either going to have to let them out or suffocate.

"What's wrong?" Cope asked when a tear trickled down Dai's cheek.

Dai shook his head as he fought for enough breath to speak. "I'm just so happy," he managed to say. Dai took a hitching breath and gave Cope a watery smile.

"Can I open my present now?" Cope asked to lighten the mood.

"It's so stupid. I'm embarrassed after your gift."

Cope dumped the contents of the bag onto his palm. "A coupon for sex on demand and a bottle of gingerbread-flavored lube." He looked at Dai from under his eyebrows. "It's just what I've always wanted."

"If you're gonna be a jerk about it!" Dai grabbed the items from Cope's hand and fled to the bedroom. Cope gave chase, and before long, each knew what gingerbread lube tasted like.

THOUGH BOTH Dai and Cope were exhausted from New Year's Eve revels, neither wanted to sleep yet. They'd seen the New Year in with the friends who'd become their family and returned home for a private celebration. Drained but satisfied, they lay in bed in each other's arms, telling stories of their pasts.

"My dad's parents were old," Dai said in a grainy voice. "His mom had him when she was fifty-one. I remember thinking I had to be quiet and slow at their house because I was afraid I'd break one of them. They were both stick people with white hair like baby bird feathers. You could see their scalps all speckled like a brown egg. They'd been married for seventy-five years when I came along. They could communicate without talking. It was really cute. My grandad never spoke, and my grandma never shut up. But she didn't talk to him; she talked to their dog, a dachshund named Punkin."

Cope laughed softly. "Go on," he said. "It's a good story, and you tell it well."

"It was just funny to me as a kid."

"It would be funny to anyone."

"Well, Grandma would be like, 'Punkin, I think your daddy is ready for his lunch. What do you think? You think so too? I don't suppose you're hungry, you little piggie. You are? What a surprise. Do you think Daimaru is hungry? Yes, that's true. Growing boys need to eat a lot, but you're all grown, Punkin. Well, I guess we should go to the kitchen and see what we can find.' It went on like that all day." Dai smiled. "When she was upset with Grandad, she never told him to his face. She scolded him through Punkin. She would ask Punkin if he wasn't ashamed of his daddy." Dai laughed.

"They sound charming."

"They died before I got to high school. They were both in their nineties and went within days of each other."

"I hear it happens like that when one partner can't imagine living without the other one."

"To some people, my grandparents probably seemed odd, but I'd like to be like them someday."

"Me too, but I think I'd rather have a Pekingese." Dai laughed, and Cope took Dai's hand and raised it to his lips. "You've come to mean more to me than anything in my life." He kissed Dai's knuckles, darting his tongue against the sensitive web between Dai's fingers.

Dai shivered. He loved every step of the erotic dance of lovemaking, but the opening moves melted him every time. He gloried in the spark when eyes met, the teasing touches, the kisses so full of promise. When Cope touched him, the smallest caress was imbued with a deep and patient passion that enveloped Dai like a warm ocean. He hoped Cope knew that his love for him was just as boundless. "Again?" he said.

"I know it's insane, but I've got a hard-on."

Dai slid a hand under the sheet. "You're not lying," he said. "What are we going to do about this?"

Dai moved his hand up Cope's hard chest, thumbing his nipples and tracing the rungs of his abs. He walked his fingers up to stroke Cope's tumbled hair.

Cope grabbed Dai's hand and sucked each finger into his mouth one by one.

His grin was very white as he scooted up and reclined back onto his elbows. Planting his feet far apart on the wood floor, he gave his lover an unobstructed view of his crotch. Cope caught hold of Dai's foot and fondled his way up the ankle to the knee and on to the thigh. Dai moaned as Cope stroked, rubbed, and squeezed, caressing and massaging, growing ever closer to his crotch. Cope employed his mouth as well as his hands, nibbling, licking, and sucking the soft skin of Dai's belly and inner thighs. Dai moved restlessly, blissful but impatient, wanting it to go on forever but desperate for Cope to reach his goal. However, when he got there, he didn't linger.

Cope ran the flat of his tongue up the underside of Dai's cock and continued north, tracing a line up the middle of Dai's torso to the divot between his collarbones. "Want to taste all of you," he mumbled against Dai's left pec.

Dai groaned and arched his back when Cope bit down on his left nipple. Whimpering softly, he dug his fingers into Cope's hair as Cope alternated suckling with flicks of his tongue over the end of the hard nub. Cope moved to the other nipple, and Dai slid his hands down Cope's back to grip his buttocks. Lifting his pelvis, Dai rubbed his arousal against Cope's. Cope covered Dai's mouth with his, their tongues sliding together like their cocks. For several feverish moments, they moved in concert, rising and falling like waves, as the heat built ever higher.

"Hang on," Cope said breathlessly. "Just let me—" He twisted in a supple maneuver that put him face to crotch with Dai and vice versa, their heads pillowed on each other's thighs. "That's better," he said as he dove on his lover's cock.

Dai buried his face between Cope's legs, lapping at Cope's balls, shaft, and crack exuberantly. Cope matched his lover's enthusiasm, slurping loudly just to hear Dai laugh. Dai pulled Cope's thighs to his shoulders like the padded cage of an extreme roller coaster and ran his nose up Cope's cleft. Cope wriggled and tried to laugh around a mouthful of Dai. Dai reacted by thrusting deeper into Cope's mouth and darting his tongue into Cope's hole. A tremor ran the length of Cope's body as his lover circled his lower opening with a hot, wet tongue before pushing inside again. He could feel every ounce of tightness in his body unraveling in the liquid rush of heat from his core. Simultaneously, the upward spiral of impending orgasm wound a notch tighter with each passing second. Staving off his climax for the moment, Cope concentrated all his effort into driving Dai to the brink.

There was always a point when Cope knew Dai had passed fully into the realm of the senses, giving and receiving pleasure as naturally as breathing in and out. Cope cherished this unselfconscious abandon that swept him up when he made love with Dai. No one else had taken Cope to that place, and he had to believe it was love that made the difference. Otherwise, why had he never felt this transcendent passion with any of the lovers he'd had over the past decade? He'd cared deeply for one or two of them, but it was never this all-encompassing emotion that left him unsure where he ended and Dai began.

"More," Dai gasped. "I need you inside me."

Cope let Dai's balls slip from between his lips. "Yeah?"

"It's no big deal. I just want you in me when I come."

Cope kissed the tender crease where Dai's thigh connected to his torso. "Who am I to deny you?" he said as he leaned to his right to reach the nightstand. As he'd hoped and feared, the gingerbread lube was still in the drawer.

Dai ran his toes up the middle of his lover's back, stirring the long curls at Cope's nape. "I love your hair down," he purred.

"You're making it a little difficult to focus on the task here." Cope nearly dropped the small plastic bottle as Dai's toes tickled his ear lobe. "Stay still," Cope said, looking up from pouring lubricant on his fingers.

Dai flicked Cope's cock with his big toe before rolling onto his stomach. He got to his hands and knees and looked over his shoulder at Cope. Cope met Dai's molten gaze and swallowed hard. They hadn't done this before, and he had a nagging fear he wouldn't perform well enough for Dai. "I guess we could always switch if it didn't work out," he mumbled.

"What is taking so long?" Dai asked in perfect imitation of a line from *Real Genius*.

"Did it occur to you I might be savoring the moment?"

"Not really, no."

Cope chuckled. "I guess I better get back to work."

He ran a hand over Dai's firm asscheeks as he spread lube around Dai's hole with the other. Dai's breathing quickened as Cope stroked his crack and nudged gently at the puckered opening. Reaching around Dai's slim waist, Cope took hold of Dai's cock. Slowly, he shuttled his fist up and down as his forefinger sank a little deeper into Dai's ass on each stroke. Dai moaned appreciatively as the pad of Cope's finger dragged across his prostate. He began to rock gently, pushing into Cope's fist as Cope rubbed at the spot that gave him so much pleasure.

"Oh man, that feels so good." Dai's voice was raspy and languid. "But it would feel even better if it was your dick."

"You sure?"

"Yeah. What's the holdup?"

"You've never asked for this before."

"I haven't been in the mood. But if you don't want to, we can do something else. You have very talented fingers."

"And then there's my tongue."

"True, but I'm in the mood for cock."

"As you wish."

Cope licked Dai's cleft as he slowly withdrew his finger. Pouring some lubricant into his palm, he spread a coat of the thick liquid over his shaft. He nuzzled the head of his cock against Dai's glistening port, and Dai pushed back eagerly. Cope coaxed the tip of his shaft past the entrance, wrapped an arm around Dai's waist, and leaned forward. With steady pressure, he sank deeper as he fondled Dai's arousal. Dai grasped the vertical rails of the bamboo headboard and pulled up to a kneeling position. Cope splayed his hand across Dai's cobbled abdomen, holding him steady as his full length disappeared into the tight channel.

"Oh God, that's... indescribable." Dai craned his neck to look back at his lover. "You're a real smooth operator, Copeland Shore."

Cope leaned forward and managed to kiss Dai before he began to withdraw. "I wish I had the words to tell you how good this feels."

"Write me a poem tomorrow." Dai gasped as Cope pushed back in a couple of inches. "Damn! How do you know exactly the right thing to do every time?" he asked breathlessly. "Swear to God, I'm on fire."

Cope rode out the surge of pride caused by Dai's words of praise. He pulsed his hips, shunting the head of his cock in and out to a regular rhythm as he stroked Dai's shaft. "It's not my first rodeo, cowboy."

"Rodeo?" Dai scoffed. "This ride better last longer than eight seconds."

"Just tell me what you want."

"You're doing fine." Dai gasped again as the blunt tip of Cope's dick bumped over his prostate. "Just keep doing that."

"Why is it so much better with you?" Cope murmured as he did as Dai asked.

Cope thrust shallowly, hands resting on Dai's flanks as Dai rocked back against his stroke. Letting Dai set the pace now, Cope provided solid resistance and reached around for Dai's cock again. Dai rocked faster, thrusting into Cope's fist as he impaled himself on Cope's dick.

"Cope!" Dai panted. "More, Cope!"

Cope sank his length into Dai's sheath and rolled his hips as he fondled Dai's shaft. Dai mewled, clutching at the rails as Cope filled him. Cope flexed his buttocks, shifting his cock as Dai tightened and released his interior muscles. Little by little, his thrusts gained speed and depth as his hand shuttled up and down on Dai's cock. He couldn't have stopped now if a SWAT team had crashed through the windows and door. All that existed was the silken skin under his fingers, the sound of panting breath, and the delicious hot tightness that hugged his cock so sweetly. He drove Dai across the invisible line into bliss, and Dai's hoarse cry of release triggered his climax. He tightened his arms around Dai as his seed spooled out in several powerful spurts. For long moments, the only sound in the room was ragged breathing.

"Oh damn," Dai said breathlessly. "Damn."

Cope eased out of the slick passage and settled on his side. Holding out his arms, he beckoned to Dai. For a few heartbeats, Dai hung on to the headboard, gazing at Cope with love glowing in his eyes. Sinking down to face Cope, Dai stretched out, hooking a leg over Cope's hip as he nestled. Cope gathered Dai in, stroking his feathery hair.

"I really do want you in my life from now on," Cope said, his chest rumbling under Dai's ear.

"Just try and get rid of me," Dai dared him.

"I'd like to have you around all the time."

"Sounds like just the job for me. How much does it pay?"

"Surely, you jest."

"Nope, and don't call me Shirley."

"Well, rates vary." Cope smiled. "To you, I'm offering everything I have."

"Done." Dai lifted his head, finding Cope's lips with his. "I'll trade you even."

"Just one more question. Do you like gladiator movies?"

Dai's giggle was cut off by a kiss he had to admit was probably the most romantic in the history of kisses.

CONNIE BAILEY is a Luddite who can't live without her computer. She's an acrophobic who loves to fly, a faultfinding pessimist who, nonetheless, is always surprised when something bad happens, and an antisocialite who loves her friends like family. She's held a number of jobs in many disparate arenas to put food on the table, but writing is the occupation that feeds her soul.

Connie lives with her ultralight-designer husband and Ickle the Wonder Whippet at a small grass-strip airfield halfway between Disney World and Busch Gardens. Logic and reality have had little to do with her life, and she likes it that way.

Blog: baileymoyes.livejournal.com

DREAMSPUN
DESIRES

FINDING FAMILY
Connie Bailey

When you find
your family, you'll do
anything to keep it.

When you find your family, you'll do anything to keep it.

When Charles Macquarrie inherits a fortune and an international clothing company, he also inherits three young cousins he desperately needs help raising. By a stroke of luck, he discovers and hires Jonathan Lamb, who spent his life in a children's home due to chronic illness, to be his nanny.

If Jon thought a budding romance with his wealthy boss complicated his life, he has no idea of the hardships awaiting him when he's charged with embezzlement and kidnapping. But even when threatened by accounting discrepancies and mob connections, Jon and Charles won't let go of the family they've built together without a fight.

www.dreamspinnerpress.com

HUMAN
AFTER ALL

connie Bailey

In the future, corporations buy the life contracts of infants and raise them for specific careers. Jaymes, aka The Prince, is Erotic Bioware, Thoroughbred Class, trained to seduce and give pleasure in the highest tiers of society. But his latest client involves him in a political assassination, and Jaymes must flee the comforts of the city for the barbaric outlands.

With Drue the Fox, Bioware, Exotic Class, Jaymes struggles through the last wilderness on his world in his quest to return to civilization and his pampered life. The ruthless corporate mercenary on their trail should make them want to work together—but Jaymes and Drue are diametrically opposed in personality, class, and ideology and can't stop bickering about Bioware inequality.

Eventually, Jaymes's dislike of Drue evolves into something else as Jaymes wakes up to the reality of his place in society and admits that Drue is right. It will take great courage, a band of ex-military outcasts, and a sympathetic politician to clear Jaymes's name and bring about lasting changes for all Bioware. Only then can he and Drue have a life together with all the rights a human deserves.

www.dreamspinnerpress.com

Insert Here

Connie Bailey

John Garros, known to his fans as Spanish Joe for his dark good looks, makes his living as an actor in porn films. As a perfect body double for Hollywood superstar Jason Forrester, he acts in XXX-rated scenes that are inserted into Forrester's blockbuster movies. He makes good money from the profits of the modified films and spends most of it on parties and vacations, never feeling a twinge of guilt. At least not until he bumps into Jason at a party.

The two men have an instant physical attraction, and Jason surprises Spanish by calling him afterward. Spanish is even more surprised when the one-night stand turns into a budding relationship. Things are going great for him until Jason's management stumbles over the thriving traffic in "enhanced" Jason Forrester movies. When Jason tells Spanish how much the deceptive DVDs hurt him, Spanish knows he has a big decision to make: keep his mouth shut and hope Jason never sees the footage, or confess and risk losing everything.

www.dreamspinnerpress.com

www.ingramcontent.com/pod-product-compliance
Lightning Source LLC
Chambersburg PA
CBHW071006280626
47160CB00015B/1424